I0699854

CAN'T BELIEVE YOU CAME

HE'S BREAKING ALL HER RULES

MILE HIGH MATCHED
BOOK 5

CHRISTINA HOVLAND

This book is dedicated to this picture of my dog in a dress.

For rights information, please contact:
Prospect Agency
551 Valley Road, PMB 377
Upper Montclair, NJ 07043
(718) 788-3217

Cover Design: Christina Hovland

Developmental Edits: Holly Ingraham
Copy Edits and Proofreading: Shasta Schafer

CHAPTER 1
90 DAYS UNTIL ANNA
& DRAKE'S WEDDING

PIPER

A face-plant into the concrete steps would ruin both Piper Daws's dignity and her carefully calibrated timeline for the biggest day of her event planning career.

The black key fob she stumbled on skittered across the step leading to the door of her office building. The fob popped open, tossing two little circular batteries flying.

The button kind that are a total pain to find at the store.

She reached for the stair railing to catch herself before disaster really struck. Her pastel-pink fingernail polish contrasted against the chipping black paint as she grasped the warm metal rail.

"I'm not going down that easily," she muttered, steadying herself with the same resolve she used to handle difficult clients and impossible deadlines.

Not today of all days, when she finally had the contract from the Directors of Interment and Cremation Knowledge locked down for her employer, Montgomery Events. She was a junior event planner with aspirations to snag the head event planner role. Unfortunately, she wasn't the only one with the goal.

But this contract meant guaranteed *corporate* clients who wouldn't sob over wedding centerpieces or demand a last-minute dove release. Just neat, orderly, funeral professionals who appreciated her ability to organize the hell out of a conference and the occasional luncheon.

Sayonara to the bridezillas and the family drama that always paired so well with weddings. The briefest flicker of her mother's fourth wedding tickled at her memory. But she shut that shit down fast.

"Success by death." She smiled at her little joke. Smiled so wide it settled deep in her soul. Even the bright pink, yellow, and red flowers peeking through leaves seemed to cheer her on.

Piper had made her own magic happen. Unlike those ridiculous fairy tales her mother used to read her, where some born-royal prince showed up to save the day. Thanks to her hard work, this was the best day ever.

The universe clearly wanted to test her best-day-ever declaration when her right heel stuck in what was in the running for the world's stickiest wad of gum.

Okay, ew.

Balancing the found key fob on the top of a nearby trash-can lid, she pulled off her glittery gold shoe and, standing on one foot so she didn't accidentally step her bare foot into something worse, she scraped the residual gum goo through the rectangular opening into the waste bin.

Smacking the stretched Hubba Bubba against the side dislodged most of the sticky nonsense, but there was a good amount of scraping still to be done.

"Need a hand there?" a guy with a husky, deep voice asked in a tone that held entirely too much teasing given her precariously one-footed situation.

She glanced up, ready to deliver her standard "thanks, but

I've got this" speech—and promptly forgot how words worked.

Because standing there, looking like he'd just walked off a photoshoot for HotGuysinCasualWear.com, was quite possibly the most gorgeous man she'd ever seen outside of a wedding party where the groom modeled regularly for GQ.

"I'm... fine?" she forced out with only a tiny squeak.

Though—her current position with one shoe off—balancing drunken flamingo-style while scraping gum on the trash can might have suggested otherwise. "Urban bubblegum warfare. It's everywhere in Cherry Creek these days."

He chuckled at her joke, and the sound did something weird to her stomach. Weird *good*, that is.

"The Mint Gum Menace hits again. He is particularly active around corporate offices lately. The jerk." He stepped closer and she held her breath.

Not because of the proximity, but he probably smelled amazing to match the whole *thing* he had going on. She did not need that kind of distraction in her nostrils.

He reached his hand out and—

"That key's for my car."

"Oh." She glanced to where it balanced on the trash can lid. "I was just going to turn it in at lost and found. Though, technically, it found me. Attacked me. Whatever you want to call it."

"It's been known to misbehave," he said, a twinkle in his eye that made *her* suddenly want to misbehave.

His eyes were so ocean blue they made her want to jump in and go for a swim. They crinkled at the corners as he smiled. "The damn thing's never coordinated an attack with gum before. That's new."

"Clearly a conspiracy." She continued to scrape the sticky mess from the sole of her new Louboutin heel (okay, the knockoff, fast-fashion, budget-friendly version).

An awkward pause stretched between them like the big ol' wad of goo she tried to dislodge from her sole.

"I'm having a good day today," she blurted. What compelled her to share this with a hot-guy stranger? She had no idea.

"Zach," he said, those laugh lines deepening. "And clearly your day involves a battle with sidewalk hazards."

Something about his easy smile made her want to keep talking. "The gum is only a minor setback to an otherwise perfect day."

"Perfect?" He raised an eyebrow. "Now that's a dangerous word."

"I like dangerous words." She finally freed her shoe from the last of the sticky residue. "They keep life interesting."

"So does breaking from routine." He stepped closer and her breath caught. "Like helping strange women with their shoe emergencies."

"I'm not strange, and this isn't a shoe emergency." The words came out fainter than she intended.

His pupils flared. "What would you call it?"

"A temporary lapse in judgment." But she smiled as she said it.

"Temporary lapses can be the best kind of lapses." His voice dropped lower, sending a shiver down her spine. "They're the ones we don't see coming."

Their gazes tangled and, for a moment, the busy street around them faded away. Nothing existed except the electricity sparking in the air between them and the dangerous possibility of what might happen next.

Zach held his hand out for something.

She glanced to his hand. Then back to his face. Her brain short-circuited. *Obviously, the shoe. Obviously. Right?*

He moved his hand. "I'm just going to—"

On autopilot, she handed him the shoe.

"Oh." He seemed like he wasn't quite sure why it was in his hand. "Let me ... uh...?"

He sort of shrugged and then knelt to help her slip it back on like he was some kind of Prince Charming and it was a glass slipper. Instead of some random guy on a sidewalk with a knock-off pair of designer cheapies.

She was about to say something witty. At least, she hoped it would be witty, when she wobbled slightly. His free hand reached to steady her, wrapping warm and firm around her ankle.

The contact sent a little sizzle decidedly north. His thumb brushed ever so slightly against her skin as he helped slide her foot back in the now gum-free shoe.

Her breath hitched and her pulse raced inappropriately. Entirely unwelcome. And, apparently, not stopping anytime soon.

He had a knowing look, like he knew that she'd sizzled like that for a guy wearing well-worn jeans and a plain T-shirt. He stood, and it was not fair that on his athletic frame, even casual clothes seemed tailored.

"Thank you," she said, adjusting her foot. "That's so nice of you to help me out. People just... aren't nice lately. Like, at all. Seems like everyone needs a dose of happy. You know?"

"Yeah, no problem." He smirked as he reached around her and grabbed the key fob off the top of the trash, then stuffed it in his pocket.

Her smile froze.

"You weren't being nice to me, were you?" she said, the numb dose of reality taking hold. "You only wanted your key?" She said the last bit extra slowly as it sank in. "You held your hand out for your *key*. Oh my God. I swear to you I am not some kind of deranged Cinderella."

Though, if one had to announce that, then maybe she was a touch off? She melted into a puddle of embarrassment, her cheeks heating enough to likely match the color of her pink suit.

"Don't overthink it. I'm not." The slight breeze brushed his dusky blonde hair across his forehead.

"I mean, I'm not overthinking it." She totally was, but he didn't know what was going on in her brain.

"All good," he assured, carefully watching her. "I understand."

She pressed her palms along her sides to straighten her suit jacket. "What do you understand?"

"That whatever happened just now was unusual for you. It threw you off. I get it," he said, studying her with those annoyingly perceptive eyes.

"It didn't throw me off," she assured him. The words sounded flat, because they weren't entirely the truth.

"Okay," he said, moving so she could get by.

She didn't, however, move. "I feel like you're analyzing me and getting everything wrong."

"I'm not getting anything wrong."

Her lips pursed and she lifted her brows in what she hoped was a silent invitation for him to leave.

He didn't.

"You seem like the type who likes control. Prefers to manage everything so that you know where it goes. And you have no idea where to catalog… that. " He gestured to where he'd knelt to slip on her shoe.

"That?" she asked.

"The whole unexpected chemistry with strangers on sidewalks."

She bristled. Not because he was wrong, but because he wasn't. And that unsettled her more than anything. But she'd rather eat gum off the sidewalk than admit it. "I was removing gum from a shoe, not speed dating outside my office."

He smirked again, like he knew exactly how off-kilter he'd

knocked her, and worse, how she didn't hate it. A muscle twitched in her jaw as she pressed her lips together. Their odd little back-and-forth hummed under her skin, like nerves reacting to a caffeine overdose. Jittery. Persistent.

"I don't remember Cinderella dealing with gum issues, but it would've made for an interesting twist on the fairy tale," he mused.

"Cinderella stories never end like they're supposed to, gum or no gum," she replied.

She needed to get upstairs. Any second now. Right after this conversation stopped being... this.

"Not a fan of the fairy tale endings with the wedding and the happily ever after?" he asked and, for a half-second, the twinkle faded. Like maybe he'd learned that lesson the hard way.

"Well, since fairy tale endings don't exist, no." Not only no, but *hell* no. She cringed inside, and it likely showed on her face, as well.

"You don't think so?" he asked, as though this was a problem. Which was stupid because he didn't know her and she didn't know him and, dammit, she had news to tell her boss inside.

Upstairs. Away from here.

She shook out her sleeves and forced a smile on her face. "Let's just say I prefer events where the biggest drama is the decision to serve chicken or fish, and no one ends up divorced afterward."

"A nice Chamber of Commerce event dinner?" Zach suggested.

"That would be fine. Or a *funeral*," she added, a mischievous glint in her eye as she began to walk toward the front entrance. "Those are always predictable."

Zach's lips twitched and he kept stride with her. "Morbid, but efficient. I think I get it now."

Oh no, he didn't attempt to figure her out in a three-sentence sound bite. "Stop trying to put me in a box like that when you don't even know me."

He stayed with her pace.

Piper was rarely at a loss for words. They flowed freely whether she wanted them to or not. But in that second, she could not find the syllables to say anything. Surely, they were there somewhere in her brain, but they were *not* making their way to her mouth.

Her heart kind of kicked at her to say something. But… it was like someone pushed pause on her ability to speak.

And there he was, still walking with her toward the door.

"I've got a meeting happening inside I need to get to," he clarified.

Her gaze focused on the floor tiles as her shoes *click-clacked* in the otherwise silent atrium. She skirted around the fountain spitting water all over itself, and approached the elevator moving double time to… hold on, was *she* keeping up with *him*?

"Nice to meet you but I have to jet. I do have some good news to deliver. Big news. The kind that involves bonuses and promotions." She gestured vaguely toward the bank of elevators.

"Sounds exciting," Zach said, as he continued to walk with her. "Don't you want to know how the story ends? Does the key fob find true love? Does the gum exact its revenge?"

"I have a feeling," Piper said dryly, "that the story ends with us going our separate ways."

"And yet…" he loud-whispered.

Don't do it, Piper. Don't do it. Keep walking.

She totally stopped, turned around. "And yet, what?"

"You got a little tingly when I was helping you with your sticky situation. Am I right?"

"I did not." She totally did.

"It's not a big deal. This was a first for me, too. Usually, I buy a girl coffee before she lets me play Prince Charming and we get *tingly*."

Her spine stiffened. "I didn't let you play Prince anything."

Hold up, did he also feel that momentary chemistry when he touched her leg? She shook her head.

"Okay," he conceded in that way people do when they aren't actually conceding. "But you did get a little *zingy*, right?" He wiggled his eyebrows.

"Zingy?" she repeated, incredulous. "That's not even a word."

"Maybe not in the dictionary, but I know it when I see it. We're not talking a full-on lightning strike. Maybe just a little static shock. But it was there."

Damn, this guy was smoother than freshly shaved legs on satin sheets.

"Being in control isn't a bad thing," Zach said gently. Unfortunately, he also kept stride alongside her but didn't say anything more.

He did press the button with his thumb and shifted from foot to foot in that awkward way people do when they're waiting for the same elevator.

She couldn't help it; she reached out to press the already-lit call button. His gaze snagged with hers and he lifted his eyebrows slightly.

Gah, what is wrong with me?

"That doesn't mean anything," she said in a rush, gesturing to the button she'd just double pushed.

The elevator dinged, its doors about to slide open with an invitation she suddenly couldn't accept.

"You know what? I think I'll take the stairs," she announced, backing away from both the elevator and him. "It's only three flights. Good cardio. Very...*unexpected*." She emphasized the last word with enough sass to make him grin.

"Three flights in those heels?" His gaze dropped to her shoes, lingering just long enough to remind her of that earlier touch. "Seems like a lot of effort to avoid being alone with me."

"Maybe I like the exercise." She did not enjoy exercise. Not at all.

"Maybe you're running away."

"I don't run." She lifted her chin. "I make strategic exits."

"Is that what this is?" He stepped closer, right inside the edge of professional distance. "A strategy?"

The space between them tightened like the air had taken on weight she wasn't certain she could carry.

"You didn't tell me your name," he said lower.

She hadn't told her name, had she now? "Cinderella."

For a second, she almost smiled and let something subtler slip through. A crack in the fairy-tale armor.

His lips curved. "See you around, Cinderella."

For the record, she was not running away from him. She was making a strategic retreat from the terrifying little flicker of hope he'd sparked. Everyone knew hope was the most dangerous fairy tale of all.

CHAPTER 2

90 DAYS UNTIL ANNA & DRAKE'S WEDDING

PIPER

With no more time to think about Zach or the fact that she did, in fact, prefer control, Piper fixed a smile on her face. One hand on the railing, she climbed those steps with a conviction like she was climbing the last leg of Pikes Peak.

This was it. This was the contract Piper needed to prove to Aspen Montgomery that she was ready to snatch up the head event planner job and lock down any worry she wasn't the right choice.

She was the right choice. Sure, others might have had better connections than she did. Piper was new-ish to Denver. But connections could always be developed. The grit and commitment that Piper had forged through her life? Not so easy to come by.

She paused at the door to Montgomery Events, using her jacket sleeve to buff a smudge from the gold nameplate.

"Hey, Aspen." Piper called, the lush cream-colored carpet cushioning her footsteps as she stepped inside.

The reception area opened before her with recessed

lighting that cast a warm glow across the pristine white walls adorned with framed photos of past events.

And Zach-from-the-sidewalk stood near reception, casually leaning against the sweeping curve of the polished white marble reception desk. Light from the fixtures hanging above caught the rose-gold accents, as if they twinkled for him.

Piper's stride didn't falter, but her internal monologue did a full-on screeching halt. Of course, Zach was there. The universe really had a twisted sense of humor.

He glanced up and grinned like he'd won a race she didn't even know they were in. Her competitive streak flared at the loss, even if she hadn't known she was playing.

"Hello, again," he said, all casual and relaxed. "Cinderella." His eyes lingered on hers a beat longer than necessary, and that dimple in his right cheek made an appearance.

"Hi... again," she replied, still slightly out of breath from the altitude and the stairs. "Zach." A warm flutter spread across her chest, which was ridiculous considering she had other priorities right then.

Still, there was something in the way he leaned forward slightly that made her wonder if he'd been waiting for her.

"This is where you work?" he asked. His voice held the confident air of someone who either had nothing left to lose or had everything already secured.

"Uh, yeah. Who are you meeting with?" Piper replied, surprising herself with the slight hint of flirtation in her tone.

"Aspen," Zach replied. "I'm here for the meet with Aspen."

Despite his relaxed posture, Piper caught a flicker of something more calculated in his eyes. Only a brief professional assessment suggested he had more riding on this meeting than his casual demeanor let on.

But the look vanished as quickly as it appeared, replaced by that damn smile.

"I didn't realize she was having a meeting." Piper tucked

her hair behind her ear, suddenly conscious of how she must look after climbing three flights.

The elevator was clearly quicker. Noted for next time.

Also noted were the three other people in the attached waiting area, seated around the glass coffee table that held the latest issues of Vogue, Architectural Digest, and several high-end wedding magazines.

This was odd because there was no client, potential client, or any other sales meeting on the schedule for the day.

Piper glanced at Zach by the desk, at the couple sitting on the loveseat currently invested in quiet conversation, then at the lady sitting across from them.

The woman sitting across from the couple cleared her throat and gave Piper a thorough once-over. Dressed similarly in her own version of a pantsuit, she was about the same age as Piper. But where Piper was pink and fun, this woman was severe in a no-nonsense kind of way.

"That's Tess," Zach murmured close to Piper's ear, his breath warm against her skin.

"Same meeting, I take it?" Piper asked.

Zach nodded.

Tess straightened in her chair, her eyes darting between Piper and Zach with calculated interest.

"Strange that we're still waiting to begin," she said loudly enough for everyone to hear. "Aspen is usually so punctual. I wonder what's holding things up today."

Piper's pulse quickened, not just from Zach's proximity but also because Tess wasn't wrong. It wasn't normal for Aspen to keep anyone waiting. Though she had been stretched extra thin lately with her husband traveling for work.

"Oh good, Piper," Aspen said, poking her head out from the doorway to the back offices. "You're here."

"Piper..." Zach stretched her name out, his pupils flaring

as though he tasted her name for the first time instead of simply saying it.

Why did that make her feel all warm and cozy and give her a sudden need to fuss with her lipstick?

Piper glanced at Aspen, hoping the many questions she had for her boss reflected in her expression. "I'm here."

"I need a quick sec," Aspen said, tilting her head toward her office.

She had blonde hair with bangs, the kindest smile, and she always came to the office in business casual. Slacks and sweaters or, like today, a long flowing flower skirt she'd paired with a simple ribbed tee.

"Yeah," Piper said. "Of course."

She didn't have a choice; this was her boss after all.

"Just two minutes," Aspen said to the rest of the people in the room. She confidently moved down the hall and stepped into her office, making room for Piper.

Piper fought the urge to share her good news because something was seriously off here.

"I have a job for you," Aspen said, sitting on the edge of her desk. Her mannerisms were the usual calm and put together paired with perpetual smile lines around her eyes. But she also used her matter-of-fact, this-is-how-it-is tone. The one she didn't pull out often and, frankly, had never used on Piper.

"Okay," Piper said, cautiously, taking the seat Aspen waved her hand toward.

"That's Drake Wellington and Anna Dvornakov out there," Aspen said with a deep sigh.

"Oh," Piper said, the little hairs on her neck prickling because somehow, she just knew she would not enjoy what came next.

Drake was the quarterback for the Denver Stallions football team. The thing to understand about Denver was how bananas over-the-top everyone got with their football team, the players, and all things Stallions.

"I didn't catch that's who was there," Piper said.

This was a total faux pas because Denver bled gold and blue during football season. And during all the other seasons, too. This was a *football* town. Something that took getting used to when you didn't grow up here, but like the Rockies standing tall to the west? You just accepted it as how things were.

"What I mean is that the two of them were turned away..." Piper continued.

Could she blame her inattentiveness on Prince Charming and his stupid blue eyes?

"They are engaged," Aspen said like she was leading Piper somewhere she didn't want to go. Only probably with confetti cannons and fondant cake.

"No-o-o-o," Piper said, frowning. "Did it just happen?"

Aspen nodded, obviously understanding the full implication of what this meant.

"They can't do that," Piper said, quickly.

Clearly, they *could*. But the last handful of times one of the star players got engaged before the season began... well, the season flopped. Big time.

It had happened often enough that there was a solid Denver lore preventing just this kind of pre-season engagement.

With one very specific caveat: the wedding had to happen before the start of the season.

"Please tell me they're going to elope," Piper said, already understanding that would make things too simple.

"Nope." Aspen shook her head. "And I need *you* to handle their wedding."

A loud silence stretched between them for a lengthy second.

Piper didn't even have to think about it. "Aspen, no. Anyone but me."

Piper had been clear when the last wedding couple went up in so much smoke the annulment was completed before the honeymoon was even supposed to be over.

The mere suggestion of planning *another* wedding sent Piper's heart racing, her palms instantly slick with sweat.

Add in the fact that this was Denver football royalty? *Oh no.*

The memories flooded back... the Garfield wedding six months ago, when the bride had discovered her fiancé's affair during the reception. The screeching profanities, the thrown cake, the smell of buttercream and harsh perfume... the lawsuit that followed. And that one had nothing on her own parents' spree of nuptials and breakups or her own wasteland of a love life.

All other events? Fine.

Give her every corporate gala Denver could throw: the birthday blowouts, quinceañeras, even the occasional christening.

But weddings? Hard pass.

"I need you to take this one," Aspen said gently. She twirled an ink pen between her fingers, her gaze dipping before meeting Piper's again. "I really have to pare back my schedule. I can't keep working eighty-hour weeks. The kids need me to be more present—and I want to be there for them. Last night Bronson asked if I love my job more than him. He's my kid. He shouldn't feel like that. And..." she offered a small, hopeful smile, "you know I've been wanting you to step into the senior planner role."

Piper's stomach knotted. Her palms went clammy. Her chest tightened until it felt like breathing through a straw.

"It's a bad idea," she managed, her throat thick.

This wasn't just professional discomfort. After the Garfield disaster, she'd sworn off weddings forever. She didn't want to be remembered as Denver's premier *wedding ruiner*. Especially not with the quarterback golden boy's nuptials.

"I get why you'd feel that way," Aspen said gently. "But you're good at this, Piper. Better than you give yourself credit for."

"It's not that I hate weddings," Piper muttered. "I just don't enjoy watching relationships implode in real time while everyone's wearing pastels."

Aspen gave a sympathetic laugh. "Fair. But this is a big deal, and I can't handle it myself on top of everything else. I could give it to someone else, but honestly? I trust you more than anyone else. You have the instincts for it."

Piper's fingers clenched on the edge of her chair. She forced them to loosen.

"The last thing this wedding needs is another curse." She licked her bottom lip. "Every couple I've planned for has split. Every single one. If the national average is fifty percent, mine is a hundred."

"A string of bad luck isn't a curse. It's just coincidence with good catering." Aspen slid a fat binder across the desk— swatches, color palettes, vendor notes already tucked inside. "You don't break people up. You bring their vision to life. That's what you're amazing at."

"When I'm involved, the happily ever after part never loads correctly," Piper whispered. "I'm the common denominator in a series of romantic disasters. This is just a bad idea."

"Maybe this is the one that proves you wrong." Aspen's voice softened further. "And I'll be here in the background however you need me. You're not alone in this."

Gah. Ugh. Piper's stomach did another unhappy twist.

"Fine." She exhaled. "Let's just get this over with."

"Good." Aspen tapped the binder. "You know Anna and Drake—the bride and groom. The woman with them is Tess, from the Stallions' publicity department. They're footing the bill, managing the PR, and fighting the whole superstition thing so there aren't riots downtown when it gets announced. Keeping her happy is important."

"Aspen..." Piper said, flipping through the binder like it was a prison menu offering her last meal.

"You can do this," Aspen said, again.

Of course, she could do it. That was never in question. The problem came as to whether she *should* do it.

"I cleared the conference room," Aspen said, sauntering out the door and back down the hall.

Piper followed Aspen and said, almost too quiet, "I got a commitment from the Directors of Interment and Cremation Knowledge. They're having me handle all of their events."

Aspen paused, turned to Piper and smirked.

"I had no doubt you would." She hit Piper with a huge smile and clapped quietly. "As I said, you've got this."

She could scream or maybe even cry. This was supposed to be the moment she'd built her career up to, and she couldn't even enjoy it.

Blah, just because she had *that* did *not* mean that she had *this*.

CHAPTER 3

ZACH

A Cinderella moment wasn't on Zach's agenda for his sister's wedding planning meeting, but then came Piper. Her preoccupation with verbal volleying paired with her fucking-adorable control made him want more. He shook his head because he wasn't there to explore this thing between them.

Anna had asked him to be her voice of reason since they'd always done that for each other. Plus, he already had that email thread going with Tess about Wild Sacks becoming official team underwear.

So, no, he wasn't there to explore his chemistry with Piper.

Still, he caught the brief warmth in Piper's eyes before she hid it and vanished with Aspen.

Right after they disappeared down the hall, Tess's phone buzzed.

"Sixty seconds," she said, already moving toward the hall. "Hi—uh-huh—move the stadium loading dock to eleven. If it's a go, we'll need a quiet room on club level for the bride. I'm sending a dietary note to skip sushi this time, go light citrus. Put the influencer list on hold until legal clears. Text me the revised run-of-show." She ended the call, tapped a reminder, and was gone.

No wasted words. No wasted motion.

"Is she always like that?" Zach asked.

"Yup," Drake said. Super good guy who was currently digging through Anna's purse, probably for a Gatorade or crackers or something.

Anna met Zach's gaze, opened her mouth, then closed it. Her eyes widened with alarm.

Oh crap, she turned an odd shade of green he recognized from the time he'd dumped a sticky mix of Elmer's glue and cornflakes in her shoes. When they were kids, clearly.

Dammit, he knew that look.

She was gonna hurl.

Without answering his question, Anna promptly tore off in

the other direction, the back of her hand covering her mouth.

"Anna." Drake called after her, then shot Zach an apologetic look before following her like she was the ball in a playoff game, and he absolutely refused to fumble the play.

Zach blew out a breath into the sudden quiet of the room.

Anna was busy tossing her cookies from the morning sickness that had invaded her life. His sister was pregnant, and it was not going well for her.

An official underwear deal with the Stallions would be game-changing for his start-up company. After years of his family's polite confusion about why he'd chosen to design men's underwear instead of joining the family's uber successful flower business, this kind of validation would silence the doubters. The main one being his dad.

The sound of approaching footsteps in the hallway pulled him from his thoughts.

"Sorry to keep you waiting." Piper's voice preceded her

into the room, her heels clicking rhythmically until they stopped abruptly when she crossed the threshold.

She stood framed in the doorway, folder clutched to her chest, blinking at the vacant chairs. She turned to Zach. "Where'd they go?"

"Anna's throwing up, Drake's probably holding her hair, and Tess went to solve three problems at once," Zach answered.

The way Piper's forehead creased with concern made something twist in his chest. "Is Anna okay, that sounds—"

The door swung open again as Tess returned, her attention still half-focused on her phone screen. She glanced up and around the room pointedly. "We're missing a bride, a groom, and the wedding planner."

"Nope. I'm right here." Piper waved. "I'm the event planner assigned to this wedding."

The words took more than a second to register fully. This was the same woman who declared her hatred of all things matrimonial earlier, yeah?

"You?" Zach asked, not totally loving the way the word came out like an accusation with a sprinkle of shock. "Not Aspen?"

"Aspen is taking more of a strategic role, so you get me." Piper tried to be chirpy, but it didn't land.

Zach couldn't help his slow smile. "The woman who thinks fairy tales are a scam is planning my sister's happily-ever-after? This day just keeps getting better."

"Professional obligations trump personal opinions," Piper replied primly. "Separating the two is part of the gig."

"Ah, so you're saying you'll plan the perfect fairy-tale wedding while internally rolling your eyes the whole time?" Zach leaned forward. "That's some next-level compartmental-ization."

"I excel at compartmentalization," she said, tapping her folder. "It's how I've survived corporate retreats where CEOs demanded live tigers as 'conversation pieces,' charity galas where donors expected their names spelled out in fireworks, and a tech conference that wanted to release five hundred butterflies in an air-conditioned convention center in January."

"Impressive résumé," Zach nodded appreciatively. "Any chance you're available to freelance? My sock drawer could use your compartmentalization expertise."

"Sorry," Piper shot back, "I only organize important things. Like seating charts that prevent family feuds and cake flavors that won't trigger obscure allergies."

"Are you implying my socks aren't important?" Zach pressed a hand to his chest in mock offense. "They're the unsung heroes of the wardrobe world."

"You seem unusually passionate about socks." Piper pointed out, a reluctant smile tugging at her lips.

"I'm passionate about many things," Zach replied, his voice dropping slightly. "Priorities being one of them."

The look that passed between them lasted a beat too long, the rest of the room seeming to fade into the background.

"You know, when I first started my business, I'd lie awake at night, worried I'd fail spectacularly. Had to learn to compartmentalize or I'd have never gotten out of bed."

Piper's eyes gentled momentarily. "The 3 a.m. entrepreneur panic? I know it well. Started planning events out of my studio apartment. First year, I organized a birthday party where the flower delivery went to Idaho instead of Indiana."

"Ouch."

"Yeah. Had to raid every grocery store within fifty miles at dawn. The bouquets were creative, to say the least."

"But you pulled it off," Zach said.

"Always do," she replied with quiet pride that resonated with something inside him.

Tess cleared her throat. "Now that we've established *that*. I have two notes. One: we need to add a quiet room to the venue plan, zero fragrances. Two: medical details stay private unless Anna and Drake approve release." Her gaze flicked to Zach—not unkind, just unmistakably in charge.

Zach blinked, the world rushing back into focus as he remembered they weren't alone. Tess had clearly observed their exchange with clinical interest. Her gaze flicked between them, a slow, deliberate assessment, as if she were scouting players for a different kind of team.

Honestly, he'd only ever seen a thorough observation of that magnitude from his babushka.

"You'll run point on logistics," Tess said to Piper. Not a question. "Be sure to secure and forward vendor NDAs to me before disclosing any details."

"Absolutely." Piper pulled the cap off her pen to take notes.

"Do you have a status on the happy couple?" Tess asked.

Piper frowned. "I understand the bride is experiencing a sort of... um... you know... a... nutritional reversal situation."

"Anna's puking and Drake's probably holding her hair," Zach clarified.

"Pregnancy can be unpredictable." Tess's expression didn't change. "Let's build buffers into the wedding schedule. Ten minutes margin per segment."

"Anna's pregnant?" Piper asked, pausing from her note taking.

"Yes," Tess said. "And it's important that all medical details stay internal unless the couple approves release."

"I've planned events with expectant mothers before," Piper assured. "There are accommodations we can make. I'll arrange seating with back support, if she needs to sit during the vows, we'll make it elegant. I'll be sure she's not on her feet all night, and water is always within reach. We'll keep restrooms close by, transportation easy, and I can even prep the wedding party to quietly step in if she needs help. It's all very doable." Her voice held genuine concern that caught Zach off guard.

"That's really thoughtful," he said, surprised by how much he appreciated someone else caring about Anna's comfort.

"My sister had hyperemesis during both pregnancies," Piper explained quietly. "I know how rough it can be."

The personal revelation felt like a small gift, something she hadn't needed to share but chose to.

"We're hoping the sickness goes away by the second trimester." Zach shrugged. "Mom had said it was the same for her, and it did eventually go away."

"Will you be participating in all wedding prep?" Tess asked.

"Anna asked me to help out, so that's the plan," he replied.

"I say the more the merrier with planning this kind of thing," Piper straightened her already-perfect posture. "Fresh perspectives can be... valuable." Her gaze flickered to Zach for just a heartbeat before returning to Tess.

Tess looked between Piper and Zach, lifting an eyebrow in that way only certain people can accomplish without looking like a super villain.

"And you two know each other?" Tess asked, glancing between Zach and Piper with curiosity.

"Not really." Piper's response collided with Zach's confident, "Yeah."

"I mean, we've met," Zach clarified.

"But it's not like we *know* each other, know each other," Piper replied.

"I mean I did help you get dressed," Zach said, a dimple appearing in his right cheek.

"Barely," Piper replied, her cheeks flushing.

Zach opened his mouth to explain their sidewalk encounter, but Tess cleared her throat, the sound more of a cue than reprimand.

"Actually, Tess, since we're already here together waiting, I wanted to talk to you about the Stallions," he said.

He didn't need long. Just enough time to confirm next steps on the official underwear conversation.

"What do you need?" Tess asked, again with the straight to the point. Her phone buzzed and she typed out a message on the phone screen before stashing it again.

He hadn't expected Piper to be there for this part of the pitch, but she didn't seem to be going anywhere until Anna and Drake returned.

He took a deep breath and dove straight into it.

"I own a brand of men's underwear called Wild Sacks and we make comfortable undergarments for men," he said to catch Piper up. "Breathable fabric, no-chafe seams, lift-and-separate pouch to reduce discomfort."

Piper seemed to choke on air, covering it with a clearly fake cough.

Tess tilted her head slightly, her gaze questioning even though her overall expression remained carefully neutral. "I recall. We've corresponded."

"Yes, and I appreciate the time you've given to the idea." He spread his hands wide, "Players stay cooler, longer. I sent your equipment manager a size run and ASTM wash-test results last week."

He forced himself not to explain exactly how he'd created a pouch to lift the family jewels and keep them nestled away from the body heat that caused them to sweat.

Sweaty balls did not make for a good sales pitch. He understood that much.

"So, this is why they call it the 'package deal'?" Piper muttered so only he could hear.

He grinned, stuffing that line away to use for a future tagline.

"Oh, shoot," Piper said, snapping her fingers with theatrical urgency. "Connor. My cactus. He needs his emotional-support spritz. It's a whole thing. You two finish up... this. Meet me in the conference room when you're through?"

She didn't make any eye contact with either of them as she gathered her folder, clutching it like a shield before heading back down the hall.

He shook his head and chuckled, letting her excuse just sort of sit in the space for a moment.

Focus, Dvornakov.

"We've got two million people following us on social media who believe in what we're building," he said, the corporate speak he'd practiced falling away into connection. "I started in my garage, selling to college buddies. Now their older brothers are buying, their dads are buying. It's not just underwear to them. It's supporting something local, something that started here."

His voice gained momentum. "I could go player by player, beg their management for endorsements. But that's not the vision. I want Wild Sacks and the Stallions to mean something together."

He met her gaze. "This isn't about quarterly projections for me, Tess. This is about proving that the little guy with the better product can make it to the championship game."

Proving that he hadn't made a mistake by going out on his own to start this company.

Validating what he'd built not only in his eyes—but his family's, too.

"Look," Tess said, sounding tired for the first time since they all arrived. "The Stallions are investing heavily in this wedding because if it goes sideways and our community dives into all the myths and legends we're up against? It will affect the entire season. This is my priority right now because it isn't just a personal event anymore. This wedding needs to be picture-perfect, and that's where my focus has to stay." She sighed. "The marketing department is willing to explore this with you. Local businesses, Colorado connections, that sort of thing. I do think that if the circumstances work, we could consider a structured pilot program for an official team undergarment."

Zach practically salivated at the carrot dangled in front of him.

"That's fantastic," he said, keeping his voice neutral despite his internal excitement.

Tess nodded. "But I want to be clear. These discussions are preliminary. Though your contributions to make this wedding a success will be noticed. The organization appreciates team players. People who understand the bigger picture. Team players who can help us craft the event to be what we both know it needs to be."

The implication was crystal clear: help make this wedding exactly what the Stallions wanted, and the underwear deal was his.

"I'm always happy to help Anna," he said carefully. "And if my help takes some of the strain off of you so you can expand your focus past the wedding? Bonus for everyone."

Including, and mostly, him.

"Great. The fact that you know the wedding planner already is very helpful." Tess leaned forward. "We need this wedding to be spectacular but controlled. You and Piper have a certain rapport." Tess studied him carefully. "She's very responsive to you."

He hesitated. He needed this deal. Needed to prove his company was worthy of the family name, even if it wasn't selling tulips and daisies.

And he genuinely liked Piper, so it wasn't like he would work her like a mark. He'd *help*, he'd be useful, and tell the truth. If that nudged things along for his company? Awesome.

"I'll do what I can." He squared his shoulders and held out his hand to shake.

"I think we both know you'll do better than that," Tess said gripping his palm.

"Then we have a deal?" he asked.

Tess tilted her head from side to side. "We have... potential."

CHAPTER 4

90 DAYS UNTIL ANNA
& DRAKE'S WEDDING

ZACH

"Let's join the others?" Tess phrased it as a question but didn't wait for an answer. She was already down the hall, the figurative sponsorship carrot glinting just out of reach.

Sure, it was close enough to taste, but not quite his to claim.

Not until he and his sister's wedding planner, the one who'd just sworn off fairy tales, delivered something picture-perfect *and* brand-smart that still felt like Anna.

No pressure there, just lots of *potential*.

Zach inhaled deeply and his stomach knotted. The soft yes he just got was fabulous, but the added-on Piper postscript gave a slight metallic tang.

But, dammit, he needed to prove the longevity of his innovative men's underwear line. He needed this boost because if there was one thing his dad—his family—would notice, it was a collab with the Stallions.

And if being a supportive brother who helped guide the

wedding planning process happened to align with his business goals... was that really so bad?

Yeah, the excuse felt flimsy even to his own ears.

He followed Tess down the corridor, the plush carpet muffling his footsteps. The conference room door stood partially open, spilling golden light into the hallway. The faint scent of coffee and expensive leather chairs wafted through the gap.

Piper sat alone, reviewing a thick binder. Her hair fell forward slightly as she leaned over the pages, creating a curtain that partially obscured her face. Something about her intense focus made him pause.

His chest tightened with a pang of guilt. Was he about to use their easy chemistry as leverage? No, if it came to that, he'd say something. He'd tell her.

Tess pushed the door all the way open and strode in.

Piper looked up, her startled expression quickly composed into professional neutrality. But when her eyes landed on Zach, they lingered for a beat too long, a flicker of warmth there that made his guilt intensify.

"How's Connor?" he asked, forcing a lightheartedness he didn't feel.

A hint of pink colored her cheeks. "He's hydrated, thank you."

Anna arrived, looking slightly less green than before, with Drake's protective arm around her waist. Her eyes, however, betrayed a mix of exhaustion and resignation that went beyond mere morning sickness. His sister's face brightened when she spotted him, and the genuine smile she gave him was a stark reminder of why he'd agreed to be there.

For Anna. This was all for Anna.

Also, for Wild Sacks. But mostly for Anna.

"You're still here," she said, sounding relieved. "I thought I'd scared everyone off."

"Takes more than a little puke to get rid of me," Zach

replied, pulling her into a gentle hug. She smelled like mint mouthwash and the faint trace of the lavender lotion she'd used since high school. The familiar scent centered him, reminding him of what mattered.

Drake clapped him on the shoulder as they all settled around the conference table. The polished mahogany surface gleamed under recessed lighting, cool and smooth beneath Zach's forearms as he leaned forward.

Piper introduced herself, gave a synopsis of her experience, and everyone settled in.

"We have a binder started with everything Anna and Drake had indicated they want for the event. Colors, favorite flowers, all that goodness," Piper said, flipping to the first page.

"Marketing's current palette is Stallions' royal blue and sunny yellow," Tess said, tapping a note into her phone before setting it aside. "If we're using team channels, we should stay in that family for anything we release."

"I really don't care what colors we have," Anna said. "I just want it to be done." The tightness around her eyes suggested she cared more than she was letting on.

"It said in the notes that you wanted to have lavender and cream as your color selections?" Piper seemed genuinely concerned about what Anna wanted.

A definite point in her favor.

Anna drew small circles on the table with her finger. "I mean, in a perfect world..."

"Lavender's beautiful." Tess slid the binder closer to scan a tab. "But it fights the palette. We'll lose cohesion on press materials."

Piper kept her tone even. "Perhaps we should get clear on the goals for this event? Generally speaking, it's about the happiness of the bride and groom. But, in this case, I'm not sure that's what we're aiming for?"

"Get these two married in a way that amplifies the Stallions brand and shows our commitment to our players and the community," Tess recited, still flipping through pages.

"You want this over fast, right?" Drake asked Anna tenderly.

"Yes," Anna agreed.

"Then we get it done so everybody can move along. Everybody wins." Zach clapped his hands together too loudly.

"Not everybody," Piper said so quietly he almost didn't hear her.

"Sorry?" he asked.

"Nothing," she said, shaking off whatever she'd been thinking about.

"You know what? Let's start at the beginning. With the engagement," Tess said, redirecting everyone's attention with the professional efficiency of someone accustomed to controlling rooms.

"Can't we just tell everyone we got engaged?" The confusion in Anna's words made her sound extra vulnerable.

"Not without inciting a Stallions-themed riot," Drake said, frowning.

"It's best to play this for the narrative, not the reality." Tess pointedly closed the binder to reset the agenda.

Piper's shoulders tensed slightly, and the fluorescent lights overhead suddenly seemed too harsh. Their quiet electronic hum became more noticeable in the momentary silence. The climate-controlled air was suddenly too cool against his skin.

"Nothing too dramatic," Anna said quickly, her fingers fidgeting with the sleeve of her blouse. "Please."

"I'm thinking an on-field proposal," Tess suggested, matter-of-fact. "Halftime fireworks, cameras, the works. Fans will Eat. It. Up. No one will even think about superstitions. And when they do? We'll be ready with the solution."

Anna's complexion lost the little color it had regained, her knuckles turning white as she gripped the edge of the table.

"No," she said quietly but firmly.

The look she exchanged with Drake spoke volumes.

"Something more subtle," Drake said, squeezing Anna's hand. The quarterback who regularly faced down 300-pound linebackers now looked distinctly uncomfortable.

"*Subtle* does not get attention," Tess countered, the gentle tap of her pen against the table punctuating her point. "On this one we're going for attention."

Anna frowned. "I feel like a prop, not a bride."

The tension in the room thickened, seeming to press against his skin.

Someone's expensive perfume (probably Tess's) hung in the air, growing cloying and overwhelming as the minutes ticked by on the sleek wall clock that punctuated each second with a barely audible click.

Somehow, he needed to steer this conversation toward a compromise that would satisfy Tess without completely steamrolling everyone else.

"Authentic is always better than staged; we can all agree on that, I think." Piper reached across the table to reclaim the binder. "This is Anna and Drake's engagement announcement, not a media stunt." She turned to face Anna directly and tapped the binder. "In your notes it says you love the botanic gardens. I think it's perfect. Intimate. Beautiful. Meaningful."

Tess's expression hardened as she listened. "That's not going to work for—"

"You know," Zach said carefully, "Piper's right. Fans will know if something's forced. Cameras don't lie." He turned to Piper, silently trying to communicate his intent. "What if we combine approaches? The gardens shoot gives us controllable visuals for the press. I'm thinking a private moment that's captured professionally for later release?"

Piper blinked, her expression shifting as she processed his suggestion. After a quick moment, she nodded slowly. "That...

could work." She glanced to the couple. "Best of both worlds, really."

They all looked at Tess for her agreement. "Private shoot at the gardens, professionally captured, released on our timeline with clean visuals, controllable message. Approved."

"And honestly," Piper added offhand, "this way we avoid all the typical engagement horror stories. No restaurant proposals where the ring gets eaten, no flash mobs of weird strangers being awkward." She tapped her pen thoughtfully against her palm. "I mean, statistically, it's a sound decision. The average engagement costs nearly four thousand dollars for what is, essentially, a glorified promise party—with a twenty percent failure-to-launch rate, so if you factor in—" She caught herself. "I mean... What I mean is..." She licked her lips. "You know what? Some thoughts are inside thoughts. I should remember that. What I should've said is, congratulations on finding a meaningful approach that honors your relationship."

Anna's mouth hung open slightly, her eyes wide with apparent shock. Drake stared fixedly at the table, suddenly fascinated by the wood grain. Tess froze mid-text, her perfectly manicured fingers hovering above her phone.

For three excruciating seconds, no one seemed to breathe.

"And that's why we keep Piper away from the greeting card department," Zach quipped, shooting his sister a wink.

Interesting that the wedding cynic from the sidewalk chose that moment to peek through Piper's professional facade.

"We're already beating all kinds of statistics," Drake assured Anna.

"And there's no way Babushka's gonna let Drake out of the engagement," Zach said wryly. "She's going to insist on being at future meetings like this."

"No," Anna said immediately, panic crossing her face. "No,

we are not involving Babushka. The last time she 'helped' with an event, the fire department showed up."

"That was a misunderstanding," Zach defended. "The flames were *meant* to be there."

"The flames, yes. The explosion, no," Anna countered.

"There was also that other thing," Drake said with a loud exhale.

"You mean the thing where she locked us in a room together?" Anna asked, pursing her lips and crossing her arms.

"You can't even be mad about that one," Zach said on a huff. "It saved your relationship."

Piper looked between the siblings with a mixture of horror and fascination. "I'm sorry, your grandmother sets things on fire?"

Of the two issues, apparently that one seemed like it was the biggest deal.

"Not intentionally," Zach said at the same time Anna said, "Always."

"Moving on," Tess interrupted. "We need to set a timeline. I'm thinking engagement shoot next week, followed by the wedding in three months."

"Three months?" Piper's eyes widened. "That's... ambitious."

"We need it before training camp," Tess explained. "And before Anna starts showing."

Anna's hand instinctively went to her still-flat stomach.

"Then we better get going," Piper agreed, diving back in.

The meeting finally wrapped up, and Tess was the first to leave, already on another call before she'd even left the room. Drake helped Anna up, his hand protectively at the small of her back.

Anna gave Zach a quick hug on her way out. "Fair warning, Mom's planning to call you tonight about the shop inventory system again."

Zach groaned. "I already told her I don't know anything about florist inventory management."

"You're the tech-savvy one," Anna shrugged. "In her mind, that means you can fix anything that comes with a power button."

Zach lingered after they left as Piper organized her notes and materials. She seemed determined to ignore his presence, though he caught her glancing his way twice.

"So," he finally said. "Weddings? *Am-I-Right*?"

Her hands stilled. "For reasons that you don't need to worry about, I need this job to go well."

Zach leaned against the conference table, studying her. "I know we barely know each other, but I'm thinking that maybe we can help each other on this one."

"How exactly?" Piper narrowed her eyes, her chin tilting slightly downward as she took a half-step back.

"The way I see it, you need a wedding that makes your boss happy. I want my sister happy."

Piper pressed her lips together, considering.

"I'm suggesting a simple partnership," Zach said. "I know my sister better than nearly anyone, I've got connections throughout the city, and I'm excellent at solving problems."

"And modest, too," Piper muttered, but the corner of her mouth inched upward.

Spending time with Piper wouldn't be a chore, either. But he didn't need to mention that.

"Look, I saw you in there. You care what Anna wants, and you fought for her. She needs that. Which puts you miles ahead of Tess. But you'll still need inside support to navigate the Stallions machine—and my, uh, *spirited* family."

Piper pushed a strand of hair behind her ear. "What do I have to do?"

"It's more about what I have to do. I help you manage my family and provide creative solutions for whatever problems come up. You help create a wedding that satisfies Tess but still feels personal to Anna. We both get what we want."

"And what exactly do you want, Zach?" Her eyes met his, direct and challenging.

"Beyond the obvious business opportunity with the Stallions?" He smiled slightly as he leaned his palms on the table to get closer to her. "Anna deserves a wedding that doesn't make her throw up more than she already is."

Something in Piper's expression gentled. "That's... actually sweet."

"Don't sound so surprised. I have my moments." He straightened up from the table. "So, partners?"

Piper hesitated, clearly weighing her options. "Fine. But I have conditions."

"Name them."

She raised an eyebrow meaningfully. "You don't interfere with my process. You can offer suggestions, and I'll consider them. *Consider*."

"That's only one condition."

"You also keep your pyromaniac grandmother away from all things wedding planning."

Zach laughed. "One, Babushka is currently on a cruise— much to all of our concern—otherwise she'd be here at this meeting and literally everything else. And two, Babushka isn't a pyromaniac, she's... enthusiastic about dramatic effects. And honestly? I think we're gonna need her," Zach said.

Babushka was the one who could ensure Anna got what she wanted, Tess didn't realize she wasn't getting what she wanted, and the damn wedding got done so he could finally shoot—and land—his shot.

"Fine." Piper caved. "But you're going to keep her in line."

Ha. As if anyone could do that.

Still, he extended his hand and, after a moment's hesitation, Piper shook it. The brief contact sent that same unexpected tingle he'd experienced with her when they were outside.

From her quickly withdrawn hand, he suspected she felt it, too.

"Let me walk you out," he said as she gathered her things.

"I'm perfectly capable of finding the elevator," she replied, but fell into step beside him anyway.

Everything about her was efficient, from her neatly organized binder to her precisely applied lipstick.

"Can I ask you something?" he said as they waited for the elevator.

She gave him a wary side-eye. "Depends on the question."

"Why do you hate weddings so much?"

The elevator doors opened, and for a moment he thought she might step inside without answering. Instead, she turned to face him.

"I don't *hate* weddings," she said carefully. "I just don't believe in the fairy tale they're selling."

"Because...?" he prompted.

She sighed. "I've seen the reality behind too many 'happily-ever-afters.'"

The answer was evasive but also revealing in its own way. Zach found himself genuinely curious about what experiences had made her so cynical.

"Well, for what it's worth," he said as she stepped into the elevator, "I think Anna and Drake are the real deal."

"That's what they all think," she replied somberly.

Zach made a mental note to text his grandmother later: *Met the wedding planner. She hates weddings. This should be fun.*

CHAPTER 5

42 DAYS UNTIL ANNA
& DRAKE'S WEDDING

*(Yes, it was 90 Days yesterday… welcome to bridal math where
schedules constantly change.)*

PIPER

Piper's phone had taken on a life of its own and was determined to drive her insane. It had been buzzing nonstop for the past hour.

Hunching over her laptop, one earbud in, Piper tuned in as the event rental vendor's voice came through her Zoom call. Overhead, the office A/C hummed away, keeping things cool enough to raise polite little goosebumps on her arms, but not cool enough to justify grabbing the emergency cardigan.

Her desk, usually a laminated shrine to productivity, now looked like a crime scene sketched by a caffeinated squirrel. Pens wandered aimlessly. Folders—color-coded, thank you very much—lay flopped open like they'd given up on life.

"You absolutely need the deposit by tomorrow," she asked, already juggling two email windows. "Not the end of the week like we originally discussed? Because Friday is what our contract says."

A text from Tess lit up her phone for the fourth time in three minutes.

> Tess: Brand consistent visual = flower girls in cleats. We'll lay turf runners to prevent scuffs, clear liability with legal, and loop equipment for sizing.

Fifth time.

> Tess: I'll cover field protection and waivers.

Lucky number sixth time.

> Tess: If it's a no, tell me fast. I'll redirect.

"I'm afraid our supplier has changed their timeline," the rep on Zoom replied apologetically. "With the current supply chain issues, we can't hold the items without a confirmed payment."

Of course they had. She took a breath. "And you're only now sharing this? Twenty-four hours before you suddenly need payment?"

The rep sounded genuinely sorry. "I understand your position. If it helps, we can offer a small discount for the inconvenience."

Well, wasn't that generous?

Piper took a sip of her long-forgotten coffee, wincing as the cold liquid hit her taste buds. "I'll get those funds transferred today. But I'll need the discount offer in writing. And confirmation once you receive payment."

One week in and she needed a pitcher of margaritas.

The call ended, so it was on to the next issue.

Flipping open her planning binder gave Piper an unreasonable sense of control.

Color-coded tabs and aggressive sticky notes were her

ride-or-die. But right now, every to-do page looked like it had been attacked with angry red tabs and neon Post-its.

The wedding timeline had compressed overnight due to a "critical team scheduling conflict." Tess had oh-so-casually announced before sunrise, like she was reading the weather.

Even worse, Drake's availability for pre-wedding publicity was now practically non-existent.

"Forty-two days out," she muttered, pressing cold palms to overheated cheeks before giving herself a good shake. "And I've got a horse as a ring bearer, a full-blown media campaign, and Tess thinking that rustic means Swarovski hay bales."

One of the other junior planners walked past her office, shot a quick look inside, then executed a flawless eye-avert per corporate etiquette.

Piper's phone blared, slicing through the low hum of her cursed career.

Oh good. The cake lady.

"Ms. Daws? I'm so sorry, but we've hit a slight, um, complication with the wedding cake design." The woman's voice wobbled dangerously. "The edible glitter—there's been some cross contamination with almond oil. I'm trying to work it out with the supplier, but the—

"Timeline," Piper finished for her, forehead thunking onto the cool laminate of her desk, which did absolutely nothing to soothe the white-hot stress pouring out of her ears. "There has to be a way to get more glitter in time."

"I've called every supplier I know. Nothing matches the Stallions' exact royal blue. There's blue...but it's lighter than you'd want. Or darker."

"Any chance we switch it up entirely? Something else with the same vibe?"

"I'm trying," the baker groaned. "It's not working."

Deep breath. Then another.

"Don't worry. We've got this," Piper said, trying to stay calm. "I'll look into it and get back to you."

Reaching for her binder yet again, her hand bumped a stack of glossy Directors of Interment and Cremation Knowledge brochures, sending them tumbling off the shelf.

Before she could wrangle them back into a stack, a knock pulled her gaze upward to Zach standing there. His navy Henley made his eyes impossibly bluer and he held what looked to be a smoothie, if she had to guess.

Her pulse did weird, unprofessional things.

Down girl.

She'd been dealing with glitter-mageddon and she hadn't exactly been in contact with the bride's hot-as-hell brother.

Maybe it was witchcraft. Maybe it was hormones. Either way, her shoulders felt noticeably lighter and the clutter manageable.

"You look like you're planning a military coup instead of a wedding," he said, eyeing her disaster-zone desk.

"At this point," Piper replied, gesturing at her phone as it buzzed again, the vibration sending a pen rolling across her desk, "a coup would be easier. At least then I'd get a cool uniform."

Zach invited himself in, dropping to the chair across from her.

Piper's eyes darted to the smoothie in his hand, lingering there like it was a long-lost love. The straw squeaked obnoxiously against the lid as he took a sip.

"What?" he asked, wiping his mouth like he hadn't committed a beverage crime in her presence.

"Nothing," she said, shaking it off.

"You were making a face," he said, cocking an eyebrow.

"I wasn't making a face," Piper lied, definitely making a face.

"You have the 'I'm so hungry I could eat my stapler' face. My sister perfected it."

Brushing his comment off, Piper folded her hands on the desk. "What can I do for you, anyway?"

"Thought you might be ready for reinforcements," he said.

"What I need is a miracle. Or a time machine." Her gaze flicked back to the smoothie again, the condensation on the cup shimmering.

"When's the last time you ate?" he asked.

She squinted, clearly grappling with the vague memory of what might have counted as her last meal.

"Here." He slid the smoothie toward her, its plastic bottom carving a charming little space through all the paperwork. "You need it more than I do."

Their fingers brushed. Just for a second. Just enough to fire off a spark right into her brain's short-circuit center. Please, oh please, let her face not be broadcasting that little zap to him.

"Blueberry kale, but it tastes better than it sounds," he said, like that was enough to sell any human on drinking juiced garden clippings.

"I don't think that would actually be hard." Her nose scrunched like it had a mind of its own.

He nudged the cup closer. Barely half an inch, but it felt a lot like pressure. "C'mon, try it. I can get something else, but you're gonna want to deal with that blood sugar crash before you yell at inanimate objects."

"I'm fine."

A hard blink from him.

The translation? Girl, no, you're not.

Truth be told, she was hungry enough that her stapler was starting to look like a snack. Blueberry kale shouldn't have sounded good, but in that moment? Even something labeled "Organic Sod Grass Delight" would've gotten a second glance.

"Fine," she muttered, giving the straw a grumpy but willing tug. Cold, sweet-tart goodness rolled across her taste buds. Shockingly tolerable. "Thanks."

Silence filled the space while she continued sipping—the

quiet disturbed only by the distant hum of office chatter. He didn't say a word, probably because he knew better. She didn't, either, mostly because she was busy trying not to inhale the whole thing in one gulp.

"Tess's mandated glitter for the cake got almond cross-contamination," she said, finally. "I freaking hate almonds."

The venom in the last part might've been too much, especially since almonds weren't the enemy. But still. Screw almonds.

Tilting her head back, she stared at the ceiling like it might cave in. When she looked down again, she expected Zach to be laughing at her, but his expression held something else.

Understanding? Maybe even admiration?

That couldn't be right.

"Can I see the binder?" he said, gently, but already reaching for it.

Their hands collided as they both moved for it at the same time. Piper pulled back quickly, the brief contact leaving her fingertips tingling in a way that was entirely too distracting, the warmth of his skin lingering on hers.

He waited a beat, letting her make the call. Could he have it or not?

Much as she wanted to snatch it back and hiss, "mine", the patience in Zach's expression lessened her resolve.

"You color-coded by urgency and vendor? That's impressive."

"Don't mock the tabs," she warned, eyes narrowing slightly.

"I'm not. I'm genuinely afraid of them."

She hated that having him there helped. Even worse, she kind of liked that he noticed she had a system.

"The DJ company just bailed on us for some influencer named—" she checked her email, the aggressive clicking of her mouse punctuating her frustration—"Kimberly Splitz."

"Ah, yes. Famous for her eyebrow tutorials and dating a C-list reality star." Zach's dimple appeared.

"I have no idea who she is."

Zach nodded at the screen. "Let me handle a replacement."

Eyebrows arching suspiciously, she gave him a once-over. "What do you mean 'handle a replacement'?"

"I mean," he said, casually flipping a plastic tab like it was no big deal, "I might know a guy. I'll check into it."

Her control freak instincts screamed, warning her not to give up the reins. But drowning with no floatie in sight, she found herself eyeing the life preserver he offered.

"A perk of awkwardly standing in the corner at my brothers' weddings."

"You're serious?"

"Totally. And before you ask: I have zero idea on the glitter sitch. Not even the edible kind. But Babushka's back in town in a few days," he said casually, snapping to the next tab with authority.

"Oh good. That's what I need. Actual fire," Piper groaned. The sparks flying anytime he was around? Already a hazard.

"She's probably not going to light actual fires," he said with a smirk. "But she is definitely going to get involved. Trust me, she has an uncontaminated edible glitter supplier."

"And how do you know that?"

"She has one of everything. Sometimes two." Zach hesitated, then added more quietly. "I don't know where she buys edible glitter, but she gets it."

"That would be great," Piper said, meaning it.

"I'm the youngest of four and I don't always feel like I'm heard. But Babushka is the one who always listens. I listen back, and that's how I know some of her tricks."

Fingers hovering over the keyboard, Piper froze. All the humming background noise landed like dust in the room.

"My mom's a professional at not listening," she murmured, more to the blinking cursor than to him. "You get really good at planning things when it's the only way to make someone hear you."

They worked in tandem for the next half hour, his presence an emotional Xanax cutting the overwhelming down to only... whelming. Somewhere during the spreadsheet-loading saga, their chairs drifted closer. Close enough that if she wanted to count his eyelashes—hypothetically—she could.

"You're kind of a genius when you're spiraling," he said smoothly. "I mean that as a compliment."

"Thanks," she replied automatically.

Honestly, though, why was that like the nicest thing anyone had ever said to her?

A sharp ping from her laptop set off a reflexive flinch.

New email from: Tess
Subject: Urgent: New Scheduling Conflict
Move the wedding to 3 p.m. instead of 6. Broadcast window shifted. Security staffing better at 3pm. Golden-hour portraits still possible with a first look.

Greaaat.

She pushed a strand of hair behind her ear.

"Zach?" she asked, closing her laptop with the delicacy of someone resisting the urge to throw it against the wall. "I'm definitely cursed."

He chuckled like she'd made a joke.

And okay, maybe it sounded like one.

But for Piper? She swallowed hard and tucked that same strand of hair again.

This wasn't a punchline.

CHAPTER 6

PIPER

Piper placed her keys on the hook by the door. The hook she'd installed after twelve separate instances of her roommate losing her keys. Then she let out an exhale that felt like it had been trapped in her lungs all day.

"I'm home," she called, toeing off her heels and lining them up perfectly on the shoe rack by her front door. Each pair in its precise spot, organized by color, then heel height. It was a small thing, but after a day of dealing with everything at her office, these little rituals of order kept her sane.

"Is that you making sensible shoe noises?" Shelby called from the living room, her voice carrying over the low murmur of the television. "Or did you go with glitter again today?"

Glitter. It'd been glitter ever since she slipped on Zach's key fob and got stuck in the damn gum.

She rounded the corner to find Shelby sprawled across their couch, surrounded by a nest of script pages, highlighters, and at least three empty mugs. The faint aroma of Shelby's citrusy perfume and the essential oils she loved to diffuse mingled in the air. As an aspiring screenwriter and part-time barista, Shelby was Piper's opposite in almost every way. Where Piper preferred control, Shelby was chaotic, spontaneous, and perpetually running late.

Yet, somehow, they'd been roommates for three years and counting.

The apartment she shared with Shelby was like a visual manifestation of their personalities. Piper had added a pale wool rug, kept her bookshelf color-coded, and kept a tidy desk where each pen had its own cup.

Everything Shelby owned was a riot of color. She had canvases leaning against the wall, bins spilling art supplies, and a jungle of plants in various stages of survival.

Somehow, the arrangement worked for them both.

"I brought you a snack." Piper held up the smoothie she'd grabbed for Shelby on the way home.

"I hope there's wine in that cup. Because if 'snack' means pureed vegetables, I'm officially disowning you as a roommate." Shelby frowned.

"It's Tuesday," Piper replied, placing the cup on her side of the coffee table.

"Wine is for Thursdays and special occasions," Shelby groaned. "You and your schedule."

As different as they were, Shelby was the only person who truly understood Piper.

Piper grabbed the bag of actual potato chips she'd hidden in a pile of Shelby's laundry last week. She dug through the pile. She figured the chips would be a little reward for Shell if she folded something.

Shelby eyed her suspiciously and moved directly in the middle of the sofa, like it was her personal mission to blur all boundaries.

"Saving for a special occasion," Piper muttered, cracking open the bag with a loud pop and releasing the salty, savory scent of the chips. "Day from hell qualifies."

"Spill," Shelby demanded, grabbing a handful of chips and biting into one with a crisp crunch. "The D.I.C.K. guys giving you shit? Or the PR lady driving you up a wall?"

Shelby closed her eyes and practically moaned as she chewed on a chip.

"The Directors of Interment and Cremation Knowledge continues to go well." Though they were seriously going to have to workshop that acronym. "And Tess continues to be Tess."

Shelby lifted her eyebrows the slightest bit. "Then what's up with the too-attractive-for-his-own-good underwear designer helper?"

"It's not him. Zach's been great." Piper paused, searching for a suitably professional description that wouldn't reveal how distractingly attractive she found Zach. "I just feel like everything's complicated."

Shelby tilted her head to the side. "Complicated like 'he wants to change all the wedding plans' or complicated like 'you want to climb him like a tree'?"

"Shelby." Piper threw the decorative pillow at her room-mate's head, a quiet thud as it missed its target.

"That's not a denial," Shelby sang, after she deftly dodged the pillow.

Piper busied herself adjusting the perfectly aligned stack of coasters on the coffee table. "He's just being so helpful and everything else is a mess."

"Oh hell, you really are totally into him." Shelby fist-pumped in the air. "Finally. It's been, what, two years since Dave the Douchebag?"

"Twenty-six months," Piper corrected automatically. "And I'm not 'into' anyone. I'm planning his sister's wedding, which makes any of my aesthetic appreciation or desired tree climbing completely inappropriate."

Anything Shelby was going to say got cut short by three sharp knocks at their door.

They exchanged glances.

Shelby raised an eyebrow. "Expecting someone?"

"Absolutely not. Tuesday is takeout and trash TV night." Piper approached the door cautiously, peering through the peephole, the cool metal circle pressed against her eye. "I haven't ordered food yet. Did you?"

Shelby shook her head.

On the other side of the threshold stood a small, silver-haired woman in an emerald green coat, carrying what appeared to be multiple Tupperware-style containers.

"Hello?" Piper called through the door. "Can I help you?"

"Open door. Arms full. Food getting cold," came the reply in a thick Russian accent, slightly muffled through the wood.

Oh no. No. No. Understanding dawned like a shovel upside the head.

Except, Zach's babushka didn't get back for three more days. Piper knew this because Zach had told her. They couldn't move forward with the stupid glitter situation until Babushka got back and…

Piper hesitated, but Shelby was already shouldering past her. "What kind of food?"

She swung the door open wide, the hinges squeaking slightly.

Zach's babushka bustled past without waiting for a proper invitation, bringing with her a wave of delicious aromas— garlic, roasted meat, and something warm and spicy that made Piper's mouth water instantly.

Piper sensed her evening plans were crumbling like a donut down the garbage disposal.

A Russian grandmother was now pushing their table from the wall to the center of the room.

"Too many stairs," the woman announced. "Building needs elevator. Not good for knees."

Shelby tossed Piper a confused glance.

"I am Nadzieja," the woman announced proudly, moving her containers onto the table.

The older woman paused her rummaging to fix Piper with an observant look. "You are Piper. The one planning my Anna's vedding."

"And you're Zach's grandmother."

The pyrotechnician and good listener.

"And Anna's grandmother. But yes. Zach is my grandson. You call me Babushka. Only people I don't like call me Nadzieja."

Piper shifted on her feet. "Um, I'm sorry, but how did you—"

"How did I know where you live? *Tch.*" Babushka waved dismissively. "I ask Anna who asks Drake who calls someone who tells him. Not difficult." She paused, once more doing that watching-Piper-closely thing that made her feel like she was getting an x-ray with no lead apron. "Zachary mentioned you. Said you are very organized. Very *interesting* voman."

Piper wasn't sure whether to be flattered or worried.

The old woman looked around the apartment, nodding approvingly at Shelby's chaotic piles. "Good. Balance."

"I like her," Shelby said, eyes bright with the kind of enthusiasm she generally reserved for characters she wanted to steal for her screenplays. Piper recognized that look. Babushka would probably end up immortalized in Shelby's next draft, quirks and all.

"You are smart girl. This is good." Babushka nodded approvingly, then reached out to pinch Piper's cheek. "Good to meet you."

Before Piper could respond, Babushka was rearranging the cushions on their couch.

"Sit," Babushka commanded, gesturing to the table. "Food first, then ve talk vedding."

"Oh, I don't—" Piper tried to protest.

"Food first," Babushka insisted, her tone not allowing for

any argument. "Hungry people make bad decisions. Ve cannot plan a vedding vith bad decisions."

"She's not wrong." Shelby had zero problem sitting down and opening the Tupperware.

"Marriage is like this apartment," Babushka observed, gesturing around. "One neat, one messy. Secret is finding person whose mess fits vith your neat."

"We're not married," Piper clarified quickly. "Only roommates."

"Piper's allergic to marriage," Shelby supplied helpfully, serving herself a bowl of stew with absolute delight. "Her parents' divorce was like the Titanic hitting an iceberg made of lawyers. And then it happened a few more times."

"Shelby." Piper hissed.

Babushka merely nodded sagely. "Parents' bad example doesn't mean the institution is bad. Just means they did vrong." She set a bowl in front of Piper with surprising gentleness. "My husband, God rest soul, ve fight like cats for over fifty years. Secret is you go to bed mad. Feel your feelings. Then get over it."

Piper shifted uncomfortably. "I'm really only the wedding planner, Ms. Dvornakov—"

"Vy do you call me 'Ms. Dvornakov' like I am a stranger at the grocery store? You don't like me?"

"Babushka," Piper amended. "I'm helping coordinate the wedding. I'm not really involved in the big-picture philosophy of marriage."

Babushka's eyes twinkled knowingly. "No such thing as 'just' vedding. You shape day that shapes lives." She settled herself into a chair, somehow making the IKEA furniture look like a throne.

That's how Piper found herself at her own dining table, watching in bewilderment as Babushka settled right in.

"This is amazing," Shelby mumbled through a full mouth. "Like, seriously, amazing."

Piper had to agree.

"Old family recipe. Secret ingredient." Babushka winked. "Now, ve discuss vedding. I have opinions."

Shelby caught Piper's eye across the table and mouthed, "She's amazing."

"Ve must have Russian traditions. Anna is sveet girl, but she knows nothing of proper celebration." Babushka leaned forward. "Drake is good boy, but American veddings? No proper customs."

"This wedding doesn't seem to be following *any* customs," Piper said carefully.

Babushka made a dismissive noise. "Young people don't know vhat makes good marriage foundation. That's vhy I help."

Funny, that sounded eerily like what Piper's mother had said around marriage number three. Turned out middle-aged people didn't know either.

"The thing is," Piper tried again, "my job is to create the wedding that *Anna* and *Drake* tell me to."

Along with their publicist, but she didn't need to mention that part.

"And they vant happy marriage, yes? This comes from proper ceremony." Babushka fixed Piper with a knowing look. "Your parents had American vedding?"

Piper blinked, caught off guard. "Yes, but—"

"And they are still married?"

The question landed like a stone in still water.

"No," Piper admitted quietly.

"Mmm." Babushka nodded, as if this confirmed every-thing. "No traditions."

Shelby's eyes darted between them, fascinated.

"My parents had a courthouse wedding and they're still disgustingly in love after thirty years," she offered.

"Exception," Babushka declared, the heavy scent of her

rose perfume fighting it out with Shelby's citrus-scented diffuser. "Not rule."

Piper took a deep breath. "Babushka, while I appreciate your insights, we've already begun making plans that—"

"Plans change. Vedding is living thing." Babushka waved her hands expressively.

Piper opened her mouth to protest that she had schedules and processes and that surprise visits from relatives weren't part of her carefully sketched timeline, when somebody else knocked on their door.

"Popular night," Shelby observed, moving to answer it.

When she swung the door open, Zach stood in their doorway, slightly out of breath. "Piper. I need to warn you about—"

His eyes found Babushka at the table, seemingly rearranging the salt and pepper shakers to demonstrate her vision for the head table, the ceramic pieces making tiny clinks against the wooden surface.

His shoulders slumped. "Fuck. I'm too late."

CHAPTER 7

42 DAYS UNTIL ANNA
& DRAKE'S WEDDING

PIPER

"Ve don't use that vord." Babushka wrinkled her nose. "Come, Zachary. You are late for dinner."

"Nobody invited me to dinner," Zach said, still standing in the doorway looking between Piper, Shelby, and his grandmother with an expression that suggested he was calculating exactly how much damage had already been done.

"Nonsense. Family alvays invited," Babushka declared. "Sit. Eat. We discuss vedding."

Piper shot him what she hoped was a desperate look. His eyes met hers briefly, and the sympathetic quirk of his mouth sent an unexpected flutter through her chest.

"Babushka," Zach sighed, stepping inside and closing the door behind him. His arm brushed against Piper's as he passed, the warmth lingering on her skin. "How did you even find Piper's apartment?"

"I have my vays," Babushka replied mysteriously, then immediately added, "Anna gave me the address. Said you might be here, too. Since you've mentioned your fondness for the pretty vedding planner many, many times."

Piper's cheeks warmed as Shelby's eyebrows migrated right up toward her hairline. The idea that Zach talked about her made her pulse go faster.

"I mentioned she is organized," Zach said quickly, giving Piper an apologetic look. "And good at her job."

"Like good Russian vorkhorse," Babushka announced.

He winced.

"Horse?" Piper repeated flatly.

"Is compliment," Babushka assured her. "Strong, proud, reliable. Not like lazy American ponies."

The not-usually cramped space of her apartment suddenly felt stifling.

"Zachary says you vill make perfect vedding for Anna and Drake," Babushka continued, patting the chair next to her. "Sit."

Zach started to sit but Babushka pulled the chair closer at the last second, nearly landing him on the carpet instead.

"Too close to corner," Babushka patted his shoulder. "Sitting at corner of the table—brings seven years vithout marriage."

"It's a silly superstition," Zach assured, sliding his chair closer to Piper's. Close enough that their knees touched under the table. Piper didn't move away, surprising even herself.

"This is problem," Babushka said firmly. "Ve need Russian traditions for proper marriage."

"I don't think—" Piper tried.

"My husband and I vere so much in love for sixty-two years until he decided to die," Babushka said. "You know vhy? Traditional ceremony."

Piper had no idea what to say to that, so she said, "My parents had a traditional ceremony the first time. It didn't stop them from divorcing when my dad decided to try yoga with the instructor in her bedroom. My mother sank his fishing boat in revenge."

Shelby choked on her stew. "You never told me about the boat."

"Not my go-to party story," Piper said entirely too chipper and painfully aware of Zach studying her with new interest.

Babushka recovered quickly. "For Anna, ve need doves. At least twelve."

"Absolutely not," Piper said firmly, sitting straighter. This was her professional territory, and animals were a hard stop. "They're unpredictable, they make a mess, and half the outdoor venues in Denver have restrictions against bird releases."

Rather than being offended, Babushka seemed pleased by Piper's pushback. "Good. You have backbone. Important for vedding planner. Vhat about vodka fountain?"

"Insurance nightmare," Piper replied automatically.

"Tablitsa Sud'by, then," Babushka countered.

"What's that?" Shelby asked.

"Traditional Dvornakov custom. The Table of Fate vhere ve seat all single friends for potential romance."

"That's actually not a terrible idea," Piper admitted, her mind already arranging seating charts. "It's essentially targeted seating arrangements. I can agree to that one."

"See?" Babushka beamed triumphantly at Zach. "She understands tradition. This is vhy I come to help."

Zach, who had been watching this exchange with a mixture of horror and fascination, finally found his voice. "Babushka, I'm sure Piper appreciates your input, but she has a process—"

"Process." Babushka scoffed. "Marriage is not process. It is a journey."

"The journey requires a roadmap," Piper insisted. "And in this case, the bride and groom create the plan."

"Vith guidance from vise elders," Babushka added.

"And the Stallions football team," Zach added.

Piper looked at Zach again, a silent plea for intervention she hoped to hell he understood.

"Babushka," Zach said gently. "Piper is very good at what she does. This is Anna and Drake's day."

"Pah. Young people need guidance," Babushka declared. She turned to Shelby, "You have good energy. Creative spirit." She gestured at Piper, "This one, she'll loosen up."

"That's what I keep telling her." Shelby agreed enthusiastically.

"I'm perfectly loose," Piper protested, painfully conscious of Zach's amusement.

The synchronized skeptical looks from all three of the others made her slightly reconsider that stance. "I mean, I'm appropriately flexible when the situation calls for it."

Zach's eyebrow raised slightly, and the hint of a smile playing at his lips made her face grow warm again.

"Like ved—" Babushka started.

"Like professional situations," Piper cut in, seizing the opportunity, "Actually, I do need your help. We're trying to find some edible glitter suppliers for the wedding cake. We need a… a very specific color. Zach mentioned something about your connections?"

Babushka's eyes lit up. "Ah. You want svyataya iskra. The holy spark. Very important. Brings prosperity to the marriage."

"It's not actually traditional," Zach clarified. "Babushka just loves anything that sparkles."

"Is beautiful, like stars in night sky," Babushka insisted. "Marriage needs little sparkle, yes? Do not vorry. I know who to call. Ve vill go tomorrow to see him."

"I can't. I'm accompanying Anna and Drake to see the potential venue tomorrow." She looked pointedly at Babushka. "Only the three of us, as planned."

"Vhat venue?" Babushka asked.

"The Falcon Hotel downtown," Piper answered before she could stop herself. "They have a rooftop terrace with mountain views."

Babushka's eyes lit up. "Perfect. I'll be there."

"That's not necessary—" Piper began.

"I insist," Babushka said firmly. "Russian mother of bride must approve venue. I'll bring Anna's mother."

"That won't work. I already have meetings scheduled there with another event," Piper said firmly. "Then I'm meeting Drake and Anna."

"Vhat event?" Babushka demanded.

"The D.I.C.K.?" Shelby asked innocently.

Zach choked while Shelby dissolved into giggles.

"It's the Directors of Interment and Cremation Knowledge," Piper clarified hastily. "And it's a completely respectable industry committee for funeral directors."

"Ah, yes. I know this group. Good people—except for Mortimer. I have things to say to that man. Lots of things." Babushka's expression darkened.

"Is that Morty? Your ex-boyfriend?" Zach asked. "Pistol Polly's Morty?"

"Pistol Polly's Morty?" Piper asked. Pistol Polly's was a local gentleman's club known for their massive steak and topless dancers.

"Story for another day." Zach shivered. "Ask Jase and Heather. They'll tell you."

"Yes. Morty." Babushka flicked her fingers and let out a sharp *pfft*. "If I see him, he vill run. And I vill catch him."

Piper resolved never to mention Mr. Thornhill—Morty—to Babushka ever again. Or allow them to be in the same room together.

"Are you certain you vant funeral directors at a vedding venue?" Babushka looked skeptical.

"It's a multi-purpose event space," Piper explained. "I'll be there for their meeting, and then I can check the terrace for Anna and Drake while I'm already on site. It's efficient."

"I like efficiency," Babushka nodded approvingly. "Though vedding and funeral in same place is not good luck. Not custom."

"It's a different floor," Piper assured her. "And churches co-mingle the two on the regular."

"Still, ve should see this place," Babushka insisted. "Make sure it has proper energy."

Before Piper could protest, Zach jumped in, his knee pressing more firmly against hers. "Actually, Babushka, I was hoping you could help me at the shop tomorrow. I've got a new design that's giving me trouble."

Babushka looked torn. "You never vant my help."

"I always want your help," Zach disagreed solemnly. "I need your eye for detail." He turned to Piper. "She's the one who taught me to sew to begin with."

Piper could have kissed him for the rescue. Not that she wanted to kiss him. Obviously.

"I cannot help you," Babushka said. "Tess is checking venue also for security and broadcast restrictions tomorrow. She told me vhen she invited your mother. Vhich means I come, too. I hope I see Morty vhile ve are there."

Piper and Zach exchanged alarmed glances.

"Morty aside, how do you know *Tess*?" Piper asked, trying to keep her voice level.

"How do I know anything? It's vhat I do," Babushka shrugged. "She says she must approve all locations for publicity reasons and security reasons and lots of other reasons. I stopped listening."

"Babushka?" Zach prodded. "How do you know her, though?"

"Her grandmother is Peggy. Ve are friends." Babushka brushed a stray crumb off the tablecloth.

"Well, that's cozy, isn't it." Piper pursed her lips. How

many more ways would her personal and professional life tangle until she couldn't tell where one ended and the other began?

"When is Tess planning to check the venue?" Zach asked.

"Tomorrow afternoon. Same time as your meeting with Drake and Anna. This is all very simple, really. You're complicating things with questions."

Piper's mind raced. She'd specifically slotted this time to hear Anna and Drake's ideas without the noise of everyone else.

"I could go with you," Zach offered suddenly, his voice dropping lower as he leaned closer.

The offer hung in the air between them.

The thought of having him there, on her side playing defense? She could use his assistance.

"That's actually a good idea," Piper admitted.

"I have them occasionally," Zach replied in a way that made Piper believe he wasn't talking about weddings or venues or any of that.

Oh. Okay, then.

"I want you to succeed," he said simply, in a voice meant only for her.

"Then it's settled," Babushka watched the exchange with obvious interest, her eyes darting between them. "Yes, good plan. Ve all go."

"We all go," Zach agreed.

"Now, dessert." Babushka clapped her hands together. "I bring ptichye moloko."

"Bird's milk," Zach translated. "It's a souffle cake."

"Sounds amazing," Shelby said enthusiastically, standing to help Babushka.

As they bustled to the kitchen, Zach leaned closer to Piper.

"I'm sorry about this," he whispered. "She's a force of nature."

"I noticed," Piper replied. "Is your entire family this invasive?"

"Afraid so. Anna and I are actually the calm ones."

"Oh," Piper muttered.

"Look on the bright side," Zach offered, his voice low and surprisingly kind. "At least Babushka likes you."

"How can you tell?"

"She fed you," he said simply. "Babushka only feeds people she approves of."

Despite herself, Piper experienced a small glow of satisfaction.

"And for what it's worth," Zach added, his voice dropping, "I never compared you to a horse. But I did tell Anna that you're the most competent person I've ever met. Also, one of the most stubborn."

"Is *that* a compliment?" Piper asked, suddenly very aware of how close they were sitting.

Their eyes met, and something in his gaze made her breath catch.

"Definitely," he replied, his fingers lightly brushing against hers again. "I enjoy knowing where I stand with someone."

"And where do you stand with me?" The words slipped out before she could stop them.

"I'm standing right here." Zach's smile turned thoughtful.

Babushka returned with dessert before Piper could respond. The stark white confection trembled slightly as she set it down, and, holy crap, Piper drew in a sharp breath. That dessert one-hundred thousand percent was shaped like a penis.

"Eat," Babushka commanded, slicing off the tip. "Then ve talk more about vedding, yes?"

CHAPTER 8

41 DAYS UNTIL ANNA
& DRAKE'S WEDDING

PIPER

"As you can see from the projections, we're expecting at least a twenty percent increase in attendance this year." Piper clicked to the next slide, suppressing a yawn that threatened to escape thanks to the late night before. "Your annual symposium has grown steadily each year and, with the addition of the new eco-burial panel, we expect even stronger numbers."

The conference room hummed with quiet approval from the twelve funeral directors seated around the polished mahogany table.

Piper had arranged them strategically to keep the more traditional directors separated from the more contemporary "green burial" advocates. She hadn't been entirely certain what to do with Mr. Thornhill—Mortimer. On the fly, she put him with the green burial group hoping to minimize pre-conference friction until they'd established more camaraderie.

Her head throbbed dully, a souvenir from Babushka's homemade vodka that had materialized from her purse after dessert last night.

What had started as a simple toast had evolved into a three-hour Russian cultural immersion, complete with toasts to Piper's 'strong legs.'

Piper refilled her water glass, willing it to be coffee instead.

"Moving on to accommodations," Piper continued, surreptitiously massaging her temple when she turned to point at the screen. "This hotel should be able to reserve our full block of rooms, including the premium corner suites for board members."

The Falcon was the perfect venue for both the D.I.C.K. symposium and potentially Anna's wedding. It was upscale but not ostentatious, centrally located, easy to work with, and featured that coveted rooftop terrace with the panoramic mountain views.

"Will we have exclusive access to the rooftop for our welcome reception?" Ms. Wilder, the association's treasurer, asked.

"Absolutely," Piper confirmed. "From seven to ten on the first night. The space will be transformed with green uplighting to match your new branding, and I've been thinking we could set up telescopes for stargazing. I like to think it'll be a subtle nod to your industry's connection to the eternal.

Eek. That earned appreciative murmurs around the table.

The little dopamine hit and internal squee Piper experienced was like a nice internal pat on the back.

This was why Piper excelled at corporate events. She understood the delicate balance between acknowledging the funeral industry's somber purpose while creating experiences that didn't feel morbid.

They broke for a quick recess. She stayed in the room while the others all stretched their legs and chatted.

Her phone vibrated in her pocket.

She discreetly checked it under the table.

Zach: Headed your way soon

Piper: Yup! See u @ 3

Zach: I'll bring you a coffee. That vodka is
no joke

Despite her headache, Piper felt her lips twitch. She liked him. Really liked him.

Piper: Unprofessional to mention my
hangover

Zach: Practical to treat it

Piper: Skinny vanilla latte as big as they can
make it

Zach: See you at 3, Cinderella.

That nickname again. Piper felt a little flutter of... something she wasn't going to analyze during a professional meeting.

"Ms. Daws?" Mr. Martin called to her. "What are your personal thoughts on the memorial technology showcase?"

Piper smoothly pocketed her phone. "I believe it's essential. The digital afterlife management platforms are revolutionizing your industry. I think you should consider allocating the entire west wing of the exhibition hall for interactive demonstrations."

Piper circled the table, distributing folders containing the information they needed to review for the next part of their session together.

The familiar rhythm of a well-organized corporate event settled her.

This was where she belonged—managing conferences with clear objectives and predictable outcomes. Here in this space, there were zero chaotic wedding spectacles or emotions running high with family members showing up at all hours with purse vodka.

"Once we're all settled again let's discuss options for the keynote speakers," Piper continued, advancing to the next slide for when they regrouped. "I thought we would invite Dr. Montgomery from the university's Thanatology Department, and Jake Winters, founder of Forever Digital Footprint? If they're available, they would be phenomenal."

"I'm so glad we made the right choice in hiring you." Mortimer flashed a huge toothy grin that sort of made her squirm uncomfortably.

While the directors all poured water and ate their snacks, she finished up her room reset. She refused to let her mind wander to the upcoming wedding venue assessment with Zach and his gallon of coffee.

She didn't think about how she needed to be thorough—checking sunset angles, acoustics, capacity, and power outlet access. No, she didn't think about that because after Babushka left last night, she'd created a comprehensive checklist that accounted for all Tess's requirements while still prioritizing Anna and Drake's preferences so she wouldn't *have* to think about it.

The rest of the D.I.C.K. planning session went smoothly, and it was nearly two when Piper moved on to finalizing the budget options.

"Now, if you'll direct your attention to page seven of your packets, you'll find the budget breakdown from last year's—" Piper's sentence died as movement at the conference room's glass door caught her eye.

Through the frosted logo of The Falcon, she made out a familiar silhouette in the lobby.

Tall. Athletic build. Casual stance that somehow managed to look both relaxed and purposeful.

Zach.

Way too early.

Her headache intensified as she watched him charm the receptionist at the front desk, who was now pointing in the direction of her meeting room.

"Ms. Daws?" Mr. Martin prompted. "The budget?"

"Yes," Piper nodded, dragging her attention back to the meeting.

No. Absolutely not. This is NOT happening right now.

"I think we can negotiate a five percent reduction in the audio-visual package while actually upgrading the equipment." She continued the discussion on autopilot while keeping her eye on Zach through the glass.

The D.I.C.K. board members nodded approvingly at her budgetary thoughts when Zach finally turned toward the conference room.

His eyes met hers through the glass, and his face broke into that infuriatingly fascinating smile that had been forefront in her mind since their first sidewalk encounter.

He held up what was clearly a coffee carrier in one hand and mimicked knocking with the other. Then he winked at her, and Piper's stomach did a completely unprofessional flip.

"Is everything alright, Ms. Daws?" Mr. Martin asked, following Piper's distracted gaze.

Piper fixed her professional smile. "Absolutely. I just... I know we're nearly done here today, but there's someone I need to... there's just a little..." She swallowed past the sudden nervous lump in her throat. "I need a five-minute recess."

Thankfully, they all agreed, and Piper adjusted the blazer on her sea-foam-green pantsuit, mentally checking off the final items on their meeting agenda as she marched toward Zach.

"You're early," she said when she reached him, trying to keep her voice low.

Zach held up the coffee like a peace offering. Or a bribe.

Honestly, with this headache, Piper was tempted to accept either.

"Early bird gets the rooftop," he said, holding out a coffee for her. He flashed a grin like they were sharing a private joke and not standing ten feet from a room full of death-care professionals.

She reached for the cup. "You're not funny."

"I am a little funny."

Piper scanned the lobby behind him for any sign of an early Tess. Or worse—Babushka.

Zach leaned in slightly, dropping his voice. "Relax. Tess and Babushka aren't here yet. I wanted to get here and watch the door in case they come early. Your other meeting with the dead people club seemed really important and I'm pretty sure I can *accidentally* delay Babushka if I tell her I have a girlfriend."

"You have a girlfriend?" Piper asked, her heart not liking that thought one bit.

"No, but Babushka doesn't know that."

"You think that'll stall her?"

He gave her a look. "You've met Babushka."

Piper took a long, blessed sip of her latte and closed her eyes for half a second. Heaven. Liquid life support.

"Okay," she muttered, voice tight. "I have approximately three minutes before I need to herd my D.I.C.K.s back to their seats, so if you're going to be helpful, be helpful and *go watch the door.*"

"I'm going to go do that. I'm going to be *extremely* helpful," Zach said the words like a caress.

That gave her pause as her tummy fluttered at all the helpful things this man could probably do for her.

Mortimer strolled by, flanked by two other D.I.C.K. members. All three of them obviously eavesdropping.

Zach straightened instinctively, and as soon as Mortimer

saw him, the guy frowned and scurried back to the conference room.

What on earth was that all about?

"Ah, Ms. Daws," Mr. Martin said, eyeing Zach with the wary politeness reserved for unexpected guests and shopping mall Santas. "Is this a…colleague of yours?"

Piper swallowed her concern about Mortimer. "Yes. Sort of. This is—" She turned to Zach with a desperate look. "This is Zach. He's, um… a vendor?"

That should not have sounded like a question.

"Oh? What sort of vendor?" Ms. Wilder asked, peering at Zach like she was already suspicious of his lack of a tie.

Piper opened her mouth to invent a sort-of-truth. Something safe. Something bland.

Zach beat her to it.

"I specialize in bespoke men's undergarments," he said cheerfully. "Luxury-level support for your most personal needs."

Piper coughed. Hard. "He's *kidding*. He runs a, uh, IT consulting firm. Very discreet. Helps events run smoothly behind the scenes."

Mr. Martin chuckled. "Always good to see our event coordinator so… resourceful. We'll head back in."

As the board members returned to the conference room, Piper let her forehead drop to the lid of her coffee cup.

Zach leaned in beside her. "Too much?"

"Too much," she muttered. "Definitely too much."

"Good news is, they'll never forget me."

Piper didn't respond. She simply took another sip of her coffee and sighed.

He was right. They wouldn't forget him. And, heaven help her, neither would she.

CHAPTER 9

PIPER

The Falcon Hotel's rooftop terrace sprawled with sophisticated luxury beneath a sky of blue as clear as Zach's eyes. Glass barriers edged the perimeter, offering unobstructed views of the city skyline, while strings of light bulbs crisscrossed overhead, waiting to illuminate the space after dark. Potted olive trees and lavender plants created natural dividers throughout the space, their subtle fragrance mingling beautifully with the late-afternoon air.

Piper moved toward the bar area, clipboard in hand, mentally cataloging every detail. Once the sun set, the space would transform from elegant to magical.

"So?" Zach asked as they took in the scene. "What do we think?"

Before Piper could respond, the rooftop doors swung open again.

"Sorry we're late," Drake announced, striding onto the outdoor area with a confidence that somehow made the space seem smaller. "Babushka wasn't ready."

His arm wrapped around Anna as her eyes went wide,

taking in the view. Behind them followed Tess, tapping furiously on her phone, and Babushka, who carried what appeared to be a large picnic basket. A blonde woman who must've been Zach's mom slipped through last. She was the same height as Anna and had a solid motherly presence about her. Gentle, even. She wore a comfy cardigan over a matching blouse, had florist's hands with neat crescent nails, and the kind of calm that settled a room.

"Ceremonial bread." Babushka proclaimed, holding the basket aloft. "Ve must test acoustics vith traditional Dvornakov sourdough."

"What kind of sourdough tests acoustics?" Piper asked.

"Borodinsky," Zach said as though that was an actual answer.

Anna pursed her lips. "Babushka, we talked about this..."

"I could eat." Drake raised his hand.

"You can always eat," Anna muttered, but the fondness in her voice was unmistakable.

"This is gorgeous," Anna and Zach's mom—Diana, her name was Diana—said. "It's perfection."

They did quick introductions and, while Piper braced herself for Diana to say or do something, well, *Dvornakovesque*, she didn't. The woman seemed totally normal.

"This space has several advantages," Piper began, stepping right into presentation mode. "It accommodates up to two hundred guests with the current configuration, though we could increase capacity with some adjustments to the seating arrangement."

Tess glanced up quickly from her phone. "Plan for at least two hundred to be safe. You figure with teammates, plus-ones, coaches, and staff we're already nudging that number. We can still design the aesthetic to seem intimate in photos."

"We agreed it would be intimate," Anna said, her tone tempered.

"Intimate is relative," Tess said without missing a beat. "In celebrity terms, two hundred is practically eloping."

Babushka snorted. "Elopement means bad luck. Vedding needs family vitnesses. Many, many vitnesses."

Piper caught the subtle tightening of Anna's shoulders and the way Drake automatically moved his hand up and down her back in response.

Honestly, the whole dynamic with this group was fascinating: equal parts earnest and dramatic.

"We can layer lounges and vignettes, so it photographs more intimately," Piper suggested.

"Piper's right," Diana assured. "We can make two hundred feel like eighty with the right clusters. I've squeezed receptions into tighter greenhouses. It's a great idea."

Piper couldn't help it: she preened under Diana's praise.

"The afternoon sun creates shadows that might be problematic," Tess said, slicing through the moment. "I'm thinking we add a light scrim on the west side or shift the ceremony by twenty minutes. Easy enough to solve."

"Perhaps we should discuss the *pros* and cons?" Piper suggested, attempting to steer the conversation. "The location offers incredible views and natural light for photography. The indoor ballroom connected to it gives us flexibility in case of weather issues. And I've talked to the hotel about bringing in your personal caterer. There are fees, of course, but nothing out of the ordinary."

"Food very important," Babushka nodded. "No skimpy American portions."

People said a lot about American portions, but calling them skimpy was not generally the issue.

"What about the cons?" Drake asked, his focus surprisingly sharp for someone who'd been eyeing Babushka's breadbasket since she arrived.

"Aside from the lighting issue, privacy could be a problem," Piper admitted. "The dance floor is visible from some of the higher floors of the neighboring buildings."

"I think we can make that work in our favor. We'll want to engineer at least one dance moment that invites teammates onto the floor," Tess suggested. "Those clips perform well on social channels. And having the neighbors help with the filming from their windows isn't a bad angle at all."

"Perhaps we should get a feel for the space," Zach suggested, moving away from the group toward the edge of the venue. "Everyone spread out and see how it flows."

A good suggestion. They all dispersed.

Drake led Anna toward the far corner, speaking quietly. Tess wandered off to take light measurements with an app on her phone. Babushka gravitated to the bar area with her basket.

Zach drifted toward Piper, casually sitting on the edge of a table. "So, on a scale of one to homicidal, how are you handling the committee approach to wedding planning?"

"I'm fine," Piper said automatically, then caught his knowing look. "Fine. Seven out of ten. But I'm managing."

"For what it's worth, you're doing great."

Something about the way he said that made her want to puff out her chest and grin. Instead, she glanced over to Anna, as she traced the pattern on a marble tabletop.

"It's a good sign when the bride can envision herself in the space," Piper said, tilting her head in that direction.

"Is that wedding planner wisdom or Piper intuition?" Zach asked.

"Both," she admitted. "I think this space is a good fit. Special without being intimidating."

"Like a good first date venue," Zach mused, looking out at the mountains. "Not too formal, great view, natural conversation starters."

"I wouldn't know," Piper said dryly. "My dating history

mostly features chain restaurants and one memorable outing to a monster truck rally."

Zach's eyes widened. "Monster trucks? That doesn't seem very... you."

"It wasn't. He thought it would be 'quirky.'" She made finger quotes on the last word.

Zach's laugh was sincere. "Was it?"

Piper shook her head. "Nope."

Zach adopted an exaggerated seriousness as he puffed out his chest. "What are we looking for here exactly? Flower capacity? Champagne logistics? Optimal positions for the release of Babushka's definitely-not-happening pigeon-doves?"

Piper practically had to smother her smile. "Actually, I'm thinking about sight lines, sun angles at different times of day, and whether the electrical capacity can handle both a DJ and proper lighting so Tess can get the after-dark pictures she wants of the dance floor."

"Of course you are," Zach said, but there was no mocking in his tone, just a tender appreciation that made her stomach flutter.

"We have an audience," she murmured, looking toward Anna and Drake again.

Zach glanced over his shoulder. "Ah. The happy couple seems quite invested in our conversation."

"They probably think we're discussing wedding details."

"Or they're watching their wedding planner hitting it off with the bride's charming brother," Zach suggested, eyes twinkling.

"We are not 'hitting it off,'" Piper protested, though her traitorous cheeks warmed again. "We're having a very profes-sional discussion."

"Very professional," he agreed solemnly. "So, *professionally,* what do you think of their relationship?"

The abrupt change of subject caught Piper off guard. "Anna and Drake?"

"Yeah. You've seen a lot of couples in your line of work, right? Even if you avoid weddings."

Piper gazed across the terrace where Drake was now carefully tucking a strand of hair behind Anna's ear, his expression tender. "They seem... real," she admitted. "The way they look at each other when they think no one's watching. It's not performative."

"But that doesn't mean it will last," Zach observed, studying her carefully.

"No. It doesn't."

"No faith in happily ever after?"

Piper shrugged. "Statistics don't lie."

"Statistics don't account for everything," Zach countered. "Sometimes it's about choice. Every day choosing each other, even when it sucks."

The conviction in his voice was surprisingly moving.

"Anna likes it," Zach said with confidence. "I can tell. She keeps looking at the sunset and smiling that little secret smile she gets when she's imagining possibilities."

"You know her well."

"She's my sister. I've been reading her facial expressions since I was in diapers."

The fondness in his voice made Piper curious. "Were you close growing up?"

"Always, though we're pretty different. Anna's the steady one. Predictable career, stable relationship. I'm more..." he trailed off, searching for the right word.

"Unpredictable?" Piper suggested.

"Experimental," he corrected as his lips curved up. "I like trying new things, finding unconventional solutions. It makes me a good designer but sometimes a frustrating brother."

"And yet she clearly adores you."

"The feeling's mutual," Zach said simply. "Which is why I

want this wedding to be what *she* wants, not what's best for team publicity or team tradition."

The sincerity in his voice touched something in Piper.

"We'll make it work," Piper found herself promising, despite the committee approach.

"I believe you," Zach said, his voice dropping slightly as he moved closer. "You're pretty convincing when you get that determined look."

She became acutely aware of how close they were standing, the warmth of his arm nearly touching hers. The setting sun cast his face in a golden glow that softened his features and brought out flecks of amber in his blue eyes.

For a breathless moment, the entire venue seemed to fade away. There was just Zach, looking at her with an intensity that made her usual defenses falter. Made her want to lean in and take a taste.

He glanced briefly to her lips.

"Piper..."

Before she could reply, a sharp voice cut through their conversation, "The social media optics are excellent," Tess announced, heading for Babushka and the breadbasket.

"I'm sure the hotel will be thrilled." Piper scribbled a note on her clipboard.

"Zachary, come try bread." Babushka called from across the space where she served Drake a big slice of brown bread with butter.

"Duty calls," Zach sighed. "Somebody better save me if she tries to perform a blessing ritual with vodka like she did at Jase's wedding. I smelled like a distillery when we left."

The easy way Zach interacted with his family and the sincere affection behind his teasing increased his attractive quotient by a solid 20. Piper's focus lingered on him longer than strictly necessary as he strode toward his grandmother and Tess hustled behind.

"I think he likes you, you know," Anna said beside Piper, a knowing smile playing at her lips.

"I... that's not..." Piper fumbled.

"Of course," Anna agreed smoothly. "I just thought you should know. As his sister, I feel obligated to mention he hasn't stopped talking about 'the wedding planner with the impressive organizational skills' to anyone who will listen."

"Oh." Piper wasn't sure what else to say. "That's professional of him to notice."

Anna's laugh was gentle. "Sure, let's call it business interest. I haven't seen him this 'professionally interested' in anyone... before... ever."

Zach seemed to be attempting to translate between Babushka and Tess about something that involved a great deal of hand motions and frowning that even got Drake's attention away from the butter.

"I'm going to go... help Drake." Anna beamed as she walked toward her fiancé.

Piper moved to the quietest corner of the terrace to compile some notes, but it took no time for Tess to grab her attention and pull her from one corner to another with increasingly specific questions.

Every time she tried to rejoin Anna and Drake to get their unfiltered opinion on the various aspects of the venue, Tess intercepted with another concern about lighting, acoustics, media positioning, or how Babushka wanted the tables to be rounds while Tess preferred rectangles. Tablitsa Sud'by didn't work with rectangles, apparently. Tess didn't work with rounds.

So, there they were, at a stalemate of shapes.

Tess's phone rang.

"Legal needs me," she said, already walking away to take the call. "You've got this under control, Piper?"

Piper nodded. Of course, she had this.

Zach caught Piper's eye and gave a subtle nod toward a quiet spot by the potted palms.

The setting sun cast his profile in golden light. For a moment, she allowed herself to appreciate *that* view before clearing her throat.

"Rescue mission?" she asked.

"Something like that." He shifted to make room for her beside him. "I figured you might need a breather from Tess the Taskmaster."

"Is it that obvious?"

"Only to someone who's been watching you try to escape for the last..." He checked his watch. "Twenty-seven minutes."

The casual admission that he'd been observing her sent an unexpected flutter through her chest. "I need to get honest feedback from Anna and Drake," she explained. "Without Tess's industrial-strength filter."

Before he could respond, Anna and Drake made their way across the room toward them. Piper straightened. With Tess nowhere to be found—probably plotting world domination with legal—this was her shot.

"So, what do we think?" Piper asked.

"I like it," Anna said with a quick glance to Drake. "I think this is it."

"If Anna says this is it, then this is it," he replied staring at Anna in that gentle way of couples in love.

They seemed so real together. The kind of real Piper was terrified of breaking.

"Fabulous," Piper grinned huge instead of thinking more on that. "Then I *think* we should sit and go through the rest of the binder."

Drake and Anna exchanged glances that screamed "emergency exit strategy."

"Right, yes. We have that thing we have to get to," Anna said, already stepping toward the door.

Probably best that they took off before Tess got back with more ideas and more to-dos.

"I'll join you," Diana added, with a pointed look to Babushka.

"Don't vant to be late," Babushka agreed.

"Late for what?" Zach asked.

"Anything," Babushka answered with a wave of her hand.

The four of them made a hasty exit, leaving Piper and Zach alone.

"You can take off if you need." Piper shifted her weight from one foot to the other. "I still need to check out the audio-visual setup."

"Want company?" Zach asked, hands in his pockets. His casual stance did nothing to diminish the intensity of his attention as it rested on her.

The silence stretched between them uncomfortably.

"Don't you have underwear to design or something?" she asked, but there was no bite to her words.

"I'm multitasking. Besides, I'm good with tech stuff." He moved to stand beside her. "I'll have you know I once built a custom inventory management system for my family's flower shop and installed new sound systems in all the shops. Before I found my true calling in men's supportive undergarments, of course."

Piper rolled her eyes but couldn't suppress a small laugh. "Fine. You can help me check the AV closet." She pointed toward a discreet door near the bar area.

They crossed the space together, an evening breeze beginning to stir. The door was tucked almost invisibly into the wall's paneling. Piper tested the handle as Zach snagged the basket Babushka left behind.

The door turned smoothly, revealing a small, climate-controlled room lined with equipment racks. The space was cramped but efficiently organized, with digital mixers, amplifiers, and various control panels mounted in neat rows.

Zach followed her inside, pulling the door shut behind them.

"Impressive setup," Zach said, tracing his fingertip along a touchscreen controller.

Piper nodded, making notes on her clipboard. "Good capacity, state-of-the-art equipment. If Anna wants music during the ceremony, we'll need to run tests for sound bleed, but—"

A sharp click interrupted her mid-sentence.

They both turned toward the door.

"Did that...?" Zach asked, already moving toward the handle.

"It couldn't have," Piper said, but the sinking feeling in her stomach told her otherwise.

Zach tried the handle, then tried again with more force. It didn't budge.

"We're locked in," he confirmed, giving the door another futile tug.

Piper stared at him; clipboard clutched to her chest. "That's impossible. These doors don't automatically lock from the outside."

"And yet..." Zach stared down at the door handle.

"This is ridiculous. There has to be another way out."

"No windows, no second exit," Zach observed, running his hands along the walls as if hoping to discover a secret passage. "Just us and about a million dollars' worth of sound equipment."

"No signal in here," Zach said, checking his phone.

"Mine, either," Piper sank down onto the only chair in the small room. "How did this even happen? These doors are designed specifically not to lock people inside. It's a safety hazard."

Zach rested his shoulder against the equipment rack, a suspicious frown forming on his face. "Unless someone deliberately locked it from outside."

Their eyes met in sudden understanding.
"Babushka," they said in unison.

CHAPTER 10

41 DAYS UNTIL ANNA
& DRAKE'S WEDDING

PIPER

"But how would Babushka even lock this?" Piper strode to the door and tried it again. Nope. Nada. It wasn't moving.

"Trust me, never underestimate Babushka's abilities," Zach sighed, running a hand through his hair. "If she wants something to happen, she'll find a way."

"Why would your grandmother want to lock *us* in a closet?" Piper demanded, the absurdity of the situation finally hitting her. "What could she possibly gain from that?"

Zach hesitated, looking suddenly uncomfortable. "She's an enigma, that one."

"This is what she did to Drake and Anna," Piper said. Not a question, a statement.

Zach confirmed, his pulse visible along the line of his neck.

"So, your grandmother thinks that trapping two adults in small spaces is the path to true love?" Piper's voice rose incrementally with each syllable. "That's—that's—"

"Effective, apparently," Zach admitted with a sheepish smile. "I mean, it worked for Anna and Drake."

Piper sat in one of the folding chairs she found against the back wall, her palms pressed to her cheeks. Her throat tightened with the familiar feeling of dread. "How bad was it? Between Drake and Anna before the big lock-in?"

"What do you mean?"

"Couples that have serious problems before marriage? Those problems don't magically disappear after the wedding." Piper's voice sounded tight even to her. "If anything, they get worse."

Maybe the point of this whole thing wasn't to push her and Zach closer together. No, maybe it was to remind her that *they* were a bad idea in the first place.

Zach straightened, his expression growing serious. "Anna and Drake are solid. Like, really solid. They just had a communication hiccup during a stressful time. Every couple has rough patches."

"That's what they all say," Piper muttered, shaking her head. "Until it all falls apart."

"Nah." His voice wrapped gently around the last word as he crouched in front of where she sat. "Not every relationship is doomed because it hits a bump. Not Anna's, not..."

Ours.

He let that unspoken word hang there in the air between them. And all she could focus on were the flecks of green in his eyes she'd never noticed before.

The intensity between them had her squirming in the seat. And the knowingly perceptive way he acted like he could see right through to the raw hurt underneath did not help the situation.

Piper stood abruptly, forcing him to step back. "This isn't about philosophy. This is about getting out of here before I miss my movie marathon." A tangle of wires blurred in her vision as she blinked, trying to focus on something—anything

—other than what had just happened. "Maybe we can patch into one of the event rooms and call for help?"

Silence stretched as he studied her before finally replying, "Good thinking. Let me see what we've got."

They worked side by side in tense silence, Piper focusing all her attention on the control panel while trying to ignore both Zach's proximity and the unsettling revelations she needed to totally pretend had not happened.

She stared at the mess of wires and switches. Was the electrical system they were trying to hack into as hopelessly crossed as her own professional boundaries? Because each connection she traced seemed to lead somewhere unexpected, just like her feelings for Zach.

The small space made it impossible not to be aware of him—the faint smell of his cologne, the warmth radiating from his body, the brush of his arm against hers as they hunched over the equipment.

She looked up to find his face much closer than she'd anticipated, his eyes darkened with an emotion she wasn't ready to name. Dim overhead lights cast long shadows over stacked equipment. The air, warm and dry, crackled with unspoken things.

"Piper," he breathed, her name almost a question.

She couldn't look away. Couldn't step back. Couldn't remember why she should want to.

His attention lingered on her mouth, and she gravitated toward him, drawn by some invisible force she couldn't, and seriously didn't want to, resist.

"Zach."

Their breaths mingled, ragged and uneven, as the distance between them narrowed to almost nothing.

He waited, leaving that slip of a space there. He didn't move. Didn't take his eyes off hers.

No, that was her. She closed that space and pressed her

lips to his, testing the feel as her whole body seemed to melt against him.

He let her take control of the kiss, until he didn't. He opened for her when she moaned a quiet sound and that was the end of that.

His hands were in her hair, and he devoured any protests she couldn't think of anymore. Heat pooled low in her belly, and it didn't matter that they were locked in a closet. It didn't matter that she didn't believe in love.

No, all that mattered was the spark deep inside he was fanning with whatever the hell that was he could do with his tongue.

She gripped his shoulders and let him do what he wanted to because he definitely knew his way around a kiss. That was for damn sure.

Her heart hammered against her ribs as panic and desire fought it out inside. This wasn't supposed to happen. She didn't blur the lines. Didn't risk her reputation with personal entanglements.

Her brain was a fogged-over windshield, logic smeared useless beneath all that heat, by the time he pulled away a fraction of an inch. She was out of breath and a solid four miles past sanity.

Carefully, he moved her to the chair where she'd been before. This time he pressed the pad of his thumb against her lips, soothing the fire that still made her want to jump him right there, professionalism be damned.

"We're gonna come back to this, yeah?" he asked.

She nodded since she couldn't form a syllable at that moment.

He seemed to understand that he'd totally wrecked her ability to communicate because he grinned like he walked straight out of a Warner Brothers' cartoon. Which was apt, given she probably had red hearts dancing around her head.

All she could do was watch him as he cataloged the wires and followed them to the black box on the wall.

"Here." He pointed to a series of labeled buttons at the back of the panel. "These control the microphone system for each event space. If we can patch through to the main ballroom then—"

"They'll hear us," Piper finished, already standing to reach for the controls.

Their fingertips bumped over the panel, and for a moment, neither moved away. His warm fingers gripped hers, his skin slightly rough as he squeezed her palm.

"This one connects us," he said, his voice rough as he reached past her to press a button. "Should connect us."

The spell broken, Piper blinked rapidly, trying to regain her composure as he gestured toward the microphone.

"Press this when you're ready to speak," he instructed, not quite meeting her eyes.

She steadied herself before pressing the button.

"Hello? This is Piper Daws. I'm trapped in the audiovisual room on the rooftop terrace. If anyone can hear this, please come help. The door is locked from the outside."

They waited in tense silence for several seconds before a subtle electronic whine filled the room. Suddenly, Piper's message boomed back at them, echoing through the small space at deafening volume. Her amplified voice declared to no one in particular, "...PLEASE COME HELP. THE DOOR IS LOCKED FROM THE OUTSIDE."

Piper winced, covering her ears as her distress call reverberated.

Two seconds later, the same message echoed from outside the door.

"Did that go through the entire hotel?" Piper asked, moving her gaze from the door to Zach then back to the door.

"I think," Zach said carefully as the announcement finally,

thank God finally, ended, "I maybe might have patched into the wrong system."

"You think?" Piper stared at him in horror. "What exactly did you connect us to?"

"If I had to guess..." He rubbed the back of his neck.

"Guess away."

"The emergency broadcast system."

Piper groaned, dropping her head into her palms. "So now everyone in the entire building knows we're stuck in a closet together."

"You didn't mention me, so they only know about you." Zach shrugged. "Look at the bright side. Someone's bound to come get us now."

As if on cue, rapid footsteps approached, followed by the sound of rustling from the outside and the door opening.

The hotel manager stood there, his expression a mixture of concern and irritation as he took in the sight of them. His name tag read "Marcus," and his perfectly pressed suit somehow managed to look even more formal than Piper's. She could appreciate that in a fellow professional.

"Ms. Daws," he said stiffly, apparently recognizing her from the D.I.C.K. meeting. "Would you care to explain why you've activated our emergency announcement system to broadcast your predicament to our guests? *All* of our guests."

Before she could form a response, Zach spoke first, "Actually, that would be my fault. However, you might want to be more concerned about why your audiovisual room locks from the outside with no internal release. Had there been a fire, we would have been trapped with no way out."

"Yes," Piper said. "That's a serious safety violation."

"I'm sure the fire marshal would be very interested to hear about a hotel trapping guests in rooms they can't escape from." Zach's tone sharpened from casual to authoritative in an instant.

Marcus visibly paled. "I assure you; these doors do not lock this way."

"But they did," Zach said.

"Something must have been tampered with." Marcus toyed with the doorknob, pressing the lock and turning the lever to release it.

At Marcus's mention of tampering, a flicker of suspicion passed instantly between her and Zach.

"Tampered with?" she asked. Also, go her, because it sounded like the thought hadn't occurred to her until Marcus mentioned it right then.

"All the more concerning." Zach kept his stare on Marcus. His easygoing charm transformed into commanding and confident. A glimpse, perhaps, of the businessman beneath the casual exterior? "But, for now, I'm simply relieved that someone heard Piper's call for help," he finished.

"Of course, of course," Marcus stammered.

"Piper?" Tess called, hurrying behind Marcus. "Are you okay? I was on the phone with legal when the whole thing came over the intercom."

"That's basically what happened," Piper said. "Marcus came to let us out."

"Legal?" Marcus blanched. "Please accept our most sincere apologies. I'll have maintenance check every door immediately. And perhaps we could offer you both a complimentary dinner at our restaurant this evening? To make amends?"

Piper crossed her arms, glancing at the now-unlocked door, not entirely trusting it. "That won't be necessary."

"Thank goodness you're both okay," Tess said, side-eyeing Marcus. "Loop me in on the report and facilities audit. I'll walk with you now while you start the paperwork."

Piper felt a little bad for Marcus as Tess steered him toward the elevators.

They made their way back across the now-empty terrace.

How she could be embarrassed and relieved and a little turned on? Well, that was anyone's guess.

"Oh, wait," Zach said, turning back toward the audiovisual room. He ducked inside and emerged with the small wicker basket of bread.

Piper raised an eyebrow.

"It's *really* good bread," he said with a grin as they reached the exit.

A laugh escaped her lips before she could stop it.

The sun had begun its descent toward the mountains, bathing everything in a muted golden light that made the city skyline shimmer.

Piper caught herself studying Zach's profile and the strong line of his jaw, the way his eyes crinkled slightly at the corners even when he wasn't smiling. Like he laughed so often the lines were already permanent.

"Thank you," she said suddenly. "For handling that with the manager. You were impressive."

With a smile that tugged a little too knowingly, he said, "High praise from someone who intimidates funeral directors for fun."

"I do not intimidate them," she protested. "I organize them. There's a difference."

"If you say so."

They reached the parking garage level in comfortable silence. As they stepped out, Zach hesitated.

"Speaking of organizing," he said, falling into step beside her. "What would you say to celebrating our daring escape from audiovisual imprisonment? I've got an in with Brek at Brek's Bar. He always has good bands."

"That's Aspen's brother's bar." Piper paused by her car. "I've never been."

It never felt like a place she'd fit in, honestly.

"Come with me, then," Zach said.

Key fob in hand, every instinct crafted from years navigating delicate client relationships and steering clear of drama warned her to shut it down. To maintain the separation between work and pleasure. To keep the damn walls firmly in place.

But Zach had already started to pull those walls down and something—an openness, a genuine interest that went beyond mere flirtation? Whatever it was, she was reconsidering.

"Just to celebrate our escape?" she asked cautiously.

"Absolutely," he assured her, though the slight twinkle in his eyes suggested more. "Plus, I owe you because that had Babushka written all over it in giant red Sharpie with exclamation points."

"The thing is, I've been running the whole thing in my brain and Babushka left long before she could've done anything to the lock."

"If there's one thing I've learned," Zach said. "It's that you should never underestimate what that woman can do."

Piper smirked. "Noted."

"A drink?" Zach said, his eyes sparkling.

Piper bit her lip, mentally running through her evening schedule. No urgent deadlines. No early meetings tomorrow. Only a movie marathon that could wait for another night.

There really was no valid excuse, even if she'd wanted one.

"Okay," she said. "But absolutely no talk about weddings."

The smile that spread across Zach's face was like watching the sun. She could almost convince herself this was simply a friendly, professional outing. A simple celebration of surviving a bizarre situation.

But the flutter in her stomach said it was so much more.

CHAPTER 11

41 DAYS UNTIL ANNA
& DRAKE'S WEDDING

ZACH

The glow of neon beer signs bathed Brek's Bar in a kaleidoscope of colors, transforming the dive-bar atmosphere into something unexpectedly inviting.

They walked in together, Zach still carrying the breadbasket as Piper took in the mismatched furniture, vintage concert posters, big stage, and the eclectic crowd that seemed perfectly at home mixed together.

"This is..." Piper hesitated, clearly searching for the right word as she adjusted the collar of her blouse, still looking every inch the polished professional he really wanted to see relax, not rush.

"Not quite what you expected?" Zach offered with a hint of amusement playing across his features.

She nodded, seeming slightly uncomfortable as she surveyed the room.

"It's got character," she finally said, her posture still rigid.

Zach leaned in slightly. "You're allowed to relax, you know. No clipboard police here."

Something in his gentle teasing seemed to reach her. Piper

took a deep breath, removed her tailored blazer and draped it over her arm. With a determined motion, she pulled the elastic from her hair, letting it cascade in waves around her shoulders. The transformation was subtle but immediate—like watching a tightly wound spring uncoil slowly.

"Better?" she asked, a challenge in her eyes.

"Much," Zach said, his gaze lingering perhaps a second longer than strictly necessary. "Come on, let's grab a booth."

In the corner, a four-piece band was setting up equipment. The guitarist tuned strings while the drummer assembled his kit. The crowd was diverse with professionals unwinding after work mingling with tattooed artists, college students, and neighborhood regulars. Above the well-worn bar, neon signs advertised various beers alongside quirky slogans that had probably hung there for decades.

Zach led the way through the crowd, with Piper trailing behind him. He nodded at a couple of guys he knew as they hollered greetings, threw up a hand for a quick high five here, bumping fists there.

Piper carried herself like she was on a site visit. Out here, he was in his element. Piper? Piper was learning the room.

"Zach, my man," Brek, the owner and bartender with a closely trimmed beard and sleeve tattoos, called out. "The usual?"

"Yup," Zach replied, gesturing toward Piper. "And anything the lady would like."

"I'll have a whiskey sour," Piper said.

The slight hesitation in her voice didn't go unnoticed, but he said nothing.

They slid into a high-backed booth with worn leather seats that had seen decades of patrons. The table between them bore the scars of countless beer glasses, carved initials, and what looked like a decade's worth of spilled drinks.

"This is your natural habitat, then," Piper observed, running her finger over a heart carved into the wood.

"One of them," Zach admitted with an easy smile. "I like places with stories. Every scratch on this table happened because someone was living their life. They were having a great night or a terrible one, celebrating or commiserating."

Piper looked around with new appreciation. "I don't usually frequent places with quite so much... living."

"Corporate events not known for their wild parties?" Zach teased.

"Unless you count enthusiastic karaoke at holiday parties..."

Zach nearly choked on his water. "Please tell me you take videos."

"A professional never reveals her secrets," she replied primly, but her smile gave her away.

Brek arrived with their drinks, sliding them across the table with practiced ease. "So, you finally bringing someone to meet the crew, Dvornakov? About time."

Piper twisted a strand of hair between her fingertips, slightly ducking her head.

"Brek, this is Piper. She's planning Anna's wedding," Zach clarified.

"Ah, wedding planner Piper?" Brek nodded knowingly. "Aspen's told me about you. She thinks you're the shit."

"Oh?" Piper didn't seem to know what to do with that.

"Noah was just asking about you, Zach. Said you're working on something big with the Stallions?"

Zach nodded. "Big stuff happening, man."

He didn't add that Tess had cornered him early during the venue review with one of her signature power moves.

"Things are going great with this whole thing," she had said. Followed by a loaded smile.

"Noah's here?" Zach glanced around.

"Pool tables," Brek replied before refocusing to serve another customer.

Piper took a sip of her whiskey sour, the tart-sweet balance perfect against the burn of alcohol. "Noah?"

"My business partner," Zach explained. "He's going to want to meet you. He's been following the Stallions negotiations closely."

"Wild Sacks is a real company, then?" Piper asked offhand before she could stop herself.

Zach raised an eyebrow. "As opposed to an elaborate way to make out with someone in an AV closet?"

"I just meant that… yeah, I should stop talking now."

Zach sat up straighter, his eyes brightening. "It's not only real—it's revolutionary." He leaned forward, gesturing with his hands. "Men deserve comfort, too, you know. My college roommate used to complain constantly about his underwear bunching up during games." He shook his head. "Most guys accept discomfort as the price of having a dick, but—" He slapped his palm on the table. "It doesn't have to be that way."

Piper watched as his hands danced through the air while he punctuated each point. His cheeks grew warm at the way she studied him.

"You're a comfort crusader," she said, but her tone was warm, not mocking.

"Laugh if you want," Zach said, pulling his phone out and rapidly scrolling through images. "But check it out." He thrust the screen toward her. "You'll love these illustrations. I even color-coded them by potential, like your binder." He pulled the phone back, swiping to another image. As he scrolled past a photo of him trying on a design sample, he glanced up to find her studying that one closer.

"We don't need to look at that one," he tried to swipe, but she placed her hands on his.

"No, I want to see." She leaned in.

He raised an eyebrow.

"Pfft. Not that." She rolled her eyes. "Because you are excited about the concept."

"And our designs," he said. "Piper, our designs are going to change everything."

"*Your* designs?" she clarified. "They're your designs."

"I mean, yeah. I handle that part. I started by sewing them all myself. But the company is more than just me now. That's why Noah came on. He's brilliant with the business side." He paused, thoughtful. "When I left the family business, Dad said it was a horrible idea. Jase told me I was making a huge mistake. Even Anna worried about my choices. But Wild Sacks is finally seeing some genuine movement in the industry. What we do matters."

"This is why the Stallions deal is so important," Piper seemed to finally realize.

"Yeah." Zach stared wistfully at one of the illustrations he'd swiped back to. "Being the official underwear of the Stallions validates everything." His animated expression relaxed, and he pocketed his phone. "But enough about my underwear. I asked you to come because I want to hear about you."

Piper fidgeted with her napkin. "There's really not much to tell."

"I find that very difficult to believe," Zach said, lifting his beer to his lips.

Before she could respond, Noah wove through the crowd to their booth, all six-foot-whatever of him towering over everyone. He offered Piper a quick, sincere smile.

"I thought Brek was messing with me when he said you were here," Noah said, sliding in next to Zach. "And you must be the famous wedding planner. I'm Noah." He held his hand out to her.

"Piper," she replied, shaking his offered hand.

"I think Noah was leaving," Zach said with a heavy dose of sarcasm.

Which is probably why Noah ignored him completely and turned to Piper. "He says you're the best at what you do."

"She is," Zach agreed.

"I could be modest, but why correct him when he's right," Piper teased.

"Thanks for everything you're doing with the wedding. It's taken the load off Tess, which gave her time to push our Stallions talks forward. We owe you. If this wedding goes well and we lock in this partnership? When all this falls into place like we think it will? Wild Sacks won't be a question mark anymore."

"We'll be here to stay," Zach agreed.

Here. To. Stay.

The band chose that moment to start their soundcheck.

"This place really is great," Piper said, truly relaxing against the back of the booth. "Is this your standard antidote for a day with Tess and Babushka?"

"A professional never reveals his secrets," Zach said with a grin.

CHAPTER 12

PIPER

She leaned forward, slightly, at the playful glint in Zach's eyes.

"You know, I think we know each other well enough to share a *few* professional secrets," she said.

"Only the professional ones?" A slow smile spread across his face.

"You know what?" Noah tapped out a rhythm on the table. "It's been great to meet you, Piper," he added, glancing between the two of them. "I'm going to go lose some money at pool." He slid out of the booth, shaking his head with a wry smile.

"What were we talking about again?" Zach asked, his gaze never leaving hers.

"We were talking about secrets," she said, and, damn it came out breathy.

The invisible tether between them pulled tight, even as she lifted her drink and sipped.

Brek's was nothing like the coffee shops she usually

preferred when she socialized. This place was lived in, loud, and comfortable.

For the first time since she took the Anna and Drake gig, her shoulders loosened their knot of tension, exchanging it for a warm buzz that had nothing to do with whiskey and everything to do with Zach. He became a small pocket of ease in her life that made her want to crawl inside and stay.

The music around them swelled as the band launched into their first song, a bluesy rock number with a deep groove.

"Can I ask you something?" Piper asked.

"Shoot," he said, the relaxed air around him contagious.

"Why did you bring me here tonight?" she asked, fainter than she meant to be. Vulnerable, almost.

He considered her for a moment, letting the colored lights from the stage play across his face as he seemed to search for the right words.

"Because I like you," he said simply. "And I think there's something here worth exploring outside of business deals and my sister's wedding plans."

Piper was fresh out of witty comebacks, and the taut stretch of the air around them kept her still. So she sat there, letting his words seep in. Her pulse harmonized with the lazy drumbeat coming from the stage.

"Besides," he added with a rueful smile, "you're the only woman I know who can make underwear sound like a serious career choice and wedding planning sound like a prison sentence."

She laughed, genuinely. "You're nuts."

"I prefer 'persistent,'" he corrected, opening the bread-basket and producing a serrated knife.

"I like that your persistence comes with a side of carbs."

"If we're going to be smugglers," he said, mock-grave, "we should do it properly and actually eat the contraband." He unveiled a ramekin of butter and a tiny jar of honey. "You don't need to worry, either. Brek's is known for providing diplomatic immunity for cases like this."

"Who are you, Zach Dvornakov?" she asked, seriously and, also, not.

"The hero you didn't know you needed." He folded a napkin and lifted out a fresh loaf. Malt and caraway unspooled something low in her chest.

She aimed for delicate. But the first bite drew an embarrassingly honest hum out of her. Warmth pushed up her neck.

His gaze heated, focused on her lips.

"That never happened," she said primly, pointing to the bread and then to herself.

"That absolutely happened," he said, eyes amused and intent. "Make that noise again, and I'm kissing you."

"Then stop feeding me," she muttered, already reaching for more honey. "This is carbohydrate entrapment."

"Not a chance."

"Why is this so good?" she asked.

"Because Babushka substitutes the liquid in some of her recipes with vodka. It works." He shrugged.

They fell into the rhythm of slice, butter, honey, sip, smile, laugh. The band rolled into a looser beat that made their booth a private space in the crowd of people.

"Tell me something true," he said, palm up on the table but not touching hers.

The space between their hands felt like a dare.

Piper smoothed a crumb off the table with her thumb.

"I color-code my sock drawer," she said at last. "That's why I didn't think it was funny when you teased me about doing yours."

"Does that mean you'll volunteer to adopt mine?" he asked. "They need structure. They're feral."

"They'll get a chart and a curfew. I expect a benefits package."

"Dental, vision, and naming rights to my sock bins." He

shifted toward her, his arms on the table. "Just so we're clear, organizational theory as a form of foreplay is a kink I didn't know I am into until this moment."

"Your turn," she said, grinning.

"Remember how I said Babushka taught me to sew?"

Piper nodded.

"I still like to get out my old Singer when I'm stressed. It makes my head quiet."

Something tugged hard in her chest. "You at your sewing machine is way more attractive than me with socks."

"More attractive than contraband carbs?" he asked.

"Jury's out." She angled the basket his way.

He stretched an arm along the back of the booth. "Wildly unpopular opinion?"

"Easy. Confetti is the glitter of cowards," she said confidently because she had given this a decent amount of thought.

That seemed to catch him off guard. "Explain."

"If you're going to make a mess, commit. Either go biodegradable petals or own the cleanup. Confetti is a half-measure with static cling."

"I'm learning so much." He grinned. "My turn: open floor plans ruined living rooms."

"On behalf of people who prefer doors," she said, pressing her hand to her heart, "thank you."

His expression went quiet in a way that made her chest feel too full. The conversation idled with the music, and gradually the energy shifted. Easier. Just two people talking.

"My mom insisted I had a 'natural gift' for event planning," she said.

"You mentioned your parents had multiple weddings," he said carefully. "To each other?"

Piper nodded, tracing the rim of her glass with one finger. "At first. Each time they convinced themselves that 'this time it would be different.' And each time, it wasn't."

"That's a lot for a kid to deal with," Zach observed.

"Try being appointed the wedding planner for their third attempt," Piper said with a dry laugh. "I was sixteen. My mother fired the professional because 'he couldn't understand their unique love story.'"

"Sixteen? That's..."

"Inappropriate? Traumatic? Character-forming?" Piper supplied. "All of the above. But I *was* good at it. I had a gift for creating order from messes." She lifted a shoulder.

"That's how you got into event planning professionally?"

She nodded. "Turns out the skills transfer nicely to corporate events. Better, actually, since companies don't usually divorce after the product launch."

Zach made a keep going gesture.

She swallowed, hard. "It's a pattern. My parents, my own train-wreck of a love life, even clients. I'm the common denominator. I'm the kryptonite."

Zach leaned forward, his eyes intent on hers. "You don't really believe that, do you?"

Something flashed in her eyes. Uncertainty, perhaps?

"I believe in patterns. And my pattern suggests I should stay far away from anything involving white dresses and vows no one can keep."

He gave a low whistle. "I thought my family was complicated."

Piper laughed. "I'm sorry, but nothing compares to my mom announcing her newest engagement to her divorce lawyer at my college graduation party just to piss off my dad."

He lifted his glass in surrender. "Okay, you win."

Their laughter joined the music as the band transitioned into a slower song. Couples drifted toward the dance floor, and Zach watched them before turning his gaze back to her.

"At least your family is present for you," she said. "And supportive."

He flinched at that. "They've come around. The flower business has been in the family for generations. My decision to go a different direction wasn't exactly celebrated."

"But they support you now?"

"They're still a little wait-and-see. I really think things like the Stallions deal would change that."

The band shifted to a soulful standard, the singer's voice smoothing over the clinking of glasses and buzz of conversation. Zach looked toward the dance floor and seemed to make a decision.

"What do you say?" he asked, rising and offering his hand.

Absolutely not. She didn't dance.

"I'm not good at that," she said.

"You don't have to be good at it. That's the best part."

He watched her, waiting for the wall to go up again. Instead, she paused.

"I'm really not a dancer," she warned.

"Neither am I," he admitted with a grin. "But I'm willing to risk public humiliation if you are."

"One dance," she relented, placing her hand in his.

He closed his fingers gently, but deliberately, around hers and led her toward the edge of the dance floor. The band's cover of an old soul classic filled the room, sultry and smooth. He guided her into a loose hold, his hand settling at her waist —warm, steady, lingering a moment longer than shy. There was a subtle tension in her spine, and in the way she tracked each movement carefully, strategizing not just the dance, but what it meant to let him that close.

"See? Not so terrible," he murmured, voice low near her ear.

"I like knowing what comes next," she confessed, the breath behind her words brushing across his skin.

"That's the thing about dancing," he said. "Sometimes it's better when you don't know. When you just feel it."

He led her into a simple turn and her body tensed. Then

She pressed back against him as she steadied herself. There wasn't much space between them now.

"Let me control it for a minute." He brushed his thumb over the curve of her waist. "Only for a minute. You can have all the control everywhere else."

She hesitated. Her breath caught and she forced away the flicker of resistance. And then, slowly, she gave in. Her body leaned into his more naturally, her movements trading sharpness for something fluid. Something responsive.

"There you go," he whispered, his lips shy of touching her temple. "See? The world doesn't end when you let go a little."

"The jury's still out on that," she said, the corners of her mouth twitching.

The music slipped into a slower, more intimate tempo. She slid her hand a fraction higher along his shoulder; her gaze lingered longer than casual. She pressed into him instinctively, her body fitting against his like a question waiting for an answer.

"You're getting the hang of this," he murmured, his breath grazing sensitive skin at her ear.

"Don't sound so surprised," she replied, voice lower. "I can follow directions when they make sense."

"Is that what we're doing here? Following directions?"

Her eyes met his—direct, uncertain, charged. "Isn't it?"

He smiled under the warm bar lights, his grip subtly tightening at her waist. "I think we might be improvising."

"I'm not good at improvising," she said with a hesitant smile, her mouth close enough to feel the shape of his on every word.

"Yet here you are." He turned her again, slow and deliberate, keeping her closer on the return. "Dancing with the man who makes underwear for a living."

She laughed, light and musical. "When you put it that way, this sounds like I've strayed pretty far from my comfort zone."

"The best things usually happen outside comfort zones," he replied, watching her take those words in. "I saw it on a T-shirt once, that's how I know it's true."

"This feels..." she began quietly.

"Dangerous?" he offered.

"Unexpected," she said, holding his gaze. "And the unexpected is always the most dangerous thing of all."

CHAPTER 13

ZACH

The singer's voice faded into silence, drawing the song to a close. Around them, the bar resumed its usual energy. Zach kept holding her gaze for a beat longer.

"I think I need another drink," she said, stepping back.

He gave a small nod. "I'll get them. Same as before?"

"Coke? I've gotta drive."

He nodded, and as he made his way to the bar, Zach couldn't help glancing back to where she stood at the edge of the dance floor. She was tucking a strand of hair behind her ear, her expression thoughtful as she watched the other couples around them.

"Well, well, well," Brek drawled as Zach approached the bar. "Never thought I'd see the day Zachary Dvornakov went all moon-eyed over a woman in a pantsuit. Can't help it, though. It happens to the best of us."

Brek was Zach's brother's best friend, and he'd been around since Zach was a kid. He also fell for a very organized woman who leaned professional.

"I'm not moon-eyed," Zach protested, leaning against the polished wood. "I'm being hospitable."

"Sure, and I'm running for mayor." Brek replied.

Zach put in their orders and Brek grabbed the soda gun. "She's cute, though. In that scary, could-organize-your-life-while-destroying-it kind of way. I've got one of those, too. Best thing that ever happened to me."

"Piper's not scary," Zach said automatically, then paused. "Okay, maybe a little intimidating at first, but in the best possible way."

Brek slid the drinks across the bar with a knowing smirk. "You got it bad, brother."

Zach didn't bother denying it again. There was something about Piper that had gripped him from that first sidewalk encounter.

Her sharp wit, her determination, the vulnerability she tried so hard to hide.

When he returned to their booth, Piper was already seated, her fingers absently tracing the carved heart in the wooden tabletop. She looked up as he approached, a smile spreading across her face that made his chest tighten.

"Successful mission," she said as he set the drinks down.

"Brek sends his regards," Zach replied, sliding into the seat across from her. "And his nosy curiosity."

"About?"

"You." Zach took a sip of his beer. "He thinks you're interesting."

"Like a Russian horse?" Piper pointed out, but she looked pleased.

"People are usually good judges of character on first impressions." He leaned forward slightly. "I know I was."

Piper raised an eyebrow. "And what exactly was your first impression of me?"

"That you were someone who takes herself too seriously,"

Zach admitted with a grin, "but is worth getting to know, anyway."

"Whereas I thought you were an annoying distraction who looked far too good in casual clothes," she countered, then immediately flushed as if surprised by her own candor.

Zach's smile widened. "You thought I looked good?"

"Don't let it go to your head," she warned, taking a sip of her drink. "The gum situation distracted me."

"The gum situation that brought us together," he corrected. "Some might call that fate."

Piper rolled her eyes, but her smile remained. "Some might call it poor sidewalk maintenance."

He laughed. "I prefer seeing possibilities where others see problems."

"That explains why you're so invested in this wedding," Piper observed.

Zach considered her for a moment. "Seeing what my parents have? The real deal for thirty years? I want that for Anna. My brothers? They've both found it, too."

"Thirty years," Piper repeated, something wistful in her tone. "That's rare."

"Not in my family," Zach said. "My grandparents made it to fifty-two before Babushka's 'ceremonial fire' claimed my grandfather."

Piper nearly choked on her Coke. "Wait, what?"

"I'm kidding," Zach assured her with a laugh. "He died peacefully in his sleep."

"Your family is..."

"Complicated? Completely nuts?"

"I was going to say 'passionate,'" Piper said, instead.

The band launched into a more upbeat number, and the dance floor quickly filled with a more enthusiastic crowd.

"I should probably head out," Piper said, reassembling everything back into the breadbasket. "It's getting late and all."

"Of course," Zach started to stand.

"Thank you for tonight. For the rescue from the AV room and for..." She gestured vaguely between them. "This. It's been fun."

"Fun enough to do it again sometime?" Zach asked, trying to keep his tone casual.

Her eyes met his, and for a moment, the same electric connection that had sparked between them on the dance floor flared again.

She nodded. "I'd like that a lot."

They moved through the happy disorder of the bar in a quiet space carved out just for the two of them and pushed through the heavy wooden door.

Outside, the night air was cool and crisp, a welcome contrast to the warmth of the bar. Streetlamps cast circles of light onto the sidewalk as they walked toward the parking lot.

"My car's over there," Piper said, gesturing to a sensible midsize sedan parked beneath a streetlight.

"I'll walk you," Zach offered.

They moved in comfortable silence, shoulders occasionally brushing in a way that felt both casual and charged with possibility.

At her car, Piper turned to face him, her expression unreadable in the shadows. "Well, this is me."

"Drive safe," Zach said, suddenly reluctant to end the evening. "Text me when you get there?"

She blinked, as if surprised by the request. "I will."

"The night's not over yet," he said, quickly, while he had the courage. "Unless you want it to be?"

She shook her head, pulling her bottom lip under her teeth. "Do you?"

"No," he said, then added, "You could come home with me instead?" He gestured to his car across the lot.

Piper raised an eyebrow. "That's quite the pivot. From safety PSA to sleepover invitation."

"I contain multitudes," he deadpanned, letting his gaze drag slowly over her before meeting her eyes again.

She tilted her head, playful now. "Do any of those multitudes include snacks?"

"I've got leftover Thai and a full, unopened bag of kettle corn," he said, voice casual until it dipped lower. "But if you're wondering what else is on the menu? Well, that's negotiable."

Piper raised an eyebrow, lips curving. "You should've led with the kettle corn."

He took a step closer, the corner of his mouth lifting. "You know, ever since we met, I've been curious if you take orders as well as you give them."

Her smirk was instant, and her gaze dipped to his mouth before landing squarely back on his. "Depends on the orders." She let her fingers graze down the front of his shirt, light as a tease. "But I do learn fast when there's a solid benefits package."

"I deliver excellent benefits," he said, dead serious but with a grin threatening to break through.

Piper tilted her head. "Playlist rights on the drive there? Full creative control."

His answer came with zero hesitation and a flash of excitement. "Deal." His voice turned husky. "Though, fair warning: if you keep looking at me like *that*, we might not make it through the first song."

CHAPTER 14

41 DAYS UNTIL ANNA
& DRAKE'S WEDDING

PIPER

Zach's loft shouldn't have surprised her. But, like everything about him, it did.

From the outside, Wild Sacks HQ was exactly what you'd expect. An industrial grandpa of a building sandwiched between shiny condos and edgy restaurants.

But inside—after Zach keyed them in like he was opening a secret lair, nodded to a mural with his company's logo of a super-buff squirrel wearing underwear with acorn nuts on them, and marched her up concrete stairs straight out of a gritty cop show—it turned into a whole different beast.

His apartment was peak industrial nonsense with raw brick walls that looked like they'd witnessed a hundred failed startups.

And yet. The man had pulled it off.

His kitchen was legit, not a breakroom, and the living room looked lived-in, not like a waiting area.

Functional, sure. Masculine, obviously. But not at all the frat house disaster she'd braced for.

"Well," Piper said, taking it all in, "this is not horrifying."

He laughed, tugged off his jacket, and slung it over the back of the sofa. "I do try to keep the murder-aesthetic to a minimum."

Since she was wildly committed to her reputation as a responsible adult, she sent Shelby a heads-up that she was still with Zach. Then she kicked off her heels gently, and lined them up by the door.

She couldn't exactly lose a shoe and have to pull some covert Cinderella act later, probably in front of the world's most judgmental cat.

"Do you have a cat?" she asked.

He shook his head. "No. Why?"

"Absolutely no reason at all," she said as Zach strolled to the fridge, grabbed two cans of lemon-lime sparkling water, and came back.

"How long have you lived here?" she asked.

"Since I got a loan to buy the building, I couldn't keep paying rent." He shrugged. "It can be annoying when work is right outside my door, or I've got the flu, and the employees still know I'm home. There are zero boundaries—but it works, you know?" He held out the sparkling water, and she accepted it because it was one less decision she had to make.

"Thanks," she said.

He gestured at the couch. "Sit anywhere."

She collapsed onto the sofa with a groan. She wouldn't be shocked if there was a Piper-shaped dent left behind when she finally got up.

Zach joined her, carefully giving her space. Not nuzzling, not making quippy banter, not even a suggestive twitch.

Just two people marinating in the afterglow of half a dozen almosts and one definitely illegal kiss.

The long moment stretched into two. No music, no TV, only the pensive glug-glug of the fridge and the two of them just existing together.

"I don't do this," she blurted, the words tumbling out. "The part after the not-date. The part where you roll the dice and someone turns out to be, I dunno, real. Not just a future anecdote for my next girls' night."

He didn't cut in, didn't rush with reassurance. He waited. Did the whole giving her space without making her feel like she had to do a tap number to fill it.

Honestly, it helped. Which also made it a hundred times more terrifying.

She scowled at the suspiciously distressed coffee table. "Can I say something absolutely, one million percent ridiculous?"

"Yeah. Always."

She didn't look at him as she said, "Every time I so much as think I could maybe, possibly be happy? The universe gets bored and snatches the popcorn. Like, 'Here you go, Piper, have a little hope'—and then, *boom*. Mom gets on with divorce number four. The bridesmaid just slept with the groom." She could feel a laugh trying to launch itself up her throat, except it did a U-turn somewhere near her tonsils. "I break things, Zach. I walk into anything good with relationships and *poof*—disaster confetti. I'm practically a walking curse."

She meant it as a joke. Or at least as that reliable old scar you poke just to see if it still stings. But her voice betrayed her, cracking right down the middle. For the first time, she couldn't chase it away with a laugh and a wink.

He said nothing for a second, just staring with those annoyingly stable blue eyes.

"You're not cursed," he said. Then he paused, like he needed to remember how breathing worked.

"And you're not broken." He reached over, resting his hand on hers, light as a feather but warm enough to melt chocolate. "You're just believably bruised."

Suddenly the joke wasn't a joke at all. Nope, it was a scab he lifted with impossible gentleness.

She tried to smile, but her face only managed the kind that hurts. "That's way worse, you know."

He didn't let go. Instead, he moved into her space, took the sparkling water and set it on the coffee table.

He didn't even use a coaster.

Then his hand was against her jawline, and he brushed his lips against hers.

"Being bruised shows you've fought through hard times and kept going," he said, kissing her. "It means you stuck it out when most people would've noped right out."

He laid his forehead against hers, and the silence that followed felt heavier than usual. Every cell in her wanted to run, crack a joke, do literally anything but stay put.

But instead of running, she whispered, "I don't know what you want from me, Zach."

He leaned in just a tick. "I want what you're willing to give. I want to kiss you. But only if you want me to."

She let out a laugh that came out all wet and hiccupy and mortifying, and squeaked, "I do."

His hand stayed at her cheek, sliding up into her hair, gripping it in a way that made her melt right into him. Then his body was over hers and this kiss was nothing like the closet.

The universe shrank to the heat of his mouth and the rough scrape of his thumb along her neck. The impossible safety of being right where she wanted to be with him made her wet.

Yup, there was not a single part of her that wanted to file a complaint with corporate. Hesitation melted into permission, and permission opened the door to everything else. She kissed him back.

Okay, fine, she basically attacked him.

At first, it was all trembling hands and what-am-I-doing nerves, but then those melted right into oh-yes-please permission.

And permission?

That was buy-one-get-the-entire-catalog-free, because suddenly, anything felt possible and Piper tossed her last bit of caution over her shoulder like an unwanted bra.

He reached for the hem of her shirt with all the reverence of a man about to unwrap his favorite holiday gift.

One slow tug, and it came right off.

His hands trailed along her bare sides to the spot between her legs, pressing there before unbuttoning her slacks and pulling them down.

Then with a grin that said oh-sweetheart-I've-got-this he kissed her over the fabric of her panties, looping his finger there to pull them aside and press his lips exactly where she craved him.

A low hum started in her throat—the same sound she'd made with the bread.

He chuckled.

Then he righted her underwear and kissed his way back up her body. Her hands played with his hair as he skillfully popped the clasp of her bra and flicked it—yes, flicked it— onto the nearest lamp like some triumphant lingerie flag.

"Seriously?" she said, breathless and half-laughing, "You're undressing me like you've been waiting for this moment your whole life."

He grinned, eyes wicked and dark as sin. "You say that like it's a bad thing."

This wasn't some frenzied groping behind a bar; this was deliberate and she practically sizzled everywhere he touched.

She aimed for a joke—something sassy about HR policies and CEOs of startups—but when her mouth moved, all that'd come out was a strangled little gasp that sounded desperately wanton.

"You're gorgeous," he muttered, words half-mumbled against her skin. "Not even fair, Piper."

"Oh, you noticed?" She managed a laugh, then groaned as he kissed her again.

Her hips jolted, a needy little whimper slipping out.

"Get inside me," she practically begged. "Now, Zach, please."

So much for keeping it classy.

But even her pride had run for cover with the underwear he removed so deftly.

He didn't even smirk, which would have been less mortifying than the deep, guttural groan that rumbled out of him, breath rough as sandpaper against her ear.

"Fuck, you're—Piper, you're so ready for me."

"Don't sound so surprised, Charming. This is kind of your fault."

His lips curved up against hers, and he said, "Okay, Cinderella, let's see what else I can take credit for," before lowering his head to her breast, tongue teasing her nipple until she arched back, her own hands knotted in his hair.

"Oh my God—right there—" she gasped as he sucked, gentle at first and then with more hunger. She tried to be witty; what came out was an embarrassing, "You're really good at that."

He grinned at her, all cocky and pleased.

How was he still totally clothed, and she was nearly one orgasm in?

"Don't get cocky—oh." Her words had dissolved as the two fingers inside her curled just so and her whole body went taut. She clamped a hand over her mouth and he pried it away gently, kissing her palm.

"Don't," he whispered. "I want to hear you."

Then he worked her patiently, expertly, as she tried to keep up some shred of dignity and failed spectacularly. Her thighs started to shake, hips stuttering against his hand.

She gritted out, "If you don't get inside me in the next two seconds, I swear—"

He laughed, deep and low, fished a condom from his wallet, set it on the table, and pulled his clothes off. Tearing the foil, he rolled the condom on with one hand, braced the other on the back of the sofa, and studied her face as though waiting for permission.

"Yes," she breathed, and he slid in—slow at first, stretching, filling—until her gasp broke on his name.

He rocked his hips, starting a slow rhythm that turned her bones to jelly. She dragged her nails down his back, biting his shoulder when he hit that perfect spot inside that made stars explode behind her eyes.

His voice had gone rough when he said, "Do the nail thing again."

She did as he asked because she totally could take direction. In return, he gave exactly what she needed. Hard, deep strokes, rough in all the right ways.

She tangled her legs around his waist, meeting each thrust with her own, lost to the crash and pull.

"That's it, baby, come for me," he urged, breath hot and desperate.

She shattered for him, everything clenching impossibly tight as pleasure took over—no dignity, no sass, just raw, broken cries as she came apart.

He followed with a curse and a groan, holding her tight.

"Thank you," she mumbled against his lips.

He laughed, breathless, tugging her closer. "That's my line."

He grinned into her hair, then stood up and handled the condom.

The deeply inappropriate but highly attractive idea of doing that all over again bubbled up in her mind.

Inappropriate. This was inappropriate.

Of course, he sensed that moment of hesitation from her. Of course he did.

"You're allowed to want this thing happening between us.

It's not a curse. It's just us," he said, like this—her, them—was a gift. Not a ticking clock on some inevitable heartbreak she hadn't scheduled but definitely expected.

"Just us," she echoed, wishing it could be true.

Later, after he carried her to the bedroom, they lay tangled up beneath crisp sheets that still smelled like detergent and danger.

He traced lazy patterns across her back. They didn't talk. They just breathed.

At some point—time went fuzzy when a girl kept coming —when they snuggled tight in his bed, her head tucked beneath his chin, her hand parked firmly over the steady beat of his heart like it belonged there.

He kissed her hair. Tightened his arms around her like she was something that mattered, not something temporary.

No declarations. Just safety soft as sunrise and every bit as dangerous.

When she woke with sunlight slicing through the windows and his arms wrapped around her like a human exclamation point, she just…lay there. Cocooned. Warm. One broad hand still resting at her waist like he chose her even in sleep, like his subconscious was all in.

Her brain, being the unhelpful little gremlin it was, immediately began counting the ways this could fall apart.

Don't fall.

Don't believe this is real.

Not for you.

But beneath the usual buzzing panic, something new stirred. Something quieter. A tug forward, a thread glinting in the dark.

But what if it is real?

CHAPTER 15
40 DAYS UNTIL ANNA & DRAKE'S WEDDING

PIPER

Zach's sheets smelled like linen, cedar, and a lapse in judgment so epic it deserved its own apology fruit basket. The cotton currently wrapped around her bare legs was a whispered reminder of something dangerously close to intimacy.

Not that she was panicking.

Okay. Maybe a little.

Fine. Full-blown fire drill in her frontal cortex.

Panicking, deliciously sore, and currently turned on in an entirely unacceptable, post-orgasm, post-mistake, oh-no-I-slept-with-a-man-who-might-actually-be-a-human-cinnamon-roll kind of way.

Except cinnamon rolls didn't have hands like that. Or stamina like that. Or that distracted, half-sleepy smile he'd given her sometime around orgasm number four, which had shattered her bones and any pretense that this was casual.

She blinked up at the industrial ceiling, where big metal beams seemed to hold the building together on testosterone alone. Masculine. Unapologetic.

The light angling through his monster-sized windows painted everything in an irritating, soft-focus kind of peace—like morning itself was trying to seduce her into thinking this was fine.

Like she hadn't made a reckless, half-naked, wildly pleasurable mistake that now came with consequences that smelled like his shampoo.

Because her pillow? Smelled like him. Her thigh? Draped over one of his like it'd paid rent there. And his warm, stupidly sculpted arm that had no right being this comfortable was flung around her waist with the kind of easy possessiveness you only ever saw in late-night rom-coms or nightmare commitment scenarios.

So, this was definitely a morning.

As in… the morning. After.

Her heart thudded like it realized it was late to the accountability meeting.

She was tangled in Zach's bed, blinking against the invading daylight, absolutely, positively not spiraling.

Except, oh, yep, there went her brain. Lifting the lid on the Emergency Overthink Vault like it hadn't, only weeks ago, been declared off-limits.

The list rolled out, red-carpet style. Too intimate. Too fast. Too everything.

Too close to catching feelings.

She'd done the one thing she never did. She had let her guard down. Slipped. Twice. Okay, more like four and a half times if you counted the last one.

And worst of all was how good it had been.

Capital-G, write-about-it-in-her-journal good. Memoir chapter good.

"Tell no one, and yet somehow tell everyone" kind of good.

A groan escaped her before she could swallow it, and she immediately froze, eyes flicking sideways. Zach didn't stir. He simply breathed deep. His nose nuzzled near her neck like he had every intention of making this a cozy everyday thing. As if that was a thing they did now.

Which it very much was not.

Nope.

This was the point in the story where the heroine in her head had to get out before she accidentally started naming the dust bunnies and picturing what brand of dog food they'd buy together.

Time to disengage before this turned into a montage of Sunday farmers' markets and heartfelt label-making.

Even if the bed was warm.

Even if his arm tightened when she shifted.

Even if that scent seemed to whisper something dangerous like… stay.

She carefully lifted Zach's arm from her waist, pausing when he muttered something incomprehensible in his sleep and shifted onto his stomach, burying his face in the pillow she'd just abandoned. Her escape window: officially open.

With the skill of a woman who had once escaped her ex-boyfriend's apartment using a series of rolled yoga mats as a noise buffer, Piper slipped from under the covers, padded barefoot across the fluffy rug, and gathered last night's scattered armor: bra from the lamp (eye roll), blouse tossed tastefully on the back of a chair, heels by the door, slacks still rumpled like they remembered things they shouldn't be allowed to remember.

She tiptoed to the bathroom, shutting the door behind her with a quiet, decisive click.

In the mirror, a woman who looked suspiciously like her stared back. But this person had a mess of sleep-tangled curls, remnants of yesterday's makeup whispering tales of glorious sins, and an excellent exfoliation routine.

"It was just sex," she told her reflection, which had the audacity to look both wrecked and radiant. "Great sex, sure.

With an infuriatingly sweet underwear mogul. Not a big deal."

Direct eye contact, competent tone. That's how you assert dominance over your own emotional free fall.

Sex didn't imply vulnerability. Sex didn't imply commitment or butterflies or the fact that her chest kept remembering the exact way he'd called her bruised, not broken. That line hadn't been sex. That'd been seeing her. Understanding her.

It'd been truth dipped in charm with a side of trust, and heaven help her—for five seconds last night, she'd believed him.

And that was a problem.

She scrubbed her face with cold water and finger-combed her hair. Then she pulled on her slacks, buttoned her shirt, and reattached the mental shields she'd learned to snap into place back during her parents' last divorce.

Heart locked. Exit plan secured.

Back in the bedroom, Zach was probably still out cold, one leg flung haphazardly toward the far side of the bed in carefree post-romp glory. Unreasonably attractive. Completely unconscious.

Her stomach growled a long, low protest that earned a whispered, "Even my metabolism is fucking conflicted."

And naturally, that was when Zach showed. "I can help with your metabolism problem."

Startled, Piper spun around and—yep. There he was, not asleep. No, he stood right freaking there. Arm on the doorjamb, his head tilted toward one muscular arm, lips curved in a sleepy, satisfied smile, deep-blue eyes still clouded from sleep but watching her like he was half a dream and half a memory and determined to become both.

"You're awake," she said, way too breezy.

"That's generally how talking works." He arched a brow. "Making a… what did you call it? Strategic exit?"

She shifted, clutching her shoes to her chest like they were a metaphor. "I've got a load of work."

He nodded slowly, not buying that version of the script for a second. "Is that really what you want to tell yourself?"

The words hung there, gentle but heavy.

She didn't answer.

Instead, she popped on her shoes, gripped the doorknob like it was her life raft, and tried to convince herself she wasn't cursed. Just un-caffeinated and confused.

Then she slipped out, pulled the door closed behind her, and left before she could do something ridiculous like climb back into that bed and stay.

———

Piper shoved open the apartment door with more enthusiasm than coordination, nearly stumbling over her own feet as she entered. Her keys clattered into the bowl by the door—okay, near the bowl—and she kicked it shut behind her with a little more force than strictly necessary.

She was still wearing last night's eyeliner, her phone was down to one percent, and her mouth tasted like she'd had to brush her teeth with her finger. Stellar choices, all around.

Shelby was already lounging on the couch in her usual throne-like sprawl, a vision of calm judgment wrapped in a plaid throw blanket.

"Shoes on in the house?" Shelby asked, lifting a steaming mug in her direction like it was holy communion. "Interesting."

Piper let her bag slide from her shoulder to the floor with a thud and collapsed onto the armchair like a disgraced minor royal.

"Don't start with me," she groaned. "I'm emotionally fragile and physically held together by the hope of coffee in my future."

Shelby raised an eyebrow but wordlessly extended the mug.

Piper reached for it like it was life itself. "I don't need commentary."

"I didn't say anything," Shelby said innocently. "Yet. But your hair says you did the thing. Your vibe says you caught feelings. Your whole aura is screaming mild existential crisis at me."

Piper groaned and sipped the coffee. "It was a one-time thing."

"Is that why you look like you're both ten minutes late for brunch and one epiphany away from a full-blown wedding planner breakthrough?"

"I can't catch feelings. I can't," she insisted, hoping more caffeine would hold the key to what she should do next. "He's the bride's brother. He has dimples *and* a magnetic spice rack, Shelby."

"Oh no. A spice rack?" Shelby gasped, overdramatic. "Someone fetch the elopement schedule; it is time to panic."

Piper set the mug down, not even caring about a coaster.

Then she flopped sideways, covering her face with the throw blanket. "It was everything I can't have."

Shelby pulled the blanket down and then moved the mug to a coaster for her. "You mean… warm, respectful, great in bed, and very emotionally present?"

"That's not the point."

"Then what is the point?"

"The point is," Piper said, sitting up, "I need to refocus. Anna's wedding—remember that whole career thing? The one that doesn't involve admitting I have the emotional bandwidth of a charging battery still at 2%?"

Shelby scoffed. "You didn't get caught up. Girl, you dove right in."

"And that's exactly how you drown."

Shelby eyed her. "Or it's how you plan. With intention. With heart."

Piper wasn't buying it, and Shelby could clearly tell.

"There's no curse, Piper. That's a story you use to stay safe."

Piper didn't answer.

Not out loud.

And Shelby didn't force the issue. But twenty minutes later, when Shelby headed to her shift, Piper opened her laptop and Googled:

Signs you're the problem in relationships

Then:

How to break a curse without a priest

Then:

Is emotional sabotage genetic?

She clicked into a wellness blog post titled: *You're Not Cursed, You're Attracted to Anarchy.*

She noped right out of that browser window. On that note, she slammed the laptop shut. She was officially allergic to optimism. Especially the kind cross-contaminated with internet self-help blogs and almond-laced edible glitter.

And as if the universe didn't love irony, her phone buzzed.

> Zach: Hey. My family has a dinner thing tonight to celebrate Anna and Drake's engagement being official. You should come. Low-key. A good chance to talk to Anna and Drake sans Tess.

The typing dots teased for a moment.

> Zach: And yes, I want you there. That's part of it too.

She started to type *thank you, no.*

Except this was a moment. A choice. A step.

Can we have sex after? she typed automatically.

Then deleted it.

Instead, she inhaled. Long. Steady. Then:

Piper: Sure.

It wasn't a declaration. It wasn't a promise.

But it was open.

And that, maybe, was more terrifying than any curse.

Still. She pressed send. Smiled.

And let hope sneak in just a little. Unexpected glitter in a handshake. That's all this was.

Because maybe, just maybe, she didn't have to run.

Not this time.

CHAPTER 16

ZACH

Piper's defenses sprang up the second things got real. He didn't want to push her, but he wanted her to trust that he could be a safe place to land.

Then he'd had the brilliant idea to invite her to the family dinner. Two birds, one stone, or however that went. They'd hang out, and she'd get time to talk with Anna without Tess.

Tess, who had doubled down and let him know she had a meeting with the higher-ups at the Stallions and would have news for him sometime today or tonight. Honestly, the news could be that they landed the deal… or that she got them free beer tickets for the next game.

He had no idea. But he'd mentioned it to Noah and *that* was a mistake. Noah had been on his case all afternoon for an update.

Noah: Update?

Zach: Nope. Heading to dinner with the fam.

Noah: Thought tonight was dinner w/ Piper?

Zach: She's coming too.

Zach: She needs to talk to Anna without Tess breathing down her neck.

Noah: Uh-huh. Totally just about Anna.

But as Zach straightened his collar in the mirror for the fourth time, his mind wasn't on contracts or brand expansion or the hundred other things that could go wrong.

No, it was all Piper.

The sound she made when he went down on her. How she slept so soundly curled against him. How she tried to run away that morning. With Piper, peeling back each layer only revealed another contradiction—a deeper truth wrapped in more hesitation.

The entire dinner date could end in emotional carnage. Or food poisoning.

Babushka's special borscht had been known to hospitalize weaker souls. Tonight wasn't a test to see if the family liked her, but it was a test to see if she liked the family.

He sniffed his shirt. One last swipe of deodorant, just to be sure.

It was a simple plan—introduce Piper to the Dvornakovs, extract Anna for some wedding talk, and maybe convince Piper that they could be more than what they already were.

He had this in the bag.

Zach grabbed his keys, spun them once around his finger, and slid them into his pocket.

This was either the best idea he'd ever had or a disaster that would take seven generations to live down.

It'd probably land somewhere in between.

His drive across Denver was a condensed chance for his

brain to replay the morning's full-scale Piper retreat, and a solid opportunity for him to question his confidence.

He squashed all that down as he pulled up to her apartment building, the engine humming in the quiet street.

Zach: Here.

A moment later, the front door of her building opened. She walked toward his car with a determined stride, her professional armor firmly in place. Though he caught the slight hesitation in the way she held her purse.

He got out, meeting her on the sidewalk. "Ready for this?"

A small, tight smile touched her lips. "I've reviewed the schematics. I think I can handle it."

"I have faith in you." He held the passenger door for her, a small gesture that felt weighted with all the things they hadn't said since morning. She slid into the seat, her knee brushing his hand as he closed the door, a spark of static that was becoming familiar.

He caught himself sneaking another glance at her. Then another. She didn't notice. She was too busy watching the blur of passing trees and neighborhood houses as if trying to talk herself out of something.

She probably was.

Somehow, she'd managed to look both professional and relaxed in jeans and a blouse that probably had an official color name like "seafoam" or "sage" or something equally specific that he'd never be able to identify.

He nudged the volume knob down, only enough for words to find space.

"So, my family," he started, then cleared his throat. "They're, uh—"

"Enthusiastic wedding planner helpers?" Piper offered.

He snorted. "They have zero chill and maximum opinions. I should probably apologize in advance."

"I've dealt with my family my whole life, Zach. I can handle a family dinner with yours. It'll be cake."

"Yeah, but this isn't just *any* family dinner. This is a *Dvornakov* family dinner, which means someone might interrogate you about your reproductive plans before dessert." He paused at a stoplight, turning to face her. "Just nod, eat everything Babushka hands you unless it's beets, and don't mention astrology, or American cheese."

Piper raised an eyebrow. "American cheese?"

"Trust me. My dad will spend forty-five minutes explaining why it's not real cheese, and then Jase will defend it just to piss him off, and then you'll be stuck in the middle of the Great Cheese Debate all over again."

The corner of her mouth twitched. "Noted. And astrology?"

"We don't talk about astrology." He shivered. The women in his family had strong opinions about astrological charts stronger than his dad's hatred of pasteurized process cheese.

"Want me to go over names again?"

"Nope, I've got it. I made up a little song in my head, and I've been singing it, so I don't forget."

"I want to hear it."

"No."

"Piper?"

"No."

"Piper?"

"Fine." She cleared her throat and sang, "*Sadie is Roman's wedded wife, Heather loves Jase all her life, Anna has Drake to hold on tight, Diana and Alex, Mom and Dad — so right, and Babushka lit the fires so bright.*"

"You actually wrote a song, damn." He liked it. He seriously liked it. Everything was going to be fine.

The moment they walked through the front door of his parents' house, Zach understood that everything was not going to be fine.

The wheeze of his dad's accordion hit them first, followed by the sounds of too many Dvornakovs in one room.

Someone—probably Babushka—was shouting in Russian from the kitchen. Scents of garlic and sour cream mingled in the air, thick and familiar.

Piper froze beside him.

"I warned you," he whispered.

"Don't mention cheese," she said, under her breath.

"It only works if you don't say the words," he said, making his eyes go wide.

Before she could respond, his brother Roman's, voice boomed. "They're here."

Then Jase appeared in the entryway, holding a toddler who looked suspiciously like she'd been eating chocolate with her entire face. "Finally. Nadia's been asking about Uncle Zach for the last hour."

"She can't even form full sentences yet," Zach laughed, reaching for his niece.

Piper was looking at him a little funny. Probably because he was now covered in residual chocolate.

"Nadia communicates. Loudly. Like her great-grandmother." Jase handed over the squirming child, then turned his attention to Piper. "You must be the wedding wizard who's putting up with my brother's bullshit."

"Jase," Zach warned. Growled. Same thing.

"I'm Piper," she said, extending her hand. "And I wouldn't call it wizardry. More like controlled chaos management."

"Oh, I like her. I'm Jase." He grinned and draped his arm around Piper like she was already part of the pack.

Piper allowed it. Seemed to enjoy having a brotherly hug.

And Zach? Zach didn't know what to do with that.

Nadia chose that moment to grab a fistful of Zach's hair and tug.

"Ow. Careful, tiny terror." He shifted the toddler onto his

hip. "This is Nadia. Named after Babushka. Well, Nadzieja, technically, but we call *her* Nadia."

"Because we're not sadists," Jase added.

"Nadia, this is Piper," Zach continued.

"Thank God Jase used the name," Roman's voice called as he entered from the kitchen, arm wrapped around his wife. "I'm officially off the hook."

"Piper, the guy who looks like he should probably take a day off from the gym? That's Roman. Sadie is the one making googly eyes at him."

"Hello." Piper waved.

Heather strode into the room, wiping her hands on a dish-cloth and pausing to introduce herself to Piper before saying, "You are not off the hook, Roman. Not according to Babushka. She was just telling us we need a Nadzieja Two: Electric Boogaloo."

"We're not even expecting," Sadie protested, a blush creeping across her cheeks.

Roman grinned, pulling her closer. "I mean, not yet."

"Who's not expecting what?" his mom asked, heading straight to Piper to give her a hug.

"We're not expecting a baby. Yet. But hold tight, it's not like we're being passive about it," Roman said with a shit eating grin.

"Oh my goodness," Sadie whispered, burying her face in his chest as everyone in the room erupted into cheers and exclamations in half-English, half-Russian.

"Oooh, Nadzieja two," Anna said, sauntering into the room. "Nope. That'd be three, right? Can we call her Zieja? Or Zizi? That's adorable."

"Zizi is cute," Drake chimed in from behind Anna. "What about Nads?"

"Who are we naming?" Zach's dad followed behind Drake, still carrying his accordion.

"Roman and Sadie's eventual kid," Zach said, giving Nadia a squeeze.

"Do not name her after my mother. We already have two. Try something nice like Helen."

"Or maybe Diana?" Mom asked.

"That's a good one, too," Dad agreed.

Sadie groaned with a laugh. "We are not calling our maybe-going-to-happen-someday daughter Nads. We covered this when we were dating."

"Nadzieja means 'hope,'" Roman explained over the commotion. "If it's a girl, I think we could go with Hope."

"Now that's a good name," Dad agreed, adding a few off-key notes for good measure.

Sadie lifted her head, giving her husband a sweet look. "It's perfect."

"What if it's a boy?" Zach asked. "What are you going to name him?"

Roman gave a wicked grin. "Easy. Tractor Beam Kaleidoscope. First name Tractor, middle name Beam Kaleidoscope last name Dvornakov. Very classic."

"Is he serious?" Piper asked, leaning into Zach. He did sound serious.

"I got drunk one night and agreed to it," Sadie said, pulling her lips into a tight line. "I'm totally going with the legal loophole that we cannot enter contracts while intoxicated."

"You weren't *that* drunk." Roman tsked.

"The name says she was," Zach replied, deadpan.

"If it's a boy we're gonna name him Milo," Sadie assured.

"That is really the opposite end of the naming spectrum from the other option," Piper slid her gaze to Zach.

"We should probably focus on the 'making a baby' part before the naming part." Sadie laughed.

"We should get right on that," Roman said, his voice dropping to a register that made several family members groan.

"Nope," Jase stepped in front of the door. "You do not get to leave dinner early. Because if anyone gets to leave, I'm leaving."

"He's not leaving," Heather added.

"Which means no one leaves." Jase pointed two fingers at his eyes and then back at Roman.

Zach leaned toward Piper. "The only official way to get out of a family gathering is to tie Jase to an appliance. But that has yet to happen."

As Heather whisked Nadia away for cleanup, Anna moved to give Piper a big hug. "I was worried you might decide not to come tonight."

"And miss the chance to see the inner workings of the Dvornakovs? Not a chance," Piper said smoothly.

Babushka burst from the kitchen like she was making an entrance on a Broadway stage, arms spread wide. "You brought Piper to dinner. Finally. Ve have been vaiting for you to find someone nice. Ve didn't think this day vould come."

Zach winced and pinched at the bridge of his nose. "Love you, too."

Babushka pulled Piper into a bone-crushing hug while she continued, "Sometimes he says, 'oh! Babushka! I am seeing a new voman, and then she never comes to dinner. Ve start to vonder if he even tells the truth or if he prefers to die alone with no vife or children to love him. Only under-vear. But undervear do not keep you varm and give you love."

"Fuck," Zach muttered, heat climbing his neck.

"Ve don't say that vord," Babushka tsked.

"She keeps saying that, but we keep saying it anyway." Jase shrugged.

Piper emerged from the hug looking slightly dazed. "Thank you for having me."

"Come," Babushka insisted, taking Piper by the arm. "Food is ready. Then ve talk vedding. And maybe other things." She winked at Zach with all the subtlety of a freight train. "Do you like children? They are a blessing, yes?"

Dinner was a blur of dishes being passed, conversations overlapping, and Piper somehow managing to field questions from all directions.

Jase was asking her about Montgomery Events. "You do funerals, too? That's depressing."

"Actually, memorial services can be incredibly meaningful," Piper replied. "It's about creating space for both grief and celebration. But, no, I don't plan the actual funerals, usually."

"She landed a huge account with the funeral directors' association," Zach added, pride slipping into his voice before he could stop it.

"Ve are very happy. Except she has to vork vith Morty, who deserves to regrow his bunions." Babushka said, haughtily.

"That man you gave money to?" Dad asked, frowning. "I do not like that man."

Well, this was not looking to end well.

"Pfft. He paid me back," Babushka said. "That is not vhy he deserves the gout."

Diana leaned forward, ignoring Babushka to focus only on Piper. "How's the wedding coming?"

"Really excellent," Piper said. "And once the engagement is announced in a few days and everything goes public? It'll all really start falling into place, I think."

Jase smirked. "Never mind the wedding. Mom wants to know how long you and Zach are going to keep pretending you're just colleagues?"

Zach choked on his water. "We weren't pretending—"

"We're colleagues," Piper said smoothly. "With mutual goals."

"'Mutual goals," Jase repeated, wiggling his eyebrows. "Is that what they're calling it these days?"

"Stop terrorizing them," Anna said, but she was grinning, too.

Zach looked desperately for a distraction. "Anna, you look substantially less pukey lately."

Thankfully, the conversation shifted to Anna's morning sickness, which meant babies and more Dvornakovs, which meant Zach got a moment to breathe. He snuck a glance at Piper, who was nodding along to whatever his father was saying about the stock market.

How was she doing this?

He'd expected her to be overwhelmed, maybe even want to check out. Instead, she was not just surviving but somehow charming everyone. Like right then. She'd distracted Dad from all things Babushka's ex-boyfriend. That was not an easy task, at all.

By the time they moved to dessert, Piper had the entire room engaged in a discussion about wedding traditions that had Babushka giddy with excitement.

Zach's phone buzzed in his pocket. He ignored it at first—too caught up in watching Piper somehow orchestrate his entire family like she was born to it. But when the screen lit up again, he finally slipped it out, half-expecting another nudge from Noah.

Tess: You got the green light. Let's talk fittings with Drake and the players. Details in your inbox now.

He stared at the screen.

He got the deal.

They got the deal.

That goal. The one he'd been chasing since he started the company. It was happening. His brand. The Stallions. A major marketing play.

> Tess: NDA in place. Not a whisper to anyone outside Wild Sacks until I talk to agents and arrange schedules. Then we loop everyone in.

He glanced across the table at Piper as she talked with Babushka, using her hands to explain something, her face totally animated with excitement.

The win landed with a thud in his gut. He'd just been handed everything he wanted and the one person he wanted to tell was sitting three feet away, completely off-limits.

His phone buzzed again.

> Noah: Updates from Tess? I'm dying here.

> Zach: Just heard. It's yes. NDA till briefing.

> Noah: THAT'S ALL YOU HAVE TO SAY?

> Zach: PARTY EMOJI LEVEL EXCITEMENT UP IN HERE.

> Noah: Meet after your date.. THIS IS HUGE.

"Zach?" Piper asked. "Everything okay?"

He thumbed the screen dark, every instinct shouting to *tell her*.

"Yeah," he said, and the word felt like a pebble in his shoe. "Just Noah. A work thing."

"You know, Piper, if the underwear plan doesn't work out, Zach still has his job waiting for him with the family company," Dad assured, beaming. "He's got a good future."

Thing was, Dad meant that as a compliment. But whenever he brought up that Zach still had a job waiting for him as a back-up plan? He hated how small he felt.

Piper studied him from across the table, her expression level and unreadable in the low light.

He went for the joke, the half-truth. "Don't worry, Dad. We all know that men in underwear fix everything."

"You look like you either won the lottery or ate something questionable," Roman said, laughing.

"He always looks like that," Jase added.

Zach laughed, then ribbed, "Better than looking like you."

The rest of the family went back to the conversation, but Piper studied him for a second longer. Tilting her head in question.

Dammit, he didn't understand how he was feeling.

Why? Did he want to tell her because she was a convenient audience for monumental news?

No. It was more than that.

He wanted to see that light in her eyes. The one that shone with genuine excitement and a flicker of pride *for him.*

He wanted to hear her say, "Zach, that's incredible," in that earnest way she had of making a person believe every single word. The Stallions.

It was the biggest deal of his career, a win that should have him vibrating out of his skin.

But keeping it locked inside, keeping it from *her*… it was like uncorking flat champagne. It tasted fine and it got the job done, but it wasn't the same.

CHAPTER 17

ZACH

"Now, for dress," Babushka announced, "you need something vith more sparkle. That is the Dvornakov vay. Don't be so plain vith your choices."

"I don't want sparkle, Babushka," Anna protested. "I want simple and elegant."

"Simple is for funeral, ask Piper," Babushka declared. "Vedding needs life. Excitement."

Mom nodded. "Maybe just a little beading on the bodice?"

"Or a crystal belt," Heather suggested.

"What about a statement veil instead?" Sadie asked.

"Anna, what do you envision when you picture yourself walking down the aisle?" Piper gently redirected.

Anna's face gentled. "I like my dress how it is. It flows. It's comfortable. I feel like *me* in it."

"That's exactly what you should have," Piper said firmly. "It's your day."

"Yes, but—" Babushka started.

"And," Piper continued smoothly, "I think there are ways to honor traditions that matter to your family while staying true to your vision. Maybe we incorporate something special into the bouquet? Or a piece of jewelry that sparkles? Is there something special that Anna could use?"

Babushka paused, considering. "My mother's sapphire pins. For hair."

Anna's eyes misted. "Really? You'd let me use those?"

Everyone knew Babushka didn't let anyone touch her mother's jewelry.

"For you? Of course." Babushka beamed. "See? Sparkle!"

Zach stared, slack-jawed.

"Did Piper outmaneuver Babushka?" Jase asked, so only Zach could hear.

Babushka who once convinced an entire church congregation to move a wedding outside because she didn't care for the carpet color?

"Now I just have to hope my dress will still fit," Anna said with a laugh. But she dragged her fingers through her hair like the weight of the entire wedding rested solely on her shoulders.

"Is it tight?" Piper asked.

"No. It's fine," Anna said, scrunching up her nose like the word tasted bad. "It'll be fine. I just worry my waist is getting too big too fast."

Zach studied Piper more than he participated in the rest of the evening. She remembered everyone's names. She helped his mother bring out dessert plates. She somehow wrangled the table, making room for the cheesecake and the anatomically correct pirozhki Babushka made because she knew Piper enjoyed it last time.

When his father started complaining about the neighbors' new love of blaring backyard Ed Sheeran, Zach knew deep in his gut that the good times were officially over.

"Every night. Every single night," his dad grumbled, arms crossed like a human *NO TRESPASSING* sign. "People have no concept of respect."

"Aggressive Ed Sheeran is the worst," Piper said, not dismissively but with enough interest to suggest she kept a running list of personal injustices, and this one made the cut. "This is new? Because sunset Sheeran every single night is infuriating."

Zach blinked. His father blinked harder. Someone was on his side?

"It started a few months ago, I guess," his dad said slowly, adjusting to this sudden shift in audience energy. "New owners moved in. Used to be quiet as anything next door."

"Ah. A shift in the neighborhood ecosystem," Piper mused, nodding like she wasn't just invested. No, she was emotionally drafting a proposal to the HOA. "That's the worst. I mean, they know what they're doing and still do it anyway, right?"

He hesitated, visibly wobbling between decades of practiced curmudgeon and something dangerously close to open conversation. "I mean, they're nice enough the rest of the time."

"Mmm." Piper leaned in slightly like she was sharing a secret. "What do you think? Are they being deliberately inconsiderate, or are they simply that *special* kind of clueless?"

Dad frowned, then sighed as if the question had won a small, inconvenient victory. "They might not know."

"Well, if you tell them and they keep doing it, then you'll know they're just jerks," Jase chimed in cheerfully. "Not inadvertent assholes."

"Clarity is a good thing," Anna said, pointedly staring at Piper.

There was a pause. Zach's dad glanced at Piper, still wearing his usual armor but with a flicker of something else. Consideration, maybe. Interest, possibly. Wonder, if Zach was being very dramatic—which, sadly, was his default setting with her.

She knew exactly what she was doing.

She knew how to play this family game of his.

She fits here better than me.

And that—more than anything—terrified him. Because he could have everything he wanted at the start of this gig. But it wasn't about the deal anymore. Not really.

It was her.

He stood to help clear the plates, stacking them neatly and feeling oddly domestic as he made his way to the kitchen.

"Don't screw it up," Jase whispered, suddenly beside him, so close that Zach startled, nearly dropping a fork.

"Not planning on it," Zach replied, shooting him a sideways look as he opened the dishwasher.

Even as he said that, a quiet knot tightened in his gut. He was keeping the latest Tess revelation from her, and the longer he did, the heavier it would be.

"We like her," Jase said, his voice low but firm, like he was issuing a family decree. He pointed his index and middle finger at his eyes, then at Zach's.

Zach scoffed, turning back toward the sink. "We're not—"

"Save it." Jase waved a dismissive hand. "I've seen that look before. On my own face, right before I realized Heather was it for me."

"You're totally misreading this—"

"Shh." Jase held up his fingertip dramatically to Zach's lips, ignoring the loaded dinner plate in Zach's hand. "Time for your happily married brother to dispense wisdom. Listen carefully, baby bro."

Zach swatted Jase's hand away, setting down the plate before something shattered. "Could you not do that while I'm holding our mother's good china?"

Jase pursed his lips, thoughtful. "A lesser-known sign you're falling for someone is when you start caring whether plates survive."

"You're delusional," Zach muttered.

"Well-known and documented. But this isn't about me,

this is about you and how she fits. You know how rare that is, especially with... well, all of us."

Zach dried his hands, then paused, gripping the towel a little too tightly. "I don't want to mess it up by rushing it."

Jase eased. "You're not rushing. You're feeling something real, and it scares the hell out of you. That's normal. You know what's not normal? Smiling like an idiot when someone talks about sunset Sheeran with Dad."

Zach cracked a reluctant grin.

"There he is." Jase clapped him on the back. "All you gotta do is keep showing up. Let fate handle the rest."

"Yeah?" Zach asked, his voice quieter now.

"Yeah," Jase said. "And if you ever doubt it, look around. We may be a lot, but we're fucking fantastic."

Zach didn't answer right away. But the smile stayed, lingering in the corners of his mouth as he gathered the silverware.

He wasn't ready to call it falling in love.

But maybe it was something that felt a lot like home.

"Now, first lesson from your relationship sensei," Jase said. "When you find someone who can handle Babushka without having a nervous breakdown, you lock. That. Down."

"You're getting way ahead of things. We're just working together and figuring things out."

Jase snorted. "Yeah, and I was just 'tasting the frosting' with Heather in the cookie kitchen. My point is, when you know, you know. And she's definitely the one."

The one.

"Zachary." Babushka's voice cut through his spiral. "Come. Ve need man's opinion on centerpieces and Drake doesn't care."

The rest of the night blurred together. More wedding talk. More family stories. More watching Piper seamlessly integrate herself into the controlled chaos of his life.

By the time they were saying goodbyes, Zach felt like he

was underwater, everything muffled and still but oddly urgent.

The drive back was quiet—Zach's knuckles white on the steering wheel, his mind racing.

"I got some great ideas from Anna. Thank you for this time with her," Piper said.

Zach nodded. "Of course."

"And they're amazing. Your family," Piper said. "You're lucky."

He glanced over. She was looking out the window, her profile illuminated by passing streetlights.

"They can be a lot," he managed.

"No, they're..." She hesitated. "They're connected. Present. My family is so fractured after all the divorces. My mom, dad, and sister? They're all scattered across different states, different lives."

Zach didn't know what to say about that. He'd always taken his family's closeness for granted, even when it drove him crazy.

"Babushka gave me her pirozhki recipe," Piper continued.

He tried to laugh, but it came out strangled. "Yeah, she does that."

"Are you okay? You've gotten quiet."

"I'm fine," he lied. "Tired."

Telling her was out of the question. But not telling her—keeping it locked up—felt worse.

They hesitated at the curb when he parked, neither quite ready to say goodnight. He moved closer across the console, brushing a knuckle under her chin to tilt her face toward his.

"Thanks for coming with," he murmured, his voice low. Her eyes flicked to his mouth.

He leaned in slowly, giving her the chance to turn away if she wanted.

She didn't. Their lips met in a kiss that began muted, careful, then found its gravity.

No rush. There was time in it, weight, the press of everything unsaid. Her hand slid to his chest, steadying herself as the kiss lingered on, breath shared between them.

When they finally separated, it was with a quiet exhale, like they'd both been holding their breath.

He smiled, brushing an errant strand of hair behind her ear.

"Do you want to come in?" she asked.

"Yes," he said without any pause. Then he exhaled and pulled back. "But I can't. Noah's waiting at the shop to go over shit with me."

Shit he wanted to tell her all about.

She nodded once, then looked down. "Right. Of course."

She hesitated only slightly before starting to open the car door.

No, he couldn't do this. He couldn't keep it from her.

"Wait," Zach said, his voice rough.

Piper paused, and turned, questioning.

"I want to tell you something," he said, his hands sweaty.

"Okay?"

"I'm not supposed to tell anyone outside Wild Sacks, but..." He shrugged, meeting her gaze. "You're not just anyone."

That bought him a grin.

"Hire me. Then it's legal," she said, offhandedly.

"The pay is crap, and the hours are nothing," he teased.

She turned slowly and waved her hand like she had a magic wand. "I can live with that. Consider me having applied with HR."

"Great. You're hired." He leaned back, resisting the urge to touch her. "We got the Stallions deal."

Piper blinked, processing. Then grinned huge. "Really? That's amazing."

She moved in to give him a big hug before pulling back.

"Yeah. It's happening." He ran a hand through her hair. "And I just... I just had to tell you."

"I can tell. That hiring paperwork is a nightmare." She moved forward and kissed him again. "Zach?" she asked with a quirky grin.

"Yeah?"

"I quit. I can't be sleeping with my boss." She wrinkled her nose. "It's tacky."

He chuckled. "We're gonna have a meet at the shop with Tess. I'll text you a random time. You can swing by and *accidentally* find out for yourself," he offered. His tone was hopeful.

"Consider it done." She opened the door and stepped outside. "Goodnight, Zach," she said before closing the door behind her.

Business: secured.

The deal: done.

His family: happy.

And Piper?

She was the one variable he hadn't accounted for. The one thing he'd refused to examine too closely. Because once he did, he knew the weight of it would shift everything.

But it turned out that he didn't need to examine it to make it matter. She mattered all on her own. And his world was all tangled now. Piper. The deal. His feelings.

He closed his eyes and let his head fall back against the seat, the car quiet around him. Everything he'd ever wanted was in motion, each domino exactly where it needed to be.

But all he could think about was her.

CHAPTER 18

35 DAYS UNTIL ANNA
& DRAKE'S WEDDING

PIPER

Anna and Drake's engagement shoot at the Denver Botanic Gardens was gorgeous. Sunlight shone through the leaves of a solidly old-as-hell oak, reflecting over Anna in a glow that had nothing to do with light staging.

"Get closer," Tess called, standing behind Roman.

"Like you actually tolerate him, Anna," Roman added, playfully.

Since Roman was a photographer, *and* the bride's brother, he got drafted to help. Also, he was amazingly good at what he did and ridiculously hard to book without a long lead time.

"The light through the conservatory glass is perfect." Tess glanced to the sky. "But we'll need to move with those clouds. I'll go get the next spot prepped to take advantage of the shadows." She was a bundle of busy, juggling ten invisible balls at once.

Meanwhile, Drake couldn't seem to take his gaze away from Anna. He stared with the stunned, giddy expression of a man who'd just found that a winning lottery ticket wasn't paper, it was her.

Even Anna's mom drifted at the edge of the group, tilting a peony in its container.

"Just a little this way," she whispered, her gaze then fixing on her daughter. "Oh, Piper... the light." A cascade of gold reflected in Anna's hair that was, frankly, unfair.

Roman took the shot and Piper had no doubt he'd nabbed it perfectly.

"Um... have you heard from Babushka?" Piper asked as Diana and Roman moved more potted peonies into the walkway. "I half expected her to show up with a ceremonial breadbasket to test the lighting."

"I could go for bread," Roman admitted.

"Of course you can, you're a Dvornakov." Diana chuckled, a warm, motherly sound. "Babushka's off with Zach. He's been busy with something important lately. He won't tell any of us what it is." She waved a dismissive hand, a gesture of fond exasperation. "That's how he gets with his projects."

"No kidding," Roman agreed. "One minute he goes silent, the next he's started his own company. Who knows what he's got going down this time?"

"Since Babushka's involved, I just hope it's legal." Diana sighed. "But it's Zach, of course it's legal."

Piper tucked a little bit of pride against her ribs, a secret warmth. She was the one he'd trusted. The invisible thread that had been spooling out between them for weeks gave a distinct, satisfying tug.

Her gaze drifted to the entry.

She should have been focused entirely on the details, on the laminated schedule, on the photographer's cues. But her focus kept going to the door to see if Zach showed. This was a ridiculous, unprofessional habit she couldn't seem to shake today.

The strange sort of unfamiliar ache of hope that Zach would pop by just to say hello was driving her crazy.

Zach wasn't coming. He'd been swallowed whole by the Stallions deal. While the rest of the world, including his own family, saw him as merely busy, Piper knew the truth.

The knowledge was a secret handshake, a silent pact that made her feel closer to him even when he was lost in work, wrestling with contracts and underwear prototypes.

Today, though, wasn't about missing Zach. It was about witnessing what could actually be an honest-to-goodness fairy tale. Not that long ago—heck, not even a month ago— she'd sworn this didn't exist. Not in her orbit, anyway.

With Tess working on the next stage, Piper took it as an opportunity to let Roman have some time alone with the couple, so she called Aspen.

"Aspen, hey," Piper ducked her head and stepped away.

"Surviving the vortex of true love and public relations?" Aspen asked, hopeful.

"You know what?" Piper took it all in—the gardens, the nauseatingly cute couple, the gorgeous setting. "Photos are happening. Tess has the post-announcement blitz planned, and she's doing it with a skeleton crew since the hockey team poached a bunch of her staff."

"I figure the Dvornakovs have the flowers well in hand, but how's everything else? Cake? Anything actively on fire?" Aspen asked.

"Zach's grandma was able to find edible glitter in the right color, so the cake is back on track." Piper let out a breath. Thank goodness for small miracles. "The location is a go, and I think we might actually pull this off."

"I had absolutely no doubt. And our favorite funeral direc- tors? They're happy?" Aspen asked.

"Back-burnered a bit, but they are good with that. We put in the dates for the big conference, and they've given a solid lead time for me to secure great speakers who are experts on...well, you know." Piper waved her hand dismissively, even though Aspen couldn't see it. "No worries there."

"Piper?" Aspen's voice went quiet, her teasing tone gone. "I'm really proud of you."

Piper's chest did a funny little squeeze-and-release thing. "Thanks.

"Do you like the peony placement?" Diana called from beside the walkway where the whole down on one knee bit would happen.

Piper glanced that way and gave a thumbs up.

"You're busy. I'll let you go," Aspen said, finishing up the call. "You're doing great."

Piper stuck the phone in her pocket and, clipboard in hand, forced her nerves to stay calm.

This wasn't about forever; this was only about photos. About the job at hand.

"They're sweet together," Diana said, striding toward Piper. "It makes me happy."

The reality of them was undeniable. It was in the way Anna's laugh lit her eyes, in the way Drake's hand found the small of her back without thinking.

They gazed at each other, laughed with each other, even frowned at each other over a misplaced curl, and it was all so seamless. So beautiful. A quiet part of her, the part that wasn't calloused over by her history, started to believe.

"This makes me happy, too," Piper said.

"Can I say something that I probably shouldn't?" Diana asked.

"With a lead-in like that I think you have to," Piper countered.

"Zach mentioned early on that you're not a fan of weddings." She held up her hand before she could say anything else. "And I get why that might be when it's just another day at the office. But there's so much more to a love story than the wedding. So much more." She put her hand down. "I just, I can see that you want to like it. But for whatever reason, you don't."

Piper blinked. Hard.

"I'll stop now. I like to talk too much." Diana crossed her arms around herself.

"No." Piper glanced to the concrete path, then back to Diana. "Thank you for saying that. I'm really not a fan, and I guess maybe I've started to re-evaluate that position."

"You know, it's funny, we've been through three weddings already with the kids and it just never gets boring," Diana said, wistfully. "Alex and I just love this part."

Hold on. "Three weddings?"

There were four Dvornakov children, two were married and Anna was on her way there. Which meant... the math didn't add up.

"When Jase got married the first time, they never looked at each other quite that way." Diana stayed lost in a memory. "I mean, they were in love, and it was clear, but it wasn't like this."

"Jase was married. Before Heather?" Or did he and Heather sign up for the Daws style wedding plan where they tried it a few times?

Really, it was none of Piper's business and it was her turn to hush.

Diana didn't seem to mind. She nodded. "He was. But he was military, so he was gone a lot, and she wasn't good at being alone."

Piper's stomach started to hurt.

"Sometimes everyone can do everything right and it just doesn't work," Diana mused.

Piper couldn't entirely be certain how she looked in that moment, but she would guess she'd probably turned a shade of green that matched Anna the first day they'd met. "Oh?"

"And then they meet the right person, and you can't really remember a time anymore when they weren't together."

Diana smiled, wistfully. "Except we have photos to prove it." She laughed. "The photographic evidence is where it gets you." She winked.

Her gaze drifted to the man orchestrating the magic. Roman was so muscled he was built like a tank, but he moved with the quiet grace of a predator, knelt with his camera—he called her Louise—cradled in his hands.

He was all intense focus and cropped hair, a man on a mission, but a genuine smile softened his features when he looked up from the viewfinder.

"It hasn't been easy for Roman, either," Diana said, like they were talking about the peonies again. "He and Sadie took two tries to get it right."

Two tries.

The words snagged in Piper's brain, tripping over the carefully organized files of evidence she'd been collecting her entire adult life. Her entire philosophy—the one built on the wreckage of her parents' catastrophic marriages—was predicated on a single, brutal theorem: if it failed, she was the failure. She was the curse. The common denominator.

But Jase... Roman... they'd failed and she was nowhere around.

But then they'd just... tried again? With someone new? And it had *worked*?

Diana must have seen the shock ghost across Piper's face, because she turned from watching her son, her expression gentling. "Love isn't a test you can fail, you know," she said, her voice as warm and comforting as the afternoon sun. Her gaze drifted back to Anna and Drake, who now laughed as Roman directed them into another pose. "We all think it's supposed to be a straight line, a perfect plan from start to finish. But it's not. Sometimes you have to get a little lost to find the right path." She looked at Piper then, her eyes full of a simple, profound truth that landed with the force of a revelation. "My Alex, he broke two engagements before me. Drove his mother nuts. But he told me early on that he's a terrible driver when it comes to love. I told him he just hadn't found the right road yet. The detours are part of the map, Piper."

Piper's internal ledger, with its neat columns of proof that she was wedding kryptonite, suddenly looked like nonsense.

The clipboard in her hands felt ridiculous. All her neat columns and color-coded tabs were proof of a debunked theorem.

Maybe she wasn't cursed. The paths weren't linear, and she'd thought it was her fault. But it was life. Not her. The idea was so foreign, so radically optimistic, that it stole the air from Piper's lungs. All this time she'd seen her history as a verdict, a final judgment.

But what if Diana was right?

What if it was all just… mileage? Practice?

The thought didn't settle comfortably.

"You two look like you're plotting a government takeover. What'd I miss?" Zach asked, striding toward them, his hands tucked in his pockets. He had that easy grin that always seemed to make her squirm.

No warning, no text, no explanation. One moment the world was a soft-focus memory she was observing from the sidelines, and the next, there was Zach, stepping into the middle of the shoot like he belonged there.

The sight of him was a dash of something warm and solid in the middle of her suddenly shifting universe.

Diana's smile was serene, as if she'd been expecting him. "I was just telling Piper how Roman and Sadie reconnected after all that time apart. How the second try was the one that stuck."

"She also told me Jase was married before," Piper's gaze met Zach's, and the words tumbled out before she could stop them, a confirmation of the impossible.

Zach let out a low whistle, his grin turning wry. "Wow, Mom's spilling all the family secrets today, huh?" He glanced between the two of them, his expression relaxing as he seemed to read the room. "Yeah, well. Once my brothers pulled their heads out of their asses, they finally got it right. Just took them a while to get there."

Diana made a simple noise under her breath, a fond, exasperated sound as she turned to fuss with nearby flowers. "It's not like you're winning the race when it comes to finding love, Zachary."

"Now you sound like Babushka," he said, feigning hurt.

"Take that back," Diana admonished, but her words were kind.

"And, for the record." He took Piper's hand in his. "I'd say my timing has been perfect."

Perfect timing.

Not cursed timing. Not failed timing. Perfect.

"Well, I think it's time for a break." Diana clapped her hands. "We're going to take five, everyone."

"I guess we're taking five." Piper's gaze moved from their joined hands to his face. The easy grin was gone, replaced by an intensity that stole the air from her lungs.

Roman nodded in agreement, and Anna and Drake headed inside the building.

Zach gave Piper's hand a gentle tug, leading her around the edge of the garden, toward the sprawling trunk of a large tree.

"And where are we going now?" Piper asked, playfully swinging their arms as they walked together.

"Somewhere a little more private," Zach replied, guiding her into the secluded space behind the thick trunk. He moved in front of her, so her back was to the tree and his body shielded hers.

"You know, I'm at work right now. I can't just run away," she said.

"Strategic exit during an earned break," Zach said, eyeing her carefully. "And no one is watching."

The air between them shifted to something deeper. Zach's eyes searched hers, asking for permission without actually asking. Giving her the space to say no.

"Is this also part of your 'perfect timing'?" she teased, touching her fingertip to his lips.

"It's the most important part," he said, nipping at her finger before he leaned in and kissed her.

Before Piper could form a single, coherent question, his mouth was on hers.

It wasn't a gentle kiss.

He didn't ask. He didn't hesitate. His mouth came down on hers, a firm, undeniable pressure that wasn't a question but an answer. It was the taste of a future.

CHAPTER 19

28 DAYS UNTIL ANNA
& DRAKE'S WEDDING

PIPER

Well, the engagement announcement did not go well.

Rings Before Rings? Fans Worry Engagement Will Break Super Bowl Streak

The Engagement Heard 'Round the Stadium: Fans Fear It'll Sack the Season

Tess was activating full frantic, everybody mode, Zach had been busy, and Piper's schedule hadn't slowed, either. Then she got a message:

> Zach: Stop by my place. There will be puppies.

> Piper: Is that code?

> Zach: You're gonna want to see this. Stop by when you have a sec.

Piper stepped into Wild Sacks HQ and came chest-to-pecs

with a football player wearing nothing but a pair of boxer briefs and an unapologetic grin.

Football players—real Stallions players, including Drake—walked around in their skivvies.

Bins of Wild Sacks underwear overflowed like a fabric rainbow, meticulously sorted by cut and color in a valiant attempt at order.

And a whiteboard titled The Stallion Right Up Front with exclamation points, diagrams, and hearts she suspected were ironically drawn and yet suspiciously well-balanced.

"This one? The cut is too high," Babushka pushed him away toward the back. "Leave something to the imagination," she said to another elderly woman with a bolt of fabric balanced on her walker. "Football is family friendly."

The woman nodded and shuffled behind Mr. Football and Babushka.

There were another four women of a certain age group all working together at a couple of sewing machines. The fabric practically flying.

There was definitely a vibe. A creative, weirdly energizing, scents-like-leather-glue-and-masculinity kind of vibe.

And there were puppies.

The design studio side of the industrial space had been transformed into a workshop-slash-fever dream—if said fever also came with a whole lotta puppies, a group of elderly assistants, and a minor fire code violation due to the sheer number of people present.

Zach stood nearby, mid-conversation with a tattooed tight end who looked like he could bench-press a Harley. Zach was animated and easy, gesturing toward a cluster of mannequins styled in Wild Sacks boxer briefs.

He had his sleeves rolled up and a pencil behind one ear. One of the elderly assistants handed him a binder—something suspiciously like her own—and he flipped through it like it contained the secrets of the universe.

He looked in charge. Not of people, though.

Of ideas. Of energy. Of the strange magic that came when chaos was guided by someone who genuinely believed in the madness.

The playlist in the background was a mix of hyped-up beats with basslines that lived in her sternum. It skipped once, and Babushka hollered that she "vould fix it."

"Fixing it" was apparently blaring "Pony" by Ginuwine as one of the helpers knocked over the decorative arch of footballs.

And near the food table, someone was trying to coax a puppy off a table with a food spread using what appeared to be a granola bar and whispered assurances of freedom.

Piper shook her head. "There really are puppies."

"I told you there would be," Zach mumbled, stepping toward her and staring straight at her as he said, "Hi."

"Hi," she replied staring right back.

"Hey." Tess whistled with two fingers between her lips. "When you're done with your fitting, hand off the underwear to Peggy."

"Is that her grandma, Peggy?" Piper whispered.

Zach nodded. "Babushka's friend. They're helping out given the lack-of-Tess-staff at the moment."

Tess glanced over to Zach and clearly caught sight of Piper because she immediately waved. She strode over as if nothing was remotely out of the ordinary and there weren't half-naked football players strutting everywhere.

"Piper!" she said, infusing the word with excitement. "Welcome to the cross-promotional activation for the official undergarment partner of the Denver Stallions. Wild Sacks!"

"Uh..." Piper stared at the room. There was probably something she was supposed to say here.

"She means we're the official underwear of the Stallions," Zach nudged.

Piper turned to Zach and did her best impression of utter surprise. "Get out! For real?"

"And we're being used as a distraction because nothing says ditch the superstition and look the other way quite like men in their underwear," Zach continued.

"Exactly." Tess rubbed her hands together, then hugged herself.

A tiny smirk peeked out the side of Zach's mouth. "Also, I thought NDAs were in place, Tess?"

"Piper's covered." Tess blew out her breath. "Besides, the grandmothers are all here, and I trust Piper way more than them. NDAs are the least of my concerns."

"Well, in that case, Piper, welcome to the official engagement distraction," Zach said.

"Definitely a distraction," Piper agreed.

Tess held her hands up like she was telling a story. "Imagine—"

Oh, I don't have to.

"*But* we're on the football field with a live stream."

"That sounds like… a lot of distraction," Piper said.

"Exactly. "

"We're already assuring that the wedding is going to happen fast. *Now* we inundate them with football players in the brand-new official underwear of the Stallions. And, as a bonus, if the players aren't enough—" She leveled her stare at Piper. "Puppies in mini–Wild Sacks bandanas."

"That is most definitely a distraction," Piper agreed, eyeing one of the puppies as he peed on a pair of cleats.

"The setting will be the actual field. Thank goodness, Legal cleared it. Then we're going to interview the players, showing off their Wild Sacks and holding the puppies." Tess made a ta-da gesture.

"The live stream will have links to both Wild Sacks and the puppy adoption profiles. They're rescues," Zach added.

"Noah and I agreed that a portion of Wild Sacks's sales will go to the shelter."

"That sounds like it will be..." Mayhem? Insanity? "Fun." Piper went with fun. Her voice was high and bright, like a balloon someone had overinflated.

There was a beat of silence in which Tess's overzealous smile trembled at the corners, just a little. "It's got to work. Right? You agree it's going to work?"

She looked at Piper like a magician who had pulled a rabbit out of a hat and was waiting to see whether the audience clapped or pointed out the ears sticking out of her sleeve.

Zach tilted his head. "Piper? Thoughts?"

Piper raised her chin and walked forward. "It's going to work."

Zach's smile hit her like a well-placed body shot—low, unexpected, and hard to recover from.

"For real? A sanity check," Tess said, sliding in beside Piper. "Because I feel like this is all starting to be too much."

"Adding a dozen puppies to anything will do that," Piper agreed.

"Today is fittings and pairings only," Zach said. "Ensuring fit and getting the puppy matches that work best for each player. Today's the easy day."

Babushka wailed, "Vatch out!" right before a mannequin toppled over onto a garment rack, which collapsed with a musical clang like a steel drum of despair.

"Do not vorry. It is fine," Babushka hollered.

But it didn't really seem fine.

Tess gnawed at her bottom lip. "I'm working with the one staffer who didn't bail to the hockey-team-that-won't-be-named and two interns who can't leave because they need the grade."

Now, that?

"That makes this too much," Piper said, pointing to the broken mannequin.

"We could use a hand here. Things are..." Zach ducked his chin.

Out of control? Totally obnoxious? Piper could make a long list of what *things* were there.

"Spinning," Tess admitted.

A twinge of recognition hit Piper square in the chest. Trying to balance everything, when nothing was stable, always made things harder than they needed to be.

"I can sell the vision," Tess continued. "That's what I do. But we must nail the logistics, or the field day will eat us alive."

Piper couldn't help it, she immediately started organizing the room in her mind. Making little micro-plans to ease the load.

"Piper? You're the queen of organization. Could you... maybe... add this to the list of wedding stuff that needs doing?" Zach asked, sheepish. "Only if you have time."

"I'm in over my head," Tess admitted.

Piper nodded. "If you want my help."

"Yes, please. But together," Tess added quickly. "You keep us organized. I keep the vision."

Now that? That Piper could do.

"I'm so glad you're here," shirtless Drake said, joining their impromptu tête-à-tête. "Anna doesn't want to call you but her dress is tight around the waist, and she doesn't want to bug anyone, so she's not telling anybody."

Piper exhaled. Great. "I'll check in with Anna when we're done here."

As she rolled up her metaphorical sleeves and started to audit the schedule and take notes on the current puppy assignments, something shifted. Slowly. Quietly.

What was messy became confidently checked.

"I like this." Zach came up behind her once the puppies

were loaded to go back to the shelter. "Working with you. Having you here."

He liked it. And she liked that he liked it. And she absolutely hated that she liked it.

"Okay, rapid-fire opinion time," Noah said as he pushed a rack of cast-offs by. "Are boxers-with-rhinestones tacky or genius?"

"Tacky," she said immediately. "Obviously."

"Genius," Zach said at the same time. "Obviously."

"Good to see we have a consensus." Noah nodded, smirking as he moved along.

Zach leaned in closer.

She turned to face him, inching back just enough to breathe. "Maybe they can be both."

Hold on, were they talking about men's boxers or something else?

"Fittings," Noah called. "Drake is in Flagship Black boxer briefs. Tight end over there is in compression. Rookie, you get Bolt trunks."

"Pairings," Piper echoed, scanning the kennel list. "Drake with the lab mix for steady, loyal. Tight end with the golden for camera candy. Rookie with the scrappy terrier."

"Talking points," Tess added. "Drake is team, family, and city. Tight end is strength and community. Rookie is new beginnings."

"Excellent." Zach's eyes sparkled, but the lazy smirk dissolved into something quieter. Kinder. "Thank you for coming and not immediately leaving."

Piper narrowed her eyes. "I feel slightly ambushed."

He laughed, warm and amused and—*ugh*—chest-rumbling. "Fair. I guess I owe you."

They ended up shoulder to shoulder in front of the spreadsheet displaying the player stats and which puppy they were assigned.

Nothing about this was polished or met even her vaguest

professional standards. But somehow it worked. Thoughtful. Intentional. Slightly unhinged. And still managing to hum with the possibility of magic.

She blinked at the screen, the command center inside her brain certifiably fried. She was disoriented. Not because things were wrong, but because they weren't.

"Hey," Zach said quietly. "You okay?"

Piper's throat tightened, but Zach's steady gaze held her steady, too. After a breath, she said, "This isn't what I expected. You're not what I expected."

That made him turn. "No?"

She shook her head and met his gaze, steady now. "That's the problem."

He didn't respond. Just looked at her with a slow, knowing smile that landed like a warning shot straight to her equilibrium.

And that—the way her ribcage felt like it was expanding too fast, and her brain couldn't keep pace—that was a real problem.

"I need to go check in with Anna." Piper bit at her bottom lip.

"Want me to tag along?" he asked.

Piper scanned the leftover destruction. "I think you've got quite a bit left to do here."

He nodded and gave her a quick kiss. Nothing special, just a standard goodbye-for-now kiss between two people who cared about each other.

That was the part that made her queasy. Because it was normal. Nothing unusual. And that made it extra special.

Right before she crossed the threshold, she muttered under her breath, "This is dangerous. I like this. I like him."

"Piper," Babushka caught her before she could get out the door. She patted Piper's cheek. "You are vorried. Do not vorry. You vill fix dress. You are like pretty duct tape. Ve are lucky you are here."

Piper almost laughed. Almost cried. Maybe both.

"Thank you." She went in for a hug because… well… it felt right.

Babushka caught her hands before she could back away. "And I know, your concern? It's not really about the dress. But ve von't tell Zachary."

Babushka held tight while she smiled a terrifying grin. Like she knew. She knew Piper's world was changing and, dammit, she liked it a whole lot.

"Right. Okay. I'll see you soon." Piper pulled away and she didn't stop. She shook her head and kept walking.

Because if she didn't get some distance soon, she was going to start admitting things no blinged-out boxer briefs or puppies could distract her from.

And she wasn't ready for that.

CHAPTER 20

20 DAYS UNTIL ANNA
& DRAKE'S WEDDING

ZACH

The industrial Bernina hummed, a familiar sound that usually centered him. But today, Zach's focus was shot. Every stitch on the Wild Sack prototype pulled his thoughts tighter around one thing: Piper.

This Wild Sack was starting to take shape—his fourth today—but the momentum had slowed. Not from fatigue, exactly. Though the day was as intense as the previous. This day didn't have a dozen puppies roaming his factory floor, so that was movement in the right direction.

This was more of a quiet crowd in the back of his mind, thoughts jostling for his attention all at the same time.

He leaned back for a second, rolling his shoulders. The workshop smelled like home. Fabric and oil, with a hint of dust he'd never noticed until then.

But the football field loomed larger in his mind: the upcoming live-stream, Anna and Drake's wedding... Piper. He tugged the next swath of dyed cotton into position and lowered the presser foot.

Somewhere between the stitch lines and the seam

allowance, he wasn't nervous—at least not in a traditional sense. But something hovered, right behind his usual focus.

He exhaled and ran the machine again. The fabric surged forward, the line of stitching clean and tidy. Four sacks down, two to go.

He was running a seam when his phone buzzed, Piper's name lit up the screen. The stitch went crooked.

Piper: Need your help. Can I come over?

Zach: Anytime you want to.

Piper: OMW

She showed up with Anna's wedding dress in a garment bag, another brown sack filled with white cloth, and an expression that only prompted lots of questions and zero answers.

"What's up?" he asked, eyeing the bag.

"Hear me out, before you say no," Piper said, laying it across one of the huge pressboard tables they used to cut material.

"Always a great start to any conversation." He crossed his arms.

"Anna's dress doesn't fit," Piper said, unzipping the bag so the silk fabric spilled out. "I had her try it on, and we went through everything together, and even if we let it out, it's not working."

The back of his neck went itchy. "Okay."

"I had her show me pictures of dresses she likes," Piper said. "And I don't sew, I don't know exactly what's possible, but I think we could let this one out as much as possible, then add to it from a style she likes and…somehow…make it work."

Before he could say anything, her phone was out, and she was pointing to the different styles Anna liked.

She wasn't wrong. Each of these styles would work with the dress Anna loved and would give her extra room in the midsection.

Piper ran her fingers over the line of tiny stitches. "We talked about getting a totally different dress, and she is good with it."

"Because Anna will go with most anything," Zach added.

Piper nodded. "But she worries she'll feel like she is going to be wearing someone else's story."

He nodded. "Where do I come in?"

"I think between the two of us—mostly you—we can make the dress she loves like a little hug of who she was, who she is, and who she's becoming."

The original gown was super tight through the bust and waist with a flowing skirt.

"That silk's gonna pucker like crazy if I misplace a stitch," he mused.

"I know I can go find someone to fix this, but you know what you're doing and you know the bride. Do you know enough about fashion to make it work?" She shifted her weight.

"No. I don't really know much about fashion in the runway sense, and one wrong cut? This dream dress is toast."

Piper worried her bottom lip.

"*But* I do know how to pull things apart and put them back together. And I definitely understand how to make clothing more comfortable." Zach nodded slowly, mentally dismantling the dress. "If we let it out and use as much as the dress has to give with the seams, then I can add a drape right here that will cover any of the parts that aren't perfect because of the alteration."

He pointed to the seam along the neck, flipping it over to see how much room they had to work with on the stitches. "If

I lower the neckline and add a touch of sheer overlay, we'll give some extra space in the chest area, so she can move easily."

Piper leaned in, her tone hopeful. "You could really do that?"

"I mean... yeah," he said, already reaching for a pencil. "It's fabric and a sewing machine. That's kind of my thing."

He sketched a quick idea, then quickly crumpled it. Too boxy. So he tried again.

"Anna was a stressed-out mess about this. I figure we fix it for her and then show her. Worst case? We go buy another dress off the rack because that's what we'd have to do anyway. Best case? She loves it."

"She'll love it," Zach assured, jerking his chin toward the brown paper bag. "What's in there?"

"Supplies," Piper said, pulling out lace, organza, and satin. "I stopped by the fabric store to see what they had."

"I might need her to try it on so I can get sizing and not mess it up."

"I thought of that, too, so I got her measurements." Piper pulled out her phone and held the list to Zach.

"Okay," Zach said.

"Okay?" Piper asked. "You're just good with this?"

"I mean, it needs done and I can do it, so, yeah." He shrugged, reaching for the various fabrics to get a good feel.

"Right now?" Piper asked.

"Bad timing?" Not like they had a ton of time to work with here.

"No, I can totally do it now. I just had some...."

"Some?"

"Some organization for my D.I.C.K. clients. But that can wait," Piper said, feeling the dress. "You're the absolute best."

"Let's grab that mannequin over there. The smaller one. Maybe if we stuff a bra on it, it'll be close to Anna's size?"

"Borrow mine," Piper said, already starting to undo the

clasp. Then she hesitated, fingers stalling on the clasp as though torn by whether to be professional or not.

"I was hoping you might offer, because I am fresh out," he said, and damn it came out huskier than he'd intended.

"I'm generous like that," she said with a sly smile.

———

Zach leaned back on his heels as he assessed the drape of the silk organza across the torso. Holding the folded edge in place with two fingers, he reached for a straight pin with the other hand.

Piper handed it right over. Her breath shallow and barely audible above the faint hum of the fabric iron warming on the console behind them.

"Turn it a little left," he murmured, voice low, professional.

She did as asked, the hem of the gown shifting with the movement. Her dark eyes met his in the studio mirror and held.

The chemistry had been there since day one. Volatile in all the best ways.

In the quiet studio, nothing had changed. Though, they were both giving the wedding dress the reverence it deserved since it wasn't theirs. A guy didn't make a pass at a woman while working on his sister's wedding gown. Even he knew that was wrong.

Zach swallowed and reached again for another pin, and her fingertips brushed against his palm as he handed it over.

"So?" she teased, eyebrow arched.

"So...?" he shot back, eyes locked on the fabric but grinning like he'd been caught.

She tilted her head slightly, only enough to glance back at him.

"Tess?" The name hung in the air like a dropped pin. Sharp

and precise and not something you wanted to pick up wrong and get stuck with.

He stood and stepped around to face her, his hands sliding from fabric to his pockets with practiced ease.

"She clearly needs you," he said, exhaling through his nose. "And I'm glad I told you, so you weren't totally blindsided by everything the other day."

"It was a lot," she said with a laugh. "How'd you convince Babushka to help out? And bring her friends?"

"You think she'd let us do it without her? Hell, no. As soon as she got wind that it was happening, she jumped right in and brought her friends along. That's what she does."

Piper didn't say anything. A beat passed, and then another.

He ran a rough hand through his hair.

"You know," she said slowly, "I'm impressed that you can do this. Prince Charming never made Cinderella's dress. He just showed up with a shoe."

The air between them crackled with sparks and, for a second, Piper forgot the dress wasn't hers.

Zach snorted. "Well," he said, voice low again, "Nobody's perfect. Not even Prince Charming."

She smiled up at him. He stepped closer to her, only a fraction. Enough to feel the warmth of her skin, enough to watch her pupils grow darker.

"He had a magical fairy godmother do the hard part," she murmured, her breath against his lips.

"No fairy godmother here," Zach said. "Just fabric, design, and a hell of a lot of pins."

"And," Piper said, eyes locked on his, "a guy who knows how to make a dress."

Zach sighed, breaking the silence. "I'm not perfect, Piper."

She trailed a fingertip along the bottom of his lip. "No one is."

They didn't say anything more as he finished pinning, adjusting the sleeves, modifying the neckline.

The dress looked good. They were doing this thing.

He turned to her as her arms relaxed and she let out a breath. For once, he let himself look a little longer than he should. At the subtle arch of her collarbone, the smudge of freckles across her shoulder, the rise and fall of her chest beneath her professional blazer.

He cleared his throat and stepped back.

"It's getting late. I think that's it for today," he said hoarsely. "I can start stitching tomorrow."

"I can stop by?" she asked, a sleepy end-of-the-day note to her tone.

"Or you could just stay?" he asked, trying for casual.

Her smile curved slow and sly across her face. "Now that we've done the dress. Do you want to undress me?"

He froze. Then barked a laugh and the spark between them lit brighter, pulling them together. He stole a kiss on the stairs, then another. Zach nearly tripped, too busy tasting her to watch his feet. Not like the AV closet. He grinned against her mouth. No emergency broadcast needed this time.

This wasn't fabric or pinning designs. No, this was a spark that could torch his whole loft.

They stumbled into his apartment, laughing between breaths.

Heat and fevered hands. Her fingers gripping his shirt, tugging it up and over his head with unspoken need.

He answered with his mouth on her throat, her jaw, her lips again like he couldn't handle the space between them any longer.

In the tender light of his bedroom, they left the rest of the world outside.

He slipped his hands under her shirt, grazing her skin because the bra was still downstairs.

Damn, smoother than the best cotton.

"You're killing my focus," he murmured, lips brushing her neck as he fumbled with her shirt, half expecting her to tease him for it. "I could spend hours touching you."

She giggled breathlessly, arching into him. "Hours? I don't know if I have that kind of patience."

"Mmm, but you do," he teased, nudging her onto her back and following her down. His lips took over, teasing, tongue flicking over one peaked nipple. She moaned, fingers tangling in his hair as he lavished attention on her, his free hand sliding lower to tease between her thighs.

"Someone's impatient," he teased, his finger sliding in, pulse racing as her hips shifted. She whimpered, hips lifting as he curled his finger just right, his thumb circling her bundle of nerves in slow, deliberate strokes. "Don't you dare hold back on me, Piper. I want to hear you."

Her breath hitched, her body clenching around him as he worked her closer to the edge. "Don't stop—oh, don't stop—" She came with a cry, her back bowing off the bed as pleasure crashed over her.

He didn't give her time to recover, kissing his way down her body. She gasped as his tongue flicked over her sensitive flesh, her hands flying to his shoulders.

"Too much—oh, no, never mind, don't stop—" She laughed, half-delirious, as he chuckled against her, the vibration clearly making her shudder.

He rose over her as she wrapped her legs around his hips, pulling him closer.

"You're such a tease," she accused, breathless.

"Only for you," he promised, reaching for the condom on the nightstand.

She watched his hand on his dick, breath hitching, pupils dilating, as he tore the packet open with his teeth. She trailed her fingers down his chest as he rolled it on.

His hands stilled for a moment on his shaft, his gaze darkening as her touch lingered, teasing. "Fuck, you're not making this easy."

"Good," she replied.

He stroked himself once. A slow, deliberate motion, his eyes locked on hers.

She smirked and spread her legs wide exposing herself to him.

He wanted to dive into her body. Wanted to feel her around him, hear her gasp as he drove into her.

His pulse hammered and he was so turned on he might come from another stroke of his hand. She was so open, so ready, so his.

"I love watching you do that," she gasped, her words raw and unfiltered.

"That's not very professional," he muttered, though his hips betrayed him, pressing deeper into his grip.

"We're way past that," she panted. Her nails dug into his arms, and Zach's mind flashed to that first smoothie date because she'd smirked then, too.

He groaned, easing into her because she fit him perfectly.

Damn, she's ready for me.

She made a small mewling noise at the sensation, her body stretching to take him. He stilled for a moment, to savor the feeling of her around him, her heat, her tightness.

"Fuck, you feel perfect. Think this is what they meant by a perfect fit, Cinderella?" he asked against her lips. Pulling out and then thrusting in again, more carefully this time.

She smirked, rolling her hips. "Less talking, more moving, Charming."

He laughed, catching her mouth in a kiss as he began to move, slow at first, then harder, deeper, until the only sounds in the room were their ragged breaths and the slick, wet slide of their bodies coming together.

Her nails bit into his back, urging him faster. Not their first night of figuring things out, this was them knowing each other and taking what they needed. He hit the right rhythm, her gasp sparking a grin. Their breaths tangled, peaking together in a messy, perfect rush.

She came with a shuddering cry, her body clenching around him, and that was all it took to push him over the edge, too.

With a lazy, satisfied grin, he pulled out, and reached down to remove the condom, tying it off before tossing it into the nearby trash bin. She watched him through half-lidded eyes, a smirk playing on her lips as he collapsed beside her, dragging her against his chest.

"You're *such* a distraction," he murmured, pressing a kiss to her temple.

She laughed, tracing idle patterns on his chest. "Says the man who derailed my entire evening."

He hummed, fingers tangling in her hair. "It was fun though, yeah?"

She nodded, laughing.

Later, when they lay tangled in sheets and cooler skin, she rolled toward him.

"So," she said, voice sleep-heavy and content. "Another late night at the studio?"

Zach grinned, eyes closed, one arm bent behind his head. "Never had a fitting quite like it."

Her leg slid along his beneath the covers, lazy, possessive. "Penny for your thoughts?"

Then he opened his eyes and turned his head to look at her. "I'm thinking about making you a dress."

She laughed. Quiet and low.

"And what?" she teased. "Taking it off again?"

He nodded, gaze stealing lower. "Pretty much always want to take your clothes off." His smile widened. "Even when they're made by me."

She kissed him again.

And this time, they didn't stop. They stayed tangled in sheets and each other, like the world could wait.

CHAPTER 21

14 DAYS UNTIL ANNA
& DRAKE'S WEDDING

ZACH

Zach stepped onto the Stallions' field, the turf spongy under his boots, and Anna's wedding dress tucked away in a garment bag and slung over his shoulder. The weight of it was grounding—something he was doing for family, sure. But really, it was more like a talisman from the night everything with Piper had shifted.

But those were thoughts for another time because tonight was all about Wild Sacks. The air at the stadium was electric, even without tens of thousands of fans.

The field, thick with the scent of freshly cut grass, was all about his company. Every road led… here.

He'd spent most of the day at the field finishing prep work, but once that was finished, he hurried to finish Anna's gown. Which, for the record, was more of a pain than he'd ever expected. But it was done. Complete. And ready for his sister.

Piper spun toward him, clipboard in hand, headset slightly askew, her ponytail swinging like it called plays. Her eyes locked on his and, God, that gleam unraveled him. It wasn't just a glance. It was a full-system diagnostic run by someone who already had his password.

Someone who could anticipate his next move.

Someone who saw he was cutting it close, clocked the garment bag and understood without a word of explanation, and held a spark of welcome that made the entire buzzing, brilliantly lit field fade into a muted, unimportant backdrop.

He ran a hand through his hair. The gesture felt inadequate. "I saved the hardest stitching for last, and it was a total nightmare."

"Is everything okay?" she eyed the dress bag, assessing it as a liability that might need tossed.

"It is now." He held up his hands as proof, the ghost of a needle prick on his thumb still throbbing. "I've spent the last hour with a needle and thread because the machine kept puckering the silk. Noah assured me he had everything under control here, but it looks like that's you. Not him."

"Everyone's been working together. But we're glad you're here." She leaned forward and squeezed his arm.

"We?" he asked.

"We meaning *me*. *I'm* glad you're here." Her voice was lower now, just for him, a quiet confession in the middle of a hundred other conversations.

She'd been staying over a heck of a lot more often, and he'd even stayed at her apartment a few times, learning the quirks of her coffeemaker and the exact spot on the couch that she called her "command center."

Being together just seemed… right.

Natural, like breathing.

Ever since the night he'd agreed to fix the dress, they'd been nearly inseparable. They stole moments between Wild Sacks deadlines and wedding checklists. It had become the new rhythm of his life. A steady beat beneath the noise he hadn't realized wasn't there before.

It was raw, and it was fun.

Sex that left them breathless and bantering, like their first smoothie date but with way less clothes and infinitely more at stake. It was learning the map of her skin and the cadence of her sleep-soaked voice in the morning.

And the way she looked at him right then? There on the field? Part surprise and part pure excitement? It made him want to drop the dress, dip her low, and kiss her on the spot, right in front of the players, the puppies, and the entire production crew.

"What are the odds this pre-taped shoot won't turn into a puppy riot?" Zach asked, stepping closer, his voice full of amusement.

"I don't play odds," she shot back, her grin pure mischief as she tapped her clipboard with a pen. "I go with certainty."

"And the certainty is…?"

"That it absolutely *will* turn into a puppy riot," she said, her voice dropping to a conspiratorial whisper. "And it's going to be glorious, viral, and Tess will turn it into gold for Wild Sacks and the Stallions."

"You're taming this circus like it's your day job," he said, gesturing to the… well, everything.

"It *is* my day job," Piper said, scribbling on her clipboard without looking down. "Tess wants viral gold, but since puppies don't follow scripts, I'm hoping they're good with adlibbing. Our star quarterback, on the other hand…" She trailed off, giving a pointed look toward the center of the field where Drake was being delightfully mauled by a whole pile of mutts.

"I'll take that." Piper took the dress. "And put it in the changing tent for safe keeping."

"No dogs allowed in the changing tent?"

"I mean, no actual canines I have to worry about marking it by lifting their leg," she said with a laugh as she backed away with the gown in hand.

Around him, the field buzzed, players' abs lit by stadium

lights, rocking Wild Sacks briefs in various bold colors, clutching wiggling rescue puppies.

A massive lineman was cooing in a surprisingly high-pitched voice at a chihuahua mix that fit in his palm, while a lightning-fast receiver was patiently trying to teach a beagle-mix to run a perfect post-route, his commands punctuated by yips and a wildly wagging tail

It was a beautiful, ridiculous potential disaster or potential future for him in the making.

Yeah, it was going to be the big break he needed.

Babushka, Peggy, and their friend Etta were on puppy duty near the kennels. They'd brought a few friends along, all floral prints and orthopedic sneakers galore.

Everyone whispered together like they were plotting a touchdown or a world takeover.

Zach could just make out Etta's declaration: "The little one with the spots has the soul of a dancer. He needs a sequin."

Tess paced by the 50-yard line, phone pressed to her ear, her voice sharp with vision. "Viral, people. I want tears. I want joy. Get the shots."

Zach scanned the sidelines, and a familiar jolt of warmth and slight panic hit him square in the chest. Anna, Mom, Heather, and Sadie lounged on sideline chairs, out of the fray but present enough to watch, sipping from stadium cups. There was no way they were gonna miss this.

At least that's what Mom said when she announced they'd all be there for *support*. What that really meant was 'forensic analysis of Zach's new relationship,' but he loved them for it, anyway.

What he hadn't expected was his dad tagging along, too.

Dad wasn't sitting off to the side with the others. No, he was standing near the edge of the field, arms crossed, with a funny smile on his face.

Not his usual polite, reserved smile.

It took a beat for Zach to realize his dad wasn't watching

the football players or the spectacle; he was staring right at him. And Zach was suddenly ten years old again, holding up a blue-ribbon science project, waiting for this exact look and getting a simple, "Good work, son."

The approval had always been a ghost. Now, here it was, solid and real across a football field, and Zach had no idea what to do with it.

Drake, front and center, adjusted his Flagship Black briefs, smirking like he'd thrown a game-winner. He handed a golden retriever puppy to a production assistant with the casual air of a guy who played the field even in his underwear.

"Zach." Tess spotted him, her PR grin blazing as she strode over. "Perfect. We're taping Drake's interview first, talking about community, adoption, and the unparalleled support of your briefs."

"Bold," Zach said, catching Piper's gaze. Their new secret language, a silent commentary on the absurdity of it all that made him feel like they were the only two people in on the joke. "Hope you've got a leash for this madness."

Piper snorted, scribbling again. "Spit, prayers, and a spreadsheet. The holy trinity of event production. Tess wants Oscars; I'm aiming for no lawsuits."

As if on cue, a terrier-mix—the "new beginnings" pick for the rookie—bolted from the pen, trailing a Wild Sacks bandana like a cape.

Etta dove for him, her sequined jacket gleaming under the lights, yelling, "Get back here, you tiny terror! You have not been emotionally prepared for fame!"

The crew howled with laughter, but Piper, without missing a beat, moved with fluid grace, snagging the pup mid-stride and scooping him into her arms. The terrier immediately started licking her chin, his rebellion totally forgotten.

Yeah, Zach understood how that went. He'd been there, too.

He pulled a spare bandana from his pocket, and handed it to her, their fingers brushing with a slight jolt. Just like every other time. A simple touch that felt like a lit fuse.

"Nice grab," he said, his voice a little lower than he intended. "Linebacker material?"

"Not a chance," she quipped, her eyes sparking hotter than the lights. She expertly re-tied the bandana around the puppy's neck before handing him off to a grateful assistant.

Tess clapped her hands, pulling everyone's attention. "Focus, people. We are losing the light. Drake's intro, then players. Let's go. Let's go."

Cameras rolled.

Drake stepped up, all QB charm and chiseled jaw. "Denver Stallions, meet Wild Sacks, the underwear keeping us sharp on and off the field. Because every champion needs a great support system."

He flexed, a lab mix licking his face, and while the pups didn't follow scripts, that was a well-timed, photogenic slurp.

Zach's jaw tightened as Babushka, ignoring all protocols, shoved a tray of steaming pierogies under a camera tech's nose, grumbling in Russian about young people not eating enough. The fragrant scent of fried dough, potato, and spices wafted their direction.

"What's in those, Babushka?" Piper called, her eyes narrowing as every puppy nose in the vicinity suddenly pointed in one direction, sniffing the air with frantic intensity.

Before Babushka could answer, a bulldog with the build of a tiny tank took a running start, leaped the pen with the athleticism of a seasoned hurdler, snatched a pierogi mid-air, and bolted for the end zone, dough crumbling in his wake.

One of the linemen, a giant of a man named Gus, dove for him, but the bulldog executed a perfect turn. Gus missed entirely and skidded twenty feet on the turf in his briefs, a human slip-n-slide.

Peggy cackled, thumping her cane on the ground. "Those skimpy shorts ain't hiding much, big fella!"

Zach and Piper shared a *what now* glance.

Piper didn't flinch. She raised her voice, calm and authoritative. "Noah? Grab the leashes from the sideline, now! You—" she pointed at a tech—"move the main pen to the 20-yard line, away from the food. Babushka, no more pierogies."

Babushka huffed, muttering something about the importance of carbohydrates for athletic performance, but complied.

"You're scary good at this," Zach said to Piper, half-teasing, wholly in awe.

"Terrifyingly efficient," she flashed a grin as the puppies were secured once more, the bulldog burping happily in Gus's arms.

Zach steadied a wobbly tripod, knocked askew by the bulldog's great escape.

Taping resumed, smoother this time. Drake nailed his lines, players posed with their now-leashed puppies, and the whole thing subsided into a marketable, heartwarming charm.

Etta winked at the tight end, who blushed to the tips of his ears.

The director finally called wrap, and cheers erupted. Babushka and her crew high-fived, Peggy waving a bandana like a victory flag.

From the sidelines, Anna's group clapped. And Mom stood next to Dad. She looked at Zach, then at Piper, and then mouthed the word, "Proud."

His dad just nodded, a small, unusual smile back on his face. Not just about the business, but about everything. The approval was whole.

Tess was already on her phone, confirming adoption links would be embedded in the video, set to drop tomorrow. The marketing machine was humming.

As the field cleared out, Zach and Piper lingered by the empty puppy pen, her hand finding its way into his. The stadium lights began to lower, one by one, like a cue for their private afterparty. Zach squeezed her fingers.

"You—" he said, turning to her in the growing quiet. "—continue to be terrifyingly efficient."

"You should see me with a broken printer, it's a bloodbath," she quipped.

"How do you do it? How do you constantly make madness feel like magic?'

Piper leaned in, her forehead against his. "I don't," she whispered, their breaths mingling. "The madness is just madness. The magic part... that happens when you show up."

CHAPTER 22

14 DAYS UNTIL ANNA
& DRAKE'S WEDDING

PIPER

he madness is just madness. The magic part happens when you show up. Her words echoed between them.

"Well, then I guess it's a good thing I showed up," Zach said, wrapping his arms around her.

She shouldn't have allowed it since she was working. And he was working. But then there he was beside her, unfairly attractive despite a long day.

Piper shivered, with goosebumps forming all along her skin.

"You okay?" he asked, rubbing his hands up and down her arms.

She nodded even as the Stallions' field settled into a calm that unreasonably put her more on edge.

"After every event, there's always a dip. An emotional dip. It happens. It's normal, and given the rush of the past weeks, it's not like I've had a second to stop and really prepare for it."

"But you've had two pretty major projects finish up. The engagement pictures and this… " He gestured to the stadium around them. "I don't even know what to call this."

She laughed. With the frenetic energy of the pre-taped Wild Sacks shoot fading, the stadium lights dimming, and shadows stretching across the turf, the air held onto the earthy scent that always came before the rain.

Piper shoved her clipboard into her bag; its pages crumpled from her grip during the bulldog's end-zone heist.

"Today was great." She brushed a stray piece of hair out of her face and moved with Zach toward where the puppy playpens were being dismantled since the pups were all loaded up and headed back to the shelter.

Well, except for the bulldog mix who wouldn't part from Gus. That insistence was mutual, so she had a solid hunch it would work out long term.

"You're right," Tess strode beside them. "Today was great. I couldn't have done it without your help. Thank you, Piper. Truly."

"Pfft," Peggy said as she smacked together two lengths of the plastic play area.

"Don't even start, Grams," Tess said.

"I said nothing." Peggy lifted her hands like she was the picture of innocence even though her voice was gritty, low like she'd smoked a solid carton of cigarettes each day through the 1980s.

"I know what you were going to say, and you don't need to say it," Tess countered.

"How can you know what I was going to say when I don't even know what I was going to say?" Peggy volleyed.

"You were going to spout nonsense about how there's always a price to pay for the good things that happen, but we all know that's bologna." Tess shoved her hands on her hips.

Peggy waggled her fingertip. "Young people don't understand the ways of the world. Ah, to be young and dumb again."

"I vould be young, but never stupid." Babushka shook her

head. "I vas never stupid to start. You should listen to Peggy. She's very smart."

"Did you even hear what she said?" Zach asked his grandmother.

"Nope. Didn't need to," Babushka said.

"Because I didn't say it," Peggy huffed.

"Go ahead, just get it over with so we can all move on." Tess pressed her fingertips to her forehead.

"All I would say is that when life is smooth, you better brace for what's coming." Peggy patted Tess's arm, her eyes sharp with wisdom. "That's why I always say to live in the madness. It's safer."

"Oh." Babushka shook her head. "That's no good. That is the kind of advice that makes people vorry."

"And no one needs to worry," Zach agreed. The way he'd said the words was warm and teasing.

Of course, Piper wanted to believe that he was right. But her stomach still twisted. Peggy's words were a lit match in her gasoline-soaked mind, and every attempt to douse the flame only seemed to make it hiss louder.

"Hey," Zach said, sidling up to her as she re-organized her bag. "Don't go quiet."

Piper shrugged, not meeting his eyes. "Just thinking."

About how everything could look so stunning right before it spectacularly imploded.

"This went great. Everyone's happy with how it turned out. They'll edit tonight. It'll launch right away. And Denver will stop worrying about how an engagement can wreck a season that hasn't even started. Then Drake will be on his honeymoon with my sister and life will be—" He let out a deep breath. "—calmer."

She zipped her bag with more force than necessary. "Zach?"

He waited.

"I'm trying to trust that it's okay when things get calm."

She sighed, fully meeting his gaze. "What if Peggy's right? What if when things are so easy, they only have one way to go?"

Zach's brow furrowed. "You want to call what we did here today easy? Because I have a lot of words for it, but easy isn't one." He tilted her chin up with his fingertip.

Her shoulders slumped slightly.

He let his hand sit gently against her neckline. She wanted to curl into his fingers and just let that comfort her but now was not the time.

"Did you say you needed to catch me?" Anna called over, moving toward them with the other Dvornakov girls. "What's up?"

"Yes, I did need to talk to you," Piper said, rolling her shoulders like she could undo years of conditioning and ignore Peggy's 'wisdom'. "Did Drake take off?"

Anna had made it clear that Drake could not, under any circumstances, see the dress before the big day. This wasn't a Babushka-brand superstition. This was 100% Anna's request. And Piper respected that.

"Not yet," Anna replied. "But he's going out with the guys as we speak. They invited Dad out to the afterparty. He acted like it wasn't a big deal, but it was a big deal."

"Come see us once he's gone." Piper winked in the kind of way that transmitted, *code activated*. "We've got something to show you."

Anna seemed uncertain.

"It's a surprise and it's good." Zach said, pausing to let the weight of the words sink in.

"Meet us at the changing tent in five?" Piper asked.

Diana chuckled, nudging Sadie. "Are we allowed to come, too? Or just Anna?"

"Anyone but Drake," Piper clarified.

"You should come," Zach agreed. "Definitely come."

Heather raised her plastic cup in a mock toast. "I think

that means it's about the dress, right? It's got to be about the dress?"

Sadie squealed a good kind of squeal. "Is it the dress?"

Piper mimed locking her lips and throwing away the key. "Five minutes."

She and Zach moved toward the tent to get things ready, her fingers lingering on the shoulder strap of her purse.

He stepped closer, his shoulder brushing hers as they strode together. A professional distance, sure, but close enough she could feel the heat of his body.

"Thanks for coming with," Piper said, fidgeting with the canvas bag.

"I spent way too many hours cussing at that silk to let Anna see it without me," he said.

Piper laughed, but it came out shaky, her nerves buzzing under her skin.

His hand grazed her lower back, guiding her through the maze of disassembled equipment and lingering crew.

Her chest tightened, warmth and panic tangling together. She wanted to lean into him, let his words anchor her, but that nagging voice—Peggy's voice, her own voice—whispered that this was the calm before the inevitable crash.

"You're making it really hard to stay professional," she teased.

"Good," he murmured, his eyes locking on hers for a beat too long as they entered the empty tent. "I'm not trying to make it easy."

He glanced around and then he moved quickly, not to the garment bag hanging on the rack, but to her. His palms against her cheeks as he kissed the stuffing right out of her and probably smeared her lip gloss all the way to downtown.

"What was that for?" she asked, breathless.

"Because I wanted to."

"Okay, but my lip gloss now has its own zip code. Was that strategically necessary?"

"Yes. Now, we should probably go back to being professional."

"I can't move. You're still holding my face," she said.

He chuckled and brushed the tip of his nose against hers.

Then it hit her.

She wasn't simply crushing on him. She was falling.

Like, really falling.

She was falling for awkward mornings and shared toothpaste and the way his shirts never stayed fully tucked in. She was falling for messy, inconvenient, terrifying, totally irrational love. The real deal.

Holy crap, I'm falling in love with him.

The thought froze her mid-footstep, like maybe her shoe understood the gravity of the moment.

And the thing about love? It usually came with heartbreak gift-wrapped on the side. Either his or hers. Likely his, because that would hurt the most. The universe had already played its move, and she hadn't even seen the board yet.

Stay? It gets messy and breaks her. Leave? She ruins it before it even begins.

But what if maybe love wasn't always a crash? Maybe, this time, it could be a climb?

He turned toward her, eyes tender and open.

"You know, I wanted to tell you..." she began, heart racing. "I wanted you to know that I think... um... that the thing about today was..."

"Amazing?" he asked, obviously trying to help her out. "I agree and when this works like we know it will..." His tone shifted to an all-business-inspirational-speech. His confidence at an all-time high. "Everything will be exactly what we need."

"What we need?" she echoed.

"Wild Sacks finally gets stability. And Aspen can't say you didn't move mountains to make this wedding a success for Anna and Drake. You did it, Piper. *You* did it."

Not *we* did it?

Her heart didn't sink. There was no sinking feeling here. No, this was the start of a shutdown.

This wasn't about them. *Gah.* He was talking about the deal. And just like that, the fragile, unspoken thing between them started to inch toward being a negotiation she could lose.

"Right," she said, forcing a smile so brittle it might crack with a strong breeze. "The Wild Sacks deal. My job. Total win-win. That's what I was going to say, too."

The confession lodged in her throat, a bitter pill she was forced to swallow.

For the briefest flicker of a second, something changed on Zach's face. Not easy to catch, but not nothing either.

"I mean, there's us, too…" he said, quieter now, rubbing a hand through his hair. "But, I was just also thinking—"

"You're getting everything you ever wanted. This is going to be huge for Wild Sacks. For you. And for me," she said, instead of what she really wanted to say.

Her heart raced, the confession right there on the tip of her tongue.

I'm falling in love with you, and I'm terrified I'll ruin us.

But she stopped herself.

His face flickered, a shadow of something—disappointment? —crossing it.

"Right," he said, rubbing a hand through his hair as his phone buzzed again. "Wild Sacks gets the deal. You get the corner office. Win-win." He hesitated.

"I'm ready for my surprise," Anna trilled, flipping back the curtain they used as a makeshift doorway to the tent and snapping Piper out of herself. Anna held out grabby hands like a small child awaiting cupcakes.

Piper exhaled. Time to pivot. "It's good, I think. Hopefully. No pressure, right?"

"So," she continued with a too-wide smile, "I had this idea

about your dress. We actually—" she gestured between herself and Zach "—designed something for you." She motioned toward the garment bag Zach carried.

"If you hate it, totally fine. We'll launch a Code Red and sprint to the nearest boutique. No hard feelings." She pressed the back of her hand against her forehead wishing it was an ice pack because there was definitely going to be a headache later.

Piper forced a smile, her heart hammering as the Dvornakov women crowded into the tent, their chatter filling the space like static.

She glanced at Zach, who gave her a small nod, his expression steady but laced with something comfortable. Something that made her want to spill every fear and hope she'd been bottling up.

Instead, she gripped the garment bag zipper tighter, the cool metal grounding her as she prepared to unveil the dress. Then she stopped.

"Actually." She turned to Zach. "You do it."

Anna gasped as Zach unzipped the bag inch by suspenseful inch.

"Oh," Anna whispered, fingertips sliding reverently across the fabric.

She hugged the dress to her chest and did an impromptu spin, full on tears brimming in her eyes. "It's absolutely perfect."

"You'll need to try it on," Piper said, quieter. "But it should fit."

"Hope you like it," Zach said.

"Like it? I love it," Anna said, half-laughing, half-sobbing as she pulled Piper into a smooshy, grateful hug.

Diana, Sadie, Heather, and Babushka all stood quietly, letting Anna have her teary moment.

Zach cleared his throat. "You know, Babushka always says

if you cry happy tears before the wedding, it means you'll cry unhappy ones after."

Everyone turned to him in horrified unison.

Babushka even sucked in a long breath. "I vouldn't say it at this exact moment. I vould vait until the right moment. Vhich is not now."

"Why would you say that?" Anna thwacked him on the back of the head like a seasoned sibling. "Bad vibes. Ba-a-a-ad vibe management."

"Ow." He rubbed the spot. "Hey, I don't believe it. It's just what she always says."

"It's true. I do say this. But I am not stupid vhen I say it." Babushka shook her head with grave disappointment.

Piper stayed silent.

Because unfortunately… she worried that she did believe it.

The words she wanted to tell Zach were still stuck in her chest, hot and tight and terrifying. Words that wanted out. Words she'd tried to say and failed.

That's why she said nothing as Anna tried on the dress, and it fit. Of course, it fit. She said nothing as Zach and the family headed to Brek's to meet up with the players and his dad. And she said nothing when she told Zach she wouldn't be coming to his place that night.

She didn't invite him to her apartment, either. No, because she needed a little space on her own.

By the time she made it home, Shelby was already in bed, the apartment quiet in that ambient, don't-wake-the-roomie kind of way.

Piper dropped into her desk chair, the silence pressing in from all sides. She opened her cell to text Zach. To say something.

But she stared at the screen, and then set it on her desk because she had a wedding to get done.

Because what if the problem with a curse was the unpredictability?

Because what if it waited until she was distracted, but it still came for her? And, instead of kicking in the front door like usual, this time it was taking the scenic route?

What if it had nothing to do with Anna and Drake, and everything to do with her and Zach?

Because this wasn't just a fling with him. Not anymore.

CHAPTER 23

ANNA & DRAKE'S WEDDING DAY

ZACH

They'd been busy. That's all it was.

Well, Piper had been busiest, it seemed. She wasn't intentionally blowing him off—he was certain of that, at least.

Mostly, certain.

Pretty much certain.

But while he was dealing with new Wild Sacks orders and figuring out sourcing options to meet order demands, Piper was handling wedding preparations.

They texted like nothing was wrong, still saw each other on the regular, but she stopped sleeping over. She didn't invite him to stay over at her place, either.

And, when they were together, it just... it just seemed... rushed.

"You, my brother, look like someone took a piss in your soda." Jase flopped down on the sofa in the suite at The Falcon.

They were all dressed for the wedding in their black tie,

hanging with Drake, keeping him entertained and shit. Just until it was time for him to go marry their sister.

"It's probably about Piper." Roman cracked open a beer and sat beside Jase.

"Of course, it's about Piper." Jase rolled his eyes. "The nut sack's got it bad."

Drake sat at the edge of the sofa—already in his tuxedo, just waiting for game time. "You wanna talk about it?"

"No," Zach said, meaning it.

"Too bad," Jase said. "We've got time. We need something to sort, and you've got a problem. This is what we do best before weddings."

Jase, Roman, and Drake all shared a lengthy glance that didn't sit well with him.

"Look." Drake folded his hands together. "Anna says Piper's not herself, either."

Zach nodded because, well, he knew this.

"When you've got a woman who loves you, sometimes it scares her. We're not always easy men to love," Jase said, pulling that right out of his ass.

"Speak for yourself," Roman countered.

"Dude." Jase shook his head. Then he just waved his hand along the front of Roman like that explained everything.

"Why would you say she loves me?" Zach asked, because he wasn't sure he could buy that.

"Trust me. She may not have admitted it to herself yet, and you may not have admitted it to yourself yet, but she is in love with you. And you love her, too," Drake said.

"I mean, yeah, that last part's a given," Zach conceded. "I'm so far gone for her."

"Then what we need to do is go over everything you said at the point that things went downhill so we can see where you fucked up." Jase lifted his shoulders like this was super simple.

Zach stared at the pop top on his soda can. "I don't think I did."

"And that, my brother, is how I know that you did," Jase said. "At what point did you start to feel the pull away?"

He let out a long breath. "Okay, so things were great until I kissed her in the tent when we showed Anna her dress."

Jase steepled his fingers in front of his lips. "Are you a shit kisser?"

"No." Zach shook his head.

"I mean, not that you know. No one would really tell you that. Can we call one of your exes and get them in on this?" Roman asked.

"What happened after you kissed her?" Drake countered, refocusing everyone.

Zach replayed the entire scene with them like they were in a low-budget cop movie and they were finding a serial killer instead of in his soon-to-be brother-in-law's pre-wedding purgatory suite trying to determine how he had fucked up.

Unfortunately, this method illustrated to him exactly the many, many ways he could, in fact, fuck up without even realizing it.

Option one was when he mentioned what Babushka always said in the wrong context at an inappropriate time. He'd already marked that as a high probability.

Option two was discussing how he was certain that everything was now going to work. Which, for the record, he had no idea why that would be a problem, but Roman seemed to believe that was it.

Or, option three was that Piper just wasn't that into him like he was her.

"For our purposes here, that's not an option." Jase frowned. "Because Heather and I like her, and we want her to be in the family."

"Is this whole thing entirely necessary?" Zach asked, forcing himself not to toss his hands in his hair because he didn't want to have to screw with it again, comb it to make it right.

"Are you happily married like the rest of us are?" Jase asked, stretching his arms wide. "No? Then you should sit your ass down and let us help you."

"What if it's not me? What if it's the stress of the wedding and everything else?" Zach asked, hopefully.

"Yeah, that's not it," Drake assured.

"Re-roll," Roman said. "Tell me exactly what you said again after you kissed her."

"I told her things were going amazing and that she'd done so great. That the success was all her and I was grateful."

"Why were you grateful?" Roman asked like they hadn't already been through this three times.

"Because my business is going to do well and she's gonna get her promotion. Everybody wins."

"Okay, hear me out," Roman said this like any of them were giving Zach a choice in the matter. "You said *that*." He made a circle in the air with his fingertip. "Except she wanted you to be good-kisser and 'into her' Zach and not 'TED Talk business Zach.'"

"I *meant* that the campaign helped us both. That the success should make her boss sit up and take notice," Zach clarified.

"Right. And she needed you to talk about the future. Reassure that the future is solid for you both."

"That's exactly what I said."

"Not exactly." Drake pulled his lips to the side.

"But good news, now you can fix your fuck up and Nads still gets a new kickass auntie." Jase nodded, deep in his own pride that he'd solved the riddle.

"How exactly do I fix this?" Zach asked.

"Well, first, start by telling her how you feel. Then the rest usually comes along fine," Roman assured.

"Drake, are you ready for pictures?" Mom sauntered into

the room, took one look around, clearly knew something was up, but said nothing. That's because she wasn't Babushka.

"They want to get you and your family before the wedding starts," she said instead of prying further.

"Good talk." Jase smacked Zach on the shoulder, already tying his bow tie as he moved.

Roman grunted something, but it wasn't entirely verbal.

"You got this," Drake said, like a man walking straight into a custom-made future he'd been waiting his entire life for.

And Zach? Yeah. He'd botched it. He hadn't meant for his words to land wrong with Piper.

But they had.

And he would make it right.

———

Standing at the ceremony site, Zach had one job: don't screw anything else up.

Also, show up for her.

So, really, that was two jobs. Who was counting, though?

The venue—rooftop garden-meets-ballroom fantasy—was already buzzing when they made it to the terrace.

Flower arrangements flowed from gold carts, each one perfectly matching the dusty-lavender palette Piper had fought hard for.

It was perfect without being over-the-top. Authentic in a way that slapped expectations squarely across the face.

Tess got her blue and gold for the cake and those photos, so Piper deftly negotiated lavender and cream for everything else. He had to give her that she came through for Anna.

And in the center of it all—Piper herself. Clipboard clasped under one arm, headset hanging from her grip, pushing a linen-draped table slightly to the left with her hip as she coordinated three conversations and probably solved the mysteries of the human genome on the side.

Zach grinned.

Earlier that week, he'd texted Babushka a single question because Babushka, well, she knew things.

> Zach: How do I show up for her?

> Babushka: You bring her food.

She'd followed that with a text full of fruit emojis and a Gif of a supportive panda, because Babushka.

That's why Zach had arranged for a waiter to show up with one blueberry kale smoothie before things got too crazy.

It arrived just as he did, passed quietly into Piper's hands with a small, folded note taped to the lid.

She paused. Blinked. Turned the cup slowly in one hand until the note came into view. Peeking just under the cardboard sleeve, written in Zach's messy scrawl:

You've got this. —Z

Piper stilled.

Her brows lifted, lips parting slightly before she pressed them together again. She peeled the note free, held it in fingers that always moved fast, and simply… stared at it. Like maybe the paper itself was offering a moment of reassurance.

She sipped.

Another sip.

And then, across the room, her gaze found his.

She didn't smile. Not fully. But the edges of her mouth tipped up a fraction before she mouthed it clear as day, "Thank you."

Zach's chest squeezed.

He was so in over his head. And he wouldn't change a damn thing about it.

He shuffled to his seat near the front, beside Babushka, who was already dabbing at nonexistent tears with her handkerchief.

The ceremony space had been transformed into upscale romantic rustic with just the right amount of glam football chic, if that even existed. Which, apparently, it did. And it worked.

A Stallion—yes, the literal horse—stood by with a velvet lead and a bowtie, looking oddly dignified under the fairy lights.

Piper had compromised on its presence, only if Tess agreed to babysit both the horse and his handler. Which, judging by the slightly unhinged glint in Tess's eye, had not been a relaxing arrangement.

Babushka nudged him, her eyes already misty. "She did good, your Piper," she whispered, her accent thickening with emotion.

"She's not my—" Zach started, then stopped himself. No point in lying to Babushka. She saw through everything. "Yeah, she did. My Piper."

"The flowers," she continued, gesturing to the cascading arrangements that framed the altar. "They are from the same farm that supplied your mother and father's wedding. Did you know?"

He hadn't. But of course, Piper would dig in and find that detail and then make it happen. Of course she'd make Jase track down that specific family farm, a generation later, to source these exact roses.

That was Piper. The details that no one else would think about. The connections that made everything more meaningful.

The string quartet transitioned into a slower arrangement of Drake's team's fight song and somehow made it sound elegant rather than rowdy. How much time had she spent with the musicians, finding the perfect balance between sports tradition and wedding sophistication? No wonder she'd been unavailable.

Guests murmured appreciatively at the transformation.

One of the linebackers whispered to his date, "I thought this was gonna be all footballs and beer, but this is actually nice."

Exactly what Piper had aimed for. Respecting Tess's passion without letting it overwhelm Anna's day.

The aisle glimmered with delicate lavender petals, light bouncing off gold chairs linked in symmetrical rows.

Two cakes waited in the reception space—one glitter-drenched in team colors for those pictures, and one in delicate lavender buttercream for Anna's personal photos. Because Piper thought about everything. Planned for everyone. Somehow, she even managed to get the dueling cakes to vibe together like they meshed.

"The trick," she'd muttered while sketching out the designs, not really speaking to him, "is making them look like they belong in the same universe without being twins."

The processional music swelled. First came Drake's teammates—massive men, somehow elegant in tailored suits. Then Anna's friends, each carrying a single stem of lavender and a rose bound with silk ribbon.

Drake stood at the altar.

Flashbulbs popped on the edges.

Then Anna appeared at the back of the aisle arm in arm with Dad, beaming in the custom gown Zach stitched together.

The collective intake of breath from the assembled guests sent goosebumps down Zach's arms. They'd nailed it.

The gown managed to be both classic and unexpected. Structured satin with subtle detailing in the seams.

That small moment of awe that always happens when the bride arrives, rippled through the guests as they all stood.

Before Anna could continue down the aisle, Piper nodded pointedly at Babushka. She rose slowly from her seat and shuffled toward the bride, clutching a small velvet pouch trimmed in gold thread.

She moved with purpose—quiet, reverent, leaving whispers in her wake.

As she reached Anna, she muttered just loud enough, "I get to vear the good scarf and judge people. It is a proper family occasion."

Babushka slipped the pouch into Anna's hands. The bride blinked, surprised, then carefully opened it.

Zach already knew what was inside. It was filled with pieces of dark rye bread and a pinch of salt wrapped in linen with red embroidery.

The Dvornakov family blessing.

He hadn't seen it given since his cousin's wedding years ago. No one would allow Babushka to give it. It drove her nuts.

"Na zdorovye," Babushka murmured loud enough for those closest to hear, pressing a kiss to Anna's cheek. Then, switching to English just enough to bridge traditions: "For strength, and for the sweetness after."

Anna's eyes shone immediately, the symbolism sinking in. She squeezed Babushka's hands, something unspoken passing between them.

Zach turned toward Piper, making his eyes wide like, "what the hell, you didn't say anything to me?"

She gave the faintest shrug.

And Anna? She tucked the embroidered cloth into the folds of her bouquet, right beneath the ribbon bindings to carry it with her like an anchor, a tether to something deeper.

The music began again and the ceremony continued.

And still, Zach's gaze didn't drift from the back as Anna made her way to the front.

Piper was there at the end of the aisle, framed at the far entrance, headset in place, clipboard clutched like her battle standard.

But her face? Peaceful. An unexpected smile tugged at her lips as she watched Anna stride down the aisle.

There was zero amount of jaded worry in her expression.

She hadn't only made it beautiful. She'd made it work. For everyone. The flowers were sentimental. The cakes told two stories. Even the string quartet had somehow made a football fight song weep. This was all her.

The vows began.

The horse, blessedly, didn't so much as sneeze during the big moment.

Anna let out a slow breath she'd probably been holding for ten minutes.

The music from the string quartet swelled as if it had been waiting its whole life for this cue. A warm breeze stirred the edge of the pergola, fluttering the ribbons.

Anna teared up. Drake looked like he might cry, too. Hell, even Zach was getting choked up.

The sunlight caught in Anna's veil as she laughed through a line she'd flubbed—something about sandwiches and soulmates. There was a ripple of affectionate laughter.

And, just before the vows ended, when the audience was glued to Drake's "I promise to always buy the weird pickles," Zach glanced to the back.

There stood Piper. Quietly dabbing her eye. One small tear and a smile so sure it made his heart ache.

He held that image in his mind like it was something sacred.

The reception drifted into being under the glow of string lights and champagne flutes clinking. The dance floor pulsed with first dances, then group dances, then the kind of wild cousin conga lines that would live on social media for decades.

Piper, now barefoot, tossed her shoes beside a planter and leaned against a marble column, champagne flute in hand. Her head tilted back as she sighed long and low, the picture of exhaustion laced with total joy.

Zach approached.

"Permission to request a dance?" he asked, stepping close enough that his voice dipped into the space between them like a shared secret.

She eyed him with playful suspicion, one brow arching, arms folded over her chest. "Just the one?"

He pressed a hand to his heart, eyes locked with hers, voice certain. "I'll take as many as I can get."

She shook her head, but her smile betrayed her. "You can have them all."

He offered his hand, his voice quiet but steady, "Then I'll never let the music stop."

With a roll of her eyes and a low laugh, she slid her palm into his. "Oh, you practiced that line, didn't you?"

Their fingers laced. The contact, small as it was, made all the worry and all the concern he'd been hanging onto about messing things up go still somewhere in his chest.

They drifted onto the edge of the dance floor as the song shifted to some classic love ballad lightened by strings and nostalgia. The world blurred around them in flickering lights.

Her hands settled on his shoulders as his arm slipped easily around her waist. Then, slowly, she leaned in, and her cheek came to rest against his chest like it belonged there. Her breath was steady, and the tension she carried seemed to melt as she pressed closer.

"I don't bite," he murmured, resting his chin gently atop her head.

She tilted her face just enough for her words to reach near his heart. "I know. That's part of the problem."

"We could try it if you want." He chuckled and ran his hand in a slow circle along the small of her back. The hush between them was fragile, honest.

Then he whispered, careful to speak gently into the curve of her ear, "You did it."

Her voice, warm and near and barely above the music, was a breath against his shirt. "We did it."

He turned his head, pressing a kiss to her temple, the brush of his lips lingering a heartbeat longer than casual.

Her fingers clenched lightly against his shoulder in response, and something about the quiet gesture pulled the floor out from under him. Not in fear, but in that dizzy, beautiful way when it feels like something might matter more than you're ready to admit.

His pulse thundered against the pressure of her cheek. Dangerously calm. Too calm. Say it now or lose the chance. Hell, say it wrong.

Just… say it.

He hesitated, swallowed once, then said low and close so it wouldn't scare the moment off, "Don't freak out, but… I might be in love with you."

The words weren't smooth. They tumbled out with the grace of a tipsy toddler like Nadia. They were messy and unbalanced and, honestly, too much.

Instant panic. His gut clenched.

He braced for her to bolt, or laugh, or maybe deliver one of her infamous strategic exits.

But none of that came.

She leaned back enough to meet his eyes.

"Oh." She blinked like someone who'd found herself halfway through a dream and didn't know whether to hold or run.

"Oh?" he echoed, already preparing to backpedal, to throw in a joke or excuse the confession as a momentary lapse in sanity.

And then she kissed him.

She simply leaned in and pressed her lips to his. Certain. Warm. Her hand slid up to cradle the back of his neck.

He froze for half a second, then sighed into it, kissing her back with every ounce of that tumbled truth.

When she pulled away, her smile was shy and nervous, but real.

"I might be in love with you, too," she said.

He blinked.

"Okay… I mean—great. That's great. Just for confirmation —only 'might'?"

She grinned. "I figured I'd meet you where you were, you know? Don't want to scare you off."

The music swelled around them again as he pulled her closer, swaying a little sharper now that his heart had found its rhythm.

She didn't say a word.

She simply held on. Held on like someone who knew what it was to fall and still reached, anyway. Held on like maybe she finally believed it was real.

And she exhaled against him—not a sigh but a true release, like maybe—finally—there was room to breathe because someone else could carry even a sliver of the weight she'd tucked away in silence.

Zach closed his eyes.

And in the hush between beats, in the halo of string lights and quiet hope, he let himself sway with her. Not toward an answer. Just toward something that felt like it might be okay.

Maybe.

"I'm not good at letting things be okay," she whispered. "I always expect the break."

"Then, maybe today, you just let things be whole. Just for now."

She didn't nod. Didn't speak.

It wasn't perfect.

There were cracks and doubt all along the edges.

But damn if it wasn't real.

And for the first time in a long while, real felt like enough. More than enough.

CHAPTER 24

2 DAYS AFTER ANNA
& DRAKE'S WEDDING

PIPER

Piper celebrated the successful wedding, her cautiously optimistic outlook on life, and her upcoming promotion by taking a more hands-on, mouth-on approach with her boyfriend. He seemed extremely supportive of her celebratory methods.

"Piper," he groaned, his fingers already tangling in her hair. The heat fluttering between her thighs kicked up a notch at his words. He had the kind of voice that could talk her into almost anything.

She started her work slow, lips brushing over his shaft, teasing—because restraint was sexy and, also, she'd discovered after their weekend in bed that there was an importance to pacing. He gasped when she took him deeper, her tongue swirling. She took him all the way to the back of her throat, so he'd make that groaning sound she really got off on.

"You're amazing at this," he said, with a reverence like he'd just discovered ice cream for the first time. "I'm going to make sure the only thing you can say is my name. Let's see if you can even remember yours," he continued.

Somewhere between that deeply inappropriate suggestion and the needy rumble in his chest, a fresh wave of heat flushed through her body.

She let out a hum, which turned out to be more effective than expected when it made his dick twitch. She pulled back only enough to shoot him a smug look because, hey, a girl deserved credit for her craft.

Then she went in again with slow, deliberate strokes.

Apparently, that was his breaking point.

With something halfway between a groan and a caveman grunt, he flipped her onto her back, pressing her into the bed like he was afraid she'd run away mid-kiss (she wouldn't, but it was flattering). Then his hungry mouth was on hers, all-consuming, and way less polite than usual.

"You didn't let me finish what I started," she panted, somewhere between indignation and trying not to melt.

He grinned like the smug genius he was. "You love it. Admit it."

"Absolutely not," she said, promptly arching into him as his hand slid between her legs with remarkable accuracy.

"It's going to happen," he murmured, way too sure of himself.

"You're going to kill me. Death by orgasm. The obituary will scar my family forever," she said, all drama.

"Lucky for you," he murmured, "I'm great at resuscitation."

She gasped—in the sexy way, not the scared way—as he worked her with maddening focus. She arched again, nails digging into his shoulders like she was holding on for dear life.

Which, let's be honest, she kind of was. And when her climax hit, it did so like she did everything else: graceful, loud, and totally committed.

Only then did he reach for the condom, tearing it open with his teeth.

His words from earlier hung between them, thick in the air, as he rolled it on. And then he was inside her, driving deep, making good on every word he'd whispered before.

The weekend had been a blur of tangled sheets, ordering in, and the kind of lazy exhaustion that came from being thoroughly worshipped and in love.

"Okay, but seriously," Piper murmured against his collarbone, her lips still swollen from kissing, "just because the wedding is over doesn't mean I'm suddenly free. I still have other clients, you know."

"The funeral guys." Zach chuckled, his hands sliding down to grip her hips as she shifted above him.

"Yes, they are one of my clients." She kissed his pec because she could.

He arched a brow. "What if I hired you? Then you'd *have* to stay."

Piper stilled, her fingers pausing mid-trace along his chest. She lifted her head, her expression a mix of amusement and something sharper. "That's oddly offensive."

He grinned, unrepentant. "Or romantic. You decide."

She rolled her eyes but didn't pull away, and that was answer enough.

———

Piper started the morning well-caffeinated, thoroughly orgasmed, and willing to consider believing in fairy tales.

The wedding was over. It had gone off without a hitch—unless you counted Tess trying to micromanage the band or the fact that a horse contributed an unexpected intestinal evacuation to the aisle décor.

But no last-minute cancellations.

No ominous signs.

No epic disasters involving electrical fires, allergic reactions, or emotional implosions.

Anna and Drake were all googly eyes and loving touch the entire time.

Things were… fine.

She walked into Montgomery Events feeling like she was ready for more. That she'd earned a new title and all that came with it.

Her hair was scraped into a low bun that broadcast, "competent and hydrated," and not only because she had two electrolyte packets pulsing through her bloodstream. She made it to her desk, the organized mess slowly giving way to simply… organized.

It was almost unsettling if she let it be.

She sat, opened her laptop, and began the ritual of digital triage. Returning emails and checking messages.

She clicked, scanned, replied. Usually there was a bone-deep sense of catch-up panic after any big event, but this time? Her inbox contained some gold.

Vendor confirmation. Billing queries. The occasional caps locked: *THANK YOU.*

And one subject line that made her snort out loud.

You. Are. A. Goddess. In. A. Headset.

It was from the lighting guy.

Apparently, her firm-but-fair schedule reminders and her ability to fend off unsolicited "design corrections" had earned his worship.

Piper allowed herself a small, secret smile and stared at the subject line for a second too long.

Goddess in a headset.

Not terrible. She could even get used to it. Maybe start by embroidering it on a throw pillow?

She took a slow sip of her citrus water, leaned back, and considered what it might be like taking on another wedding or two if they were like this?

Nothing crazy, just a couple of the fun ones.

And then came the ping.

No, wait, several pings.

One notification. Then three more. Then her phone lit up like a Las Vegas marquee. Her group chat with the junior planners buzzed. Her screen erupted in snippets of madness:

> CAKE LADY MAGGIE: omg did they really fight like that on the honeymoon??

Piper blinked. Clicked the first link sent with the texts. It took her straight to a gossip site blasted in a bolded red:

Trouble in Paradise? Exclusive Shots Show Stallions' Sweethearts Fighting Poolside

Her stomach dropped.

There, centered below the clickbait font, were photos of Anna and Drake on what was supposed to be their blissful, relaxing, non-chaotic honeymoon.

Except they weren't sipping mocktails or cuddling on lounge chairs. They were mid-argument by the pool.

Body language: tense.

Hands: gesturing.

Faces: not exactly adoring.

Even the tile by the pool looked familiar. Shiny, black-and-white, too perfect. Like the floor she'd stared at in the courtroom when her parents filed for divorce number two.

Her pulse skipped. She bit the inside of her cheek.

Not this again. Not again.

Piper's breath caught in her throat because it'd happened. *She* was the one constant. This was her.

Just like her parents' divorces, and the wedding where the groom was so cliché he had to sleep with the maid of honor, and the other time when the not-so-happy couple ended up annulling everything before the reception was even done.

And now? Now she was staring at photographic proof that everything—every illusion of perfect closure, of forward momentum, of curses broken—had cracked open again.

No. Wait.

She squeezed her eyes shut, forcing herself to breathe deep.

This wasn't her. Not this time. Anna and Drake had fought before the wedding. Hell, they'd bickered over napkin folds during the rehearsal dinner, and it had ended in laughter and stolen kisses.

Arguments happened. Honeymoons were stressful with jet lag, bad room service, and the weight of forever crashing down after the wedding high.

She had watched them vow their hearts out under a pergola strung with lights that she'd hand-tested for flicker.

Zach's voice echoed in her head, low and sure from that night telling her he loved her.

For one stupid, desperate second, she let herself believe in the fantasy of a happily-ever-after. Let the warmth of his hands on her hips, the way he'd whispered her name like a secret, push back the shadows.

Maybe this was just life? Messy, unglamorous, survivable.

But her chest tightened as a new wave of messages poured in.

> Shelby: I know what you're thinking. I know you. Stop it. This is not on you.

Piper didn't type back. She didn't text. Didn't call. Didn't breathe.

She sat very, very still, like movement might make it all worse.

No, no, no.

Her pulse pounded in her ears as that old familiar narrative barbed wire wove its way through her brain.

I'm the common denominator. Always have been.

A quiet sound escaped her throat—half laugh, half ache.

Of course she'd ruined it. Of course she had.

Anna had only wanted something simple and safe and real. Drake spoke his vows with fierce, teary eyes. That moment under the pergola made it all seem like it would last.

Piper dared to believe in it.

That had been her mistake.

With her record—all the parental divorces, cancelled weddings, postmarital break-ups—it didn't matter how flawless her execution was. She knew how this would end.

Why did she allow it to surprise her?

She tried to call Anna. Typed in the numbers, but went straight to voicemail.

She stood slowly. Her hands gripped with twisted resolve. A rope fraying too fast to save.

Zach's name flashed on her phone screen, calling.

She didn't answer.

Instead, she moved down the hallway like her body was separate from her logic, heading straight for Aspen where she was meeting with another junior planner in the conference room. Their murmured voices floated under the door.

It was mid-meeting, but Piper didn't care.

She knocked once, pushed it open.

"Sorry to interrupt. I'll only take a moment," she said calmly, like she wasn't unraveling from the inside out.

Aspen looked up, blinking.

She sat at the head of the conference table laying out mood boards and floral palette samples. Everything spread all over. This was for their meeting later to discuss next spring's wedding trends, including peony imports, tenting logistics, and backup rain plans.

"Piper?" Aspen asked.

"I was wrong," she said, her voice shockingly steady. "I can't do weddings. It's not a preference, it's a liability. Someone else should handle that." And leave her with the funerals and corporate galas. Safe events that don't end in heartbreak or drag anyone down.

She showed Aspen the links to the articles. Aspen's face dropped as she read along.

"I understand that not helping out with weddings means the promotion might not be mine right now, and that's okay. You need someone you can really count on for all events. You deserve that. I just—I wanted you to hear it from me."

Aspen opened her mouth, clearly caught off guard. "I— Piper, hold on—"

"I guess… I guess… that means that it's okay to select someone else. No hard feelings. But, um, I'm not feeling great. I need to take a personal day." Her chin wobbled. "Please?"

"Of course." Aspen started toward her. "Of course, take the day. Take two. But we need to talk about this."

Piper had already turned, her hands clammy.

She didn't wait, she walked straight out of Montgomery Events, past the glossy photo wall and the sparkling light fixtures and the nameplate outside the office with a new smudge near the 'M.'

She didn't fix it. Not today.

Outside, the air was cooler than expected. Sharp, like it wanted to wake her up.

Zach's voice called from behind, breathless. "Hey, Piper."

She didn't turn around.

"Piper? What's wrong?" he hurried toward her.

"I saw the tabloids."

"The Drake and Anna thing?" he asked as though it was just another morning conversation.

"What other thing is there?" she asked.

"They just had a tiff," he assured like it was no big deal.

"A tiff?" she asked.

"That's what my mom always calls it when we argue. Not a big deal, just a tiff."

She paused at the curb, her throat thick. "Zach? I'm scared it always ends and this is how the ending starts." She hiccupped.

His confidence crumbled. Like he'd finally put the dot-to-dot together and realized the finished image was once again *her* fault.

"Piper, no. This isn't the beginning of the end for them. It's not. Don't let this drag you. We broke through together. Hold onto that. I didn't realize..." He took a few steps closer, his voice easing. "No one's even talked to Drake or Anna yet. I'm not sure what's going on, but I'll tell you as soon as I know. And, if it were something big? The family would be all over my ass about it. Digging for intel. Ready to fly down and force them to make up."

She stayed still; shoulders tense.

"I stopped by because you left your binder at my place." He held out the black plastic in his hand. "Figured you'd want it for your meeting later."

She stared at it, but she didn't take it. Instead, her voice broke as she said, "I don't need it. I don't even know if I can do this job anymore. I just—"

Zach's eyes went huge. "Piper. Don't—"

"You see a tiff. I see a pattern. My pattern. How can you not see that?" How could he not get it?

He grimaced, and Piper felt that flinch of his doubt. It kicked her heart from up under her ribs.

"You're right. I don't get it because I'm not worried about Anna and Drake," Zach continued quickly. "Yeah, the pictures look bad. But those two? They love each other. Listen, every relationship struggles at some point. That doesn't mean anything. Theirs got caught in a picture. That's all."

She turned her head slightly. "You didn't see in it what I did."

He moved his palm to rest against her jaw. "Their fight is not because you worked on their wedding. I mean... it's, just, not."

She looked away again, her voice breaking. "But what if it is?"

Her throat tightened with the weight of it all.

"It's not," he said, but his voice was strained. A forced certainty that did nothing to soothe the panic clawing up from her stomach.

"This always happens," she whispered, the words trembling. Her breath caught, chest taut, heart thudding.

"That doesn't mean anything," he replied gently, but the syllables landed like stones.

She wanted to believe he was right. She really did. But evidence was not in his favor. This wasn't a theory. It was solid logic.

"I'm trying to believe in love," she said, and her mouth trembled with the effort to keep control. "But it's terrifying. I need some time to think. To figure out what I actually think without all the outside chatter." Her voice cracked on the last word, raw and exposed. "I need some space to breathe so I don't accidentally break us." She needed a minute. She needed a damn week.

Gah. The sound broke out of her, half sob, half curse.

"Running happens in fairy tales," Zach said. "But this is *us*. This is real. You don't need to run. Not when I'm right here."

She pressed her hands to her cheeks, fingers digging in like she could somehow hold herself together.

And then without waiting for answers, without waiting for mercy, she turned and walked away.

Her coat flapped behind her in the wind, unbuttoned and uncaring. Her eyes ached with tears, every blink a battle.

But her chest... her chest burned, tight and hollow all at once. She didn't look back, not until the corner loomed like a cliff she didn't want to fall from but maybe already had.

When she did turn around, Zach stood frozen, one hand half-lifted as though he were going to try to stop her. Slowly, he dropped it to his side.

His mom said that detours were part of the path.

But, what if the detour always led back to the wreckage instead?

CHAPTER 25

2 DAYS AFTER ANNA
& DRAKE'S WEDDING

ZACH

The hum of the sewing machine buzzed under Zach's fingers like it needed something to stitch more than fabric. Answers. Like him, it needed answers.

He'd settle for a goddamn glass slipper at this point. Anything to prove she was real, and she was coming back.

Outside, Denver was tucked into night. Inside, they were neck-deep in a new cut inspired by Roman gladiators.

Those were Noah's words, not his. But Zach couldn't concentrate. Not even close.

He pinched the bridge of his nose and tried not to check his phone again.

Noah sat across the worktable, poking at a pile of waistband prototypes like they might bite him.

"She's gonna call," Noah said for, oh, the fourteenth time.

Piper hadn't responded all day. Off grid. Radio-silent. Every notification on his phone triggered false hope. Every news ping made his stomach turn.

He nodded toward the prototype in Noah's hand. "That seam's off by half a centimeter. You'll feel it."

Noah gave him a look. "And you'll feel it when your heart explodes from stressing about your girl, but cool, let's focus on the elastic."

Zach scoffed.

Noah dragged one waistband across the table with the enthusiasm of a cat inspecting broccoli. "What even is this stretch blend?"

"Lycra-poly mix. Contours like butter, irritates the skin like regret." Zach's response came automatically.

"Cool. Definitely the one to go with."

"Piper said she needed space," Zach murmured.

She'd said it while seriously trying not to cry. He could still hear it on replay in his head—space—as if she hadn't just meant air but *distance*.

He hadn't known what to do then, either, except nod like he understood.

But he didn't, not really.

Zach huffed a breath, then leaned back on his stool, swallowing the emotion that had tried to claw its way up. "She thinks it's her fault. But she wasn't even there. Why the hell would she blame herself?"

"Because of a photo." Noah said. "Pretty sure it's because of the photo."

"Helpful," Zach said, dryly.

"I aim to please."

"It wasn't even a real argument," Zach pointed out. "Anna said it was about orange juice and how Drake always steals the good pillow."

Noah blinked. "The good pillow?"

"Like how in every bed there's one pillow that's always the best one? Drake steals it, apparently. Anna had enough," Zach stared at a line of broken thread on the table.

"Team Anna on this one. Drake can use the flat pillow," Noah said.

Before Zach could respond, a knock scraped sharp against the metal door.

"That better be the pizza," Noah muttered, pushing to stand.

But it wasn't.

Shelby stood under the flickering warehouse bulb like she'd been blown there by desperation. Hair up in a haphazard tower-of-terror bun, hoodie half-zipped over pajamas, and that wild look in her eyes that meant somebody was about to key a car.

"She hasn't come home," Shelby said before Zach could even ask. "Her phone's off. I've called. Texted. Pinged her location. Nothing." Her voice cracked on that last word. "She did this once before," Shelby added quickly. "Back in college. Tossed her phone in the freezer and disappeared for twelve hours. I found her sitting behind the campus library. Not crying. Not mad. Just...gone, almost. Like there was a wall she couldn't climb back over."

Zach was on his feet. Keys already in hand. That was all he needed.

"Pretty much, that. She saw the pictures," Zach said. "Didn't know the context. Just believed it was her. That she caused it. She panicked. She's not herself. We're all trying to find her."

The silence that followed was thick, choking.

"She really believes it," Zach said again, slowly, like he was convincing not just them—but himself. "It's not just a fear. It's the story she tells herself, and right now, she thinks she wrote the ending."

Because this wasn't simply needing some space.

"I already checked every coffee shop she likes. Even the ones she doesn't," Shelby said.

Zach reached for his jacket. "Okay, let's split up."

"Wait," Noah interrupted, holding a palm out. "We should think. I mean, she wasn't just upset. Which means impulsively running through Denver's most popular back alleys might not be the play."

Zach let the keys rest in his palm but didn't pocket them. A breath ticked out of him.

Shelby nodded. "She's not random when she spirals. She's precise. Logical, weirdly. We need to work backward."

"This is all because she thinks *she's* toxic?" Noah asked, carefully.

Shelby nodded. "She's said that before. That she poisons good relationships just by breathing near them."

Zach's throat dried instantly.

"She believes it," Shelby admitted.

"It's not only the belief in a curse," Zach added, quieter now. "It's her story. Every breakup, every wedding disaster in her past… it's real to her."

The urge to throw something climbed up Zach's arm.

Because he couldn't do a damn thing about any of this standing there in the shop. They needed to be out looking for her. Finding her.

"I'm gonna say something here that might make this worse." Noah ran his hand over his face. "But I'm going to say it anyway, because it needs to be said. And it might help."

Zach and Shelby both stared at him like he'd grown a second set of nostrils.

"Actually." Noah pulled out his phone. "I'm gonna loop in Tess."

He dialed the numbers and set his phone in the center of one of Zach's sewing tables, battered edges and pieces of thread still clinging to every crevice—because crisis theory always worked better with visual clutter.

Zach used a scrap of paper to start a timeline like it was a blueprint. He didn't have time to waste, but he trusted Noah. So, he rolled with it.

"Tess, hey," Noah said in an intimate kind of way that had the hairs on the back of Zach's neck prickling. "You're on speaker with me and Zach and Piper's roommate; I need you to tell Zach what you told me earlier. About the whole tabloid thing."

"Hey," Tess said, instantaneously in PR-crisis mode. "Yeah, of course. But I can't reach Piper. The photographer for the wedding isn't answering, and I want to counter all this with some reassuring dance floor photos. Is she there with you, too?"

"No," Zach said. "She's not here. She went dark. We're worried. She's got this idea that it's her fault somehow. It's a long story."

"Her parents fucked her up," Shelby said, matter-of-factly. "That's all you need to know."

"It's not her fault at all. It's my damn intern." Tess blew out a breath into the receiver.

Sorry, what?

"One of the interns figured the press would be watching the honeymoon and if there was a kiss or... something romantic between Anna and Drake, it would be good for image. Don't worry, we've discussed it. Not going to happen again."

"For fuck's sake," Zach muttered.

Tess hesitated. "It was supposed to be subtle. Carefully placed. Obviously, my team didn't pick the exact moment. The photographer went rogue, kind of."

"Apparently, this is standard PR practice." Noah pressed the end of his pen against his lips.

Tess hesitated, the line crackling with her exhale. "I didn't... It was a bad call. The intern's on coffee duty for a month, the photog's not gonna work with us again, and the oversight is mine. All mine. Damn, this is on *me*. Not her. How do we find her to tell her?"

Zach leaned into the phone, the knot in his chest loosening a fraction. This wasn't a blow-up. It was a pivot.

"Shelby's roommate intel says she holes up somewhere

logical when she spirals." Noah turned the phone his direction.

"Like where?" Tess jumped in, hopefully her PR brain was whirring productively now. "Work? The venue? Somewhere tied to the wedding?"

Shelby piped up. "Holy crap, that gives me an idea. I think she'd go where no one would look, like back to the Falcon Hotel. Closure and all that."

"I still have contacts at most hotels downtown," Tess said after a moment. "I'll make some calls, see if she's checked in anywhere. And I'll..." Tess paused, then continued with renewed determination. "...drive around the wedding venue area. She might have gone back there to process."

"I'll meet you there," Noah said, already grabbing his keys like this was just another late-night prototype run.

"And I'll head back to our apartment," Shelby stood, zipping her hoodie with purpose. "Because that's where *I'd* go if I wanted to hide in plain sight."

"Yeah," Zach said, the plan snapping into place like a well-fitted waistband. "This is good. I'll hit up her office. Maybe she stopped there? Text the group chain. First one to spot her pings everyone."

Then he paused, because whether she was ready to accept it or not, Piper was family. And his family was something special.

That's why he texted the mass family group chat and filled them in.

His phone buzzed with a text chain exploding like a string of firecrackers.

Anna: Serious? We're freaking.

Drake: Dude. Honeymoon's fine. Pillow war.
I'm wrong. Anna's right. But Tess f'd up big.
Call me.

Jase: Heather and I are in for the search party.

Beeps and dings sounded as pings flooded in from the rest of the family.

Babushka sent the same panda emoji she always did, with absolutely zero context.

Everyone agreed on search points, and Zach pocketed his phone. Grabbed his coat.

He was going to find her.

Not to fix her.

To show up. To be there so she wasn't alone. And maybe, just maybe, to remind her that some seams don't need ripping because they're meant to hold.

CHAPTER 26

2 DAYS AFTER ANNA
& DRAKE'S WEDDING

PIPER

Piper's boots scuffed against the worn wooden floor as she slid onto the barstool, her shoulders tense, fingers wrapped loosely around her chilled glass of Cherry Coke.

She hadn't meant to be there. Hadn't meant to be spilling the latest chapter of her failures to Brek Montgomery, of all people.

And, yet, this is where she found herself.

Her fingers traced the condensation down her glass as she stared past it, voice low and unsteady. "Every time I get close to something resembling a relationship—mine or anyone else's? —it crumbles. Like clockwork."

She told him all about the weddings she'd planned and how they always ended badly. She told him about her parents. About Zach.

Across the polished bar, Brek leaned in, thick forearms sinking into the edge. Tattoos curled beneath the sleeves of his worn black tee. A crooked smile played at the corner of his mouth.

"Should I worry?" he joked, backing up an inch with mock-urgency. "I might catch your bad relationship cooties."

A laugh escaped her, but it dissolved before it reached her eyes. She tapped the edge of her glass, not looking up.

Brek didn't push. Just nodded slowly.

"I'm not an expert, but I do know that if love isn't messy," he said, voice quieter now, "you're not doing it right."

"I shouldn't be doing it at all." Piper stared into the fading fizz of her soda. "That's the point."

Something in her chest tugged at the edges, stretching too wide to ignore. Maybe love was supposed to be messy. Maybe that was the point. But her brand of messy felt less like fireworks and more like the aftermath of a bad storm with scattered debris, flooding, and sirens.

The bar door creaked open twenty minutes later. Aspen strode in, her lipstick intact and concern flickering in her expression.

She scanned the bar once, eyes locking on Piper, then Brek.

Her heels clicked against the hardwood floor as she approached, her presence abrupt and inevitable, as if drawn in by Piper's bad luck. Or, more likely, a cryptic text from her bartending brother.

"I've had time to think today and while I appreciate your thoughts," Aspen said, sliding onto the stool beside her. "Only I get to choose who gets promotions at my company."

"Aspen…"

"That promotion is *yours*," she continued. "And if you can't do weddings, then we'll figure it out. Hopefully, things will change. But if tomorrow and next week you feel the same, I'll accept it."

Brek slid some kind of fizzy beverage in front of Aspen without even asking what she wanted.

"I'm sorry," Piper said, eyes fixed on the corner of the bartop. "I shouldn't have left like that. I'm sorry."

For walking out. For probably giving the junior planners nightmares about their own career trajectories.

But Aspen smiled that kind, steady smile of hers. "We all spiral sometimes, Piper. Only difference is whether we spiral alone or with people who'll catch us."

"Is that why you're here?" Piper asked. "To catch me?"

"I'm here as your boss because I want to know what happened that made you try to give up your well-earned promotion. I'm here as your *friend*, because I'm worried," Aspen said.

Piper explained it all. Everything. Just threw it all up like it wasn't messy and gross. Like shame didn't cling to every sentence. Aspen listened, never flinching, not even when Piper's voice cracked on Zach's name, or when she admitted she left her phone at home because she didn't want to hear that Anna and Drake were truly done.

Her throat burned by the end, lips trembling from too many unspoken things finally said aloud.

Aspen took it all in with grace she'd never admit to possessing.

"That is a lot for one person to carry," Aspen said, finally.

The bell above Brek's door hadn't even finished its jingle before Babushka swept in. She descended like an Eastern European snowstorm dressed for brunch at the opera. People instinctively leaned out of her orbit, either from respect or mild fear.

She wore a teal trench coat bedazzled with rhinestone roses and carried a reusable grocery bag that smelled aggressively of dill and lavender tea. Her lipstick was a violent shade of coral that worked for her, and her earrings swung like miniature chandeliers with each determined step.

"Piper," she announced, loud enough that one man across the bar dropped his peanuts. "You are not cursed. You are dramatic."

Piper blinked. "I—what?"

"I have spoken to Anna. I have spoken to Zachary. They explain everything. So, I come find you." Babushka marched behind the bar with purpose, barely acknowledging Brek, who wisely stepped aside.

"You think your life is some terrible soap opera because a couple people yelled by pool?" She plopped her bag down on the bar, then pulled out a tarnished silver flask, a handful of wrapped candies, and what looked alarmingly like laminated flashcards scrawled in hand-written Russian. "Drake and Anna, they fight, then they make up. Now they are sorry for you. Do not vorry though, there is no curse."

"I thought you believed in curses and luck and all of that," Piper managed, sitting up straighter.

"I believe in tradition." Babushka barked, as if that were the same thing. She used the bottle to fill her flask and Brek said nothing. But he did try not to smile.

He failed.

Piper frowned. "But, at the venue walkthrough, you said the wedding would be cursed if we didn't include certain traditions. Your exact words were 'do this, or the love will suffer the eternal bad luck.'"

Babushka waved a dismissive hand. "Of course, I said that. It is how I get vhat I vant."

"You... weaponize superstition?" Piper asked.

"I am Russian grandmother. That is literally my job." She arched a perfectly drawn-on brow as if daring Piper to argue. "Also, fear is more effective than inspirational quotes. Write that down."

Piper stared, speechless. Somewhere between confusion and awe.

Babushka leaned in close, tapping her ring-heavy fingers against the counter. "There is no curse. There is only the story you tell yourself to explain vhy things fall apart. You vant to believe you break things because then you don't have to build anything new. You get to keep control. Hmm?"

Piper felt her stomach dip, the words slicing through her practiced self-deprecation like buttercream. Sharp, but with enough sweetness to hit deep.

"But you say happy tears before the ceremony mean sad tears after," she said, reaching for anything that could still be real.

At that, Babushka leaned back with a snort and dramatic hand to her chest. "Oh, no—that one's real. Always has been. Never tempt fate, Piper."

Piper licked her lips. Glanced to Aspen then Brek.

Both shrugged.

"Don't look at me like that," Babushka said, sipping from her flask. "Even a curse has its rules. Now, you tell Aspen you vant your job and big promotion." Babushka pointed to Aspen. "You give it back, yes?"

Aspen nodded. "Yes."

Babushka grabbed a napkin and spit on the edge, then she sprinkled some salt there and reached over the bar to press the result against Piper's forehead.

Piper was entirely too shocked to say anything.

"The curse is now gone," Babushka announced. "I have lifted any that remains."

"You said it wasn't real to begin with?" Piper asked.

"And now you believe it, yes?" Babushka nodded. "You go to your office and you vait for Zachary. He vill be there soon."

Piper frowned. "How do you—"

"I know things because I know them." Babushka waved Piper's almost-question away.

"She does, actually," Aspen agreed. "Right, Brek?"

"I know better than to argue about anything," he said with a smirk.

Then he gave Piper a coffee to-go for the road.

"Can't have my sister's best employee wandering the streets caffeine-deprived," he said.

And then she was at Montgomery Events. Outside on the steps, anyway.

The concrete seeped cold through her slacks as Piper sat with her knees drawn up to her chest. Her hair whipped across her face in the breeze, tangling around her collar, but she couldn't be bothered to tuck it back.

She stared at the flowers in the decorative urns flanking the building entrance. They weren't blooming now—past their season, brown-edged and drooping.

Totally apt.

Piper wasn't really spiraling anymore. She didn't know what she believed, but it was good to know Drake and Anna were fine.

But now that her emotional tornado had passed, it left behind that eerie stillness that comes after destruction.

She was numb now. Numb and unsure what she was going to do next. The curse theory had felt so logical hours ago. Now it felt like a convenient excuse for avoidance.

The wind bit harder, tugging at the hem of her coat, nosing under her collar. Her hands were tucked beneath her thighs for warmth. This moment, this limbo between emotional collapse and supposed resolution, gnawed at her.

That was the cruel thing about survival. It didn't promise clarity. You made it through the wave, sure, but then you had to live in the after. With the silence. With yourself.

Was this how her love story ended? Alone, on a step, waiting.

The sound of footsteps made her tense. She didn't look up. Didn't want to hope it was him.

"Everyone's looking for you."

That voice. She'd know it anywhere, even flattened by exhaustion. Piper lifted her gaze slowly, reluctantly.

"Literally, everyone. Heather and Jase, Sadie and Roman, Mom and Dad. Babushka. Even Tess and Noah. Shelby. They're all out trying to find you." Zach stood at the bottom of the steps, hair disheveled, his blue hoodie wrinkled like he'd balled it up and shoved it in a gym bag. He held two coffees and a brown pastry bag with grease stains blooming at the bottom.

"Babushka told you where to find me?" she asked.

"No." He drew his eyebrows together. "Did you talk to her?"

"Yes."

"How did she find you?"

Piper shrugged. "How does she do anything?"

"One of life's mysteries." He didn't hesitate, just climbed the steps and lowered himself beside her like he'd done it a thousand times. Like this was their spot. Like of course he'd find her here.

"I'm not ready to be found, yet," she said, her voice small and raw.

"That's cool." He held out a coffee and the bag. "You've already got your coffee. But here's a spare."

Piper glanced at her untouched cup. "Mine's cold."

"Mine's not."

The silence between them hummed with everything unsaid. She didn't take the coffee right away. Then she did, and the bag, too. She peeked inside.

"It's a croissant but not almond. I asked twice," he said. "I figured you are still on the outs with that particular nut."

That bought him a grin. She reached in and pulled out not just the promised pastry, but a small package of bubble gum. Pink like what she'd stepped in that first day. She held it up, raising an eyebrow.

He shrugged. "Seemed like a good idea."

"I can't believe you came," she said quietly, the words scraping her throat.

Zach's eyes met hers, clear and steady. "I don't give up on the people I love, even if they want me to."

Her heart stuttered. She looked away, unwrapping the

croissant with fingers that suddenly felt clumsy. "I went to Brek's."

"Yeah?"

"He had thoughts."

"He always does." Zach's mouth curved into a small smile.

She bit into the croissant, letting the buttery flakes dissolve on her tongue.

"For what it's worth, Tess's intern arranged for a photographer to catch the honeymooners for PR. Hoping for something romantic, but the guy caught them mid-squabble about a pillow."

"A pillow," Piper repeated flatly.

"Drake stole the good pillow. Apparently, this is a thing."

Despite herself, a small laugh bubbled up. "You're making that up."

"I swear on Babushka's pirozhki." He placed his hand over his heart. "They're totally fine."

That made her look up. "That's good."

She continued eating, letting the silence settle between them like a third presence on the steps.

Finally, she said, "Why are you here?"

He shrugged. "Because you are."

She closed her eyes against the wind and let it in—his words, the quiet, the truth of being seen. The healing.

Zach didn't push. He sat, drinking his own coffee, letting his shoulder rest a whisper away from hers. The non-answer was somehow the truest answer he could have given.

"You know, I've been thinking about it. You don't break things." Zach shook his head, his voice gentle but firm. "Maybe you feel the cracks before anyone else does. But that's not a flaw. That's being brilliant."

She snorted, unconvinced.

Piper took a shaky breath, absorbing this. "Still. I just... I can't help but wait for the other shoe to drop. For something to go wrong."

"Sometimes the other shoe never drops. There's no way to know if you'll be walking around with one shoe or two."

"Well, I prefer to know," she shrugged. "Sue me."

"That's what I thought. No surprises. No..." He gestured between them. "...unexpected chemistry with strangers on sidewalks."

His words from their first meeting, thrown back at her now with such gentle precision that her eyes stung.

She closed her eyes. Held the new coffee against her chest, letting its warmth seep through her sweater. She didn't say anything else, couldn't trust her voice not to crack.

"You know," Zach added after a moment, "you aren't the only one who worries about screwing things up. I worry, too. Everyone does. That means we're people."

A breeze rustled the dying flowers in their urns.

The evening light cast long shadows across the steps where they sat side by side. No kiss. Just quiet. Real.

Piper finally leaned her shoulder into his, a silent surrender.

Zach didn't move. He stayed, solid and steady beside her.

"I love you," she whispered, the words barely audible above the city sounds.

"And I love you." He kissed her forehead, his lips lingering against her skin. "It's enough."

And for the first time in forever, Piper believed it might be.

Maybe she didn't quite know what "enough" meant.

But if it looked like this? Quiet, present, solid? It was plenty.

PIPER

Months passed as Piper and Aspen began to work closer together.

The promotion was fabulous, and Piper loved dipping into the responsibility. As she'd taken on more, Aspen had taken less. She wanted to spend time with her kids, but she didn't want to give up her company. So, Piper was her right hand.

It worked for everyone.

Piper worked on a few more weddings and the D.I.C.K. conference was coming along brilliantly.

Today, it was almost quitting time and Piper stood by the break room table in her favorite pink pantsuit and patent-leather flats. Right next to a slightly wonky cupcake tower with a glitter-glued "Wedding Survival Kit" in her grip.

There was no red carpet or giant bouquet waiting. No fanfare or ceremonial jazz hands. But this moment was special—everyone knew it.

"Okay team," she announced to the group of junior planners gathered there, "before you say thank you for the bagel spread, or the gold love-themed pens, I have a gift to distribute to Abigail."

Piper waved her forward, remembering (against her will) her first wedding that wasn't for her parents. The missing cake that got delivered to the wrong place. The best man with food poisoning. The groom late because his mother locked the keys in her minivan.

Piper hadn't had any glitter bags or sparkly morale stickers. She only had a pair of broken kitten heels, and a lunchbox full of TUMS and used-up tissues.

Abigail stepped up with that same nervous tightness Piper once carried in every shoulder muscle. The newest addition to the team was twenty-two with bangs as sharp as her Type A tendencies.

Piper held out the mesh bag to her.

"A survival kit?" Abigail asked, eyeing the glitter bag like it might be rigged to explode with heart-shaped Post-its.

Piper smiled. "You're getting your very first wedding assignment from Aspen tomorrow?"

Abigail nodded slowly. "I really don't want to screw it up."

Piper glanced down at the ground, her hair sliding across one cheek, and said, "The funny thing about screwing up is that you can usually unscrew it if you're sincere." She paused. "You should write that down."

Abigail grinned. "Noted."

"Here's what I didn't have but definitely needed when I first started." Piper handed her the pink mesh sack with ceremonial gravity. "Inside you'll find stress pucks, tissues, a sewing kit, an emergency chocolate bunny, peppermint tea, a list I made for you of 'reasons today probably isn't ruined,' fake magnetic lashes, and one extremely sparkly sticker that reads, *It's not magic. It's me.*"

"I love it." Abigail beamed, holding the kit up high while everyone else clapped and cheered.

"But be warned," Piper said, as ominously as she could. "If

you cry before the ceremony, Babushka says you might cry after, too."

No one questioned it. Babushka rules were sacred canon in the office even when they made absolutely no sense at all.

Chuckles started in the back of the group and moved all the way through.

Abigail squeezed the mesh bag like it was filled with gemstones instead of a bunch of fun stuff that didn't really matter... and at the same time mattered too much. "Thanks, Piper."

The room cleared and Piper stepped back, nibbling on a bagel.

"That was cute," Zach said, leaning against the doorframe, his hair doing its usual tousled thing.

She jumped. Caught in the act of spoiling her dinner.

"How long were you standing there?" she asked.

Zach tipped his forehead toward her. "Long enough to get emotionally invested in the survival kit's sticker choices."

She loved his voice. Loved hearing him talk. Because he always spoke like things were fine, even when they weren't. That settled her, because even if they were falling apart, they would figure it out together.

She smirked. "It was either *It's not magic. It's me.* or *Dream Day Enforcer.* Seemed on brand."

Zach crossed the room and set down his coffee. "You said pick you up at five. I'm here at five-oh-two."

"You're saying that you're late?" She tilted her head to the side.

"How's it going with Aspen gone so much?" he asked, seriously.

"Like I'm wearing high heels on an escalator. Empowering but vaguely dangerous."

He tilted her chin up with a finger. "You rocking them anyway?"

"Oh yeah," Piper murmured. "Strategic toe cramps and all."

Someone in the hallway called for Piper. Something about a linen mix-up for the Chamber of Commerce gala.

"Give me five?" she asked. "Then meet me in my office and we can go?"

"You can have ten," he teased.

She gave Zach a brief smile, excused herself, and disappeared around the corner like a woman who had actual power in her heels now.

When she made it back to her office, Zach was in her chair, feet kicked onto the edge of her desk, paging through her D.I.C.K. symposium prep files.

"You snooping or professionally vetting my funeral keynote notes?" Piper teased.

"Professionally snooping," he said agreeably.

She circled behind the desk. "Anything particularly incriminating?"

He held up a scribbled page titled: *Hot Priest Options*.

"Some questions," he said dryly. "No real answers."

Piper set down a wedding binder for one of the upcoming events she'd agreed to take on. While weddings still weren't her favorite, she had learned to enjoy them. In moderation. With lots of outsourcing.

"Do you ever think about planning your own wedding?" Zach asked, eyeing the binder.

Piper blinked hard. "Are you proposing?"

"I mean, I'm not *not* proposing." He laid his finger on the front of the binder and made small circles.

He wasn't serious. Of course, he wasn't serious.

"This is a horrible proposal. I think you can do better. Call your grandmother, she'll help." Piper popped a mint in her mouth.

"Noted." Zach shoved his hands in his pockets. "But seriously, you ever think about what you want for a wedding?"

Nope. Because she would rather just show up and have it done for her. "I'd rather show up to a well-lit party with matching napkins, walk out married, and call it a day."

Thinking about it, even casually, sent her stomach into a weird kind of somersault.

Planning events for strangers was control. Planning for herself? That was vulnerability. Suddenly it mattered if people showed up. Suddenly it mattered if she cried in the vows.

Would she walk herself down the aisle, or would she let her dad do it barefoot in flamingo trunks because he was already in Aruba?

Ew, no, thank you. Somebody else could handle all of that for her.

Zach held her gaze tight with his. Piper didn't flinch.

It wasn't that she didn't want to get married. It was that logistics felt exhausting when she spent her days turning unfiltered Pinterest moods into memories.

She grabbed her jacket and a stack of work she'd take home with her and probably not get done. "Look, if one day I show up and there's an arch already set up and champagne already chilled and Prince Charming at the end of the aisle? Well, I wouldn't be sad."

Zach shoved his hands in his pockets. "Fine. I'll rehearse it. I'll stagger in with daisies. That's how you know. Daisies are a very serious flower. Or orchids. Are those romantic or vaguely funereal?"

"You're planning my wedding with a funeral aesthetic?"

"Dual-purpose. I call it budget efficiency."

Piper giggled. "Daisies are fine. They're not tulips, but you're new at this. We'll work up to that."

"Tulips it is," he said.

She arched an eyebrow. "I get veto power on the color palette."

"Deal. If the cake is chocolate. That's non-negotiable."

"With buttercream, not fondant. I hate fondant."

"I thought you didn't care," he asked, pointedly.

"I only care about that part."

Zach leaned in, brushing his nose against hers. "I thought this was a soft proposal anyway."

"A soft proposal?"

"Yeah. Warm-up lap. Final dress rehearsal. No pressure but maybe clear your calendar in eighteen months just in case."

They were ridiculous. But some part of her? Some very traitorous, grinning part, was already picturing the whole spread.

Pausing at the Montgomery Events placard outside the door, she buffed it with her sleeve. Just for luck.

The sun slanted low over Cherry Creek, shining through the window at the end of the hall and Zach's knuckles brushed against hers like a habit. Their pinkies hooked, loosely, without thinking.

Neither of them said anything.

They didn't have to.

"I talked to my mom today," Piper said when they reached the bank of elevators.

"That's worrying," Zach replied, pushing the down button.

She pushed it again, for good measure. "She and *Dad* are going to Aruba."

"Together?" Zach's eyebrow seemed to crawl right up to his hairline.

That'd been her reaction, too.

Piper nodded. The elevator opened and Zach held his arm against the door while she stepped through first.

"And I am *not* involved. I don't care what they do. I don't care what happens." She brushed her hands together like she was done with it. "I am not planning or attending any future weddings they have."

Tender, and only for her, Zach said, "You were never the problem. You really know that now, right?"

"I know," Piper said. "I know that now."

She'd grown up believing tension was normal, peace was temporary, and anyone who didn't yell probably didn't care.

But with Zach, there had never been yelling.

Only gentle arguments and a surprising respect for color-coding.

Also, turned out that her Montgomery Events health insurance covered a whole lot of therapy. So, between that and the Dvornakov brand of therapy, she was in an excellent headspace.

Then she said, almost to herself, "I think I used to believe I had to earn everything. Even love."

Zach's hand found hers again. "Not anymore."

He slipped his fingers through hers and pulled her close while the elevator chugged to the bottom floor.

Somewhere, somehow, he slipped a diamond ring on her finger right there in the elevator between the second and first floor.

Piper held up her blinged out finger, then slowly glanced to him with all the questions to ever question in her eyes.

She twisted her wrist, admiring the diamond again.

It wasn't the kind of ring she would've picked. A little too sparkly. A little too much.

But maybe that was the point.

Zach didn't do muted colors. He did ease and effort in the same breath. Maybe she didn't need subtle? She needed sparkle wrapped in steady.

"I guess I only had to find my own kind of chaos," she said.

"You found it," he said, pressing a kiss against her hair, "and it's already planning a chocolate cake tasting so you don't have to do anything."

Piper rolled her eyes and held up her hand. "I like the ring. I get to keep it, right?"

"Yup." He kissed her.

"You're still gonna actually ask me?"

"Yup." He kissed her again. "Tonight, in bed, when you're on your second orgasm. Maybe third."

Her cheeks heated. But seriously, she wasn't gonna argue with *that*.

"Are you gonna say yes?"

"Yup," she replied. "And we won't have any doves, right?" Because that would be a hard limit for her.

"Nope." He kept kissing her, hanging on tight. "No animals are allowed. Except Jase. Maybe Roman. They can come."

She giggled.

And she didn't let go.

Not now. Not ever.

CHAPTER 28

PIPER

The box was ridiculous.

It sat on the coffee table like a prop from a lifestyle influencer's dream reel—white glossy wrapping paper, elaborate gold foil flourishes curling like vines across the surface, and with a bow so big it could've auditioned for a Lexus holiday commercial.

Piper narrowed her eyes at it, arms crossed, because there was no reason for a gift today.

She took a cautious step closer. That bow. That wrapping. It had…intent.

Did she forget something? Was this a special Dvornakov holiday she should've penciled onto her calendar?

"Zach," she called, suspicion in each syllable. "Why is there a fairy godmother's personal gift box on our coffee table?"

He appeared from the kitchen, suspiciously casual in socked feet, holding a fresh latte from their espresso machine.

He glanced to the box like it had simply occurred to him to be incredibly thoughtful on a random Tuesday.

"Oh, that? Found it hanging around. Looks like it's for you." His voice practically hummed innocence.

Piper took the fresh coffee from him, glanced from the foam heart in her cup to the gift. "What'd you do?"

Zach's shrug was infuriatingly clean. "Early anniversary. Or random Tuesday. You pick."

He took a sip of his own drink and smirked like a man confident he wouldn't be murdered in his own home.

The box made the slightest crinkle when she touched it, as if warning her. She lifted the lid slowly, certain it would release butterflies or a puppy or something.

Nestled in layers of crisp tissue was a white linen dress with pink embroidered tulips. Nothing flashy, but something undeniably special.

The fabric was light as a sigh, with delicate ribbon straps and seams so graceful they curved inward like they already knew the shape of her. The fabric whispered against her fingers as she lifted it, and she caught herself holding her breath again.

Was this one of Zach's ideas, or had someone helped? She tried to picture him, earnest with his sewing machine while he stitched together the fabric. The idea made her smile.

Just once. Quiet, involuntary. She let out a little gasp she would totally deny later.

Beneath it, folded like a secret, were ballet flats. Ivory with more tiny tulips stitched across the toe.

Zach crouched beside her, all soft knees and cocky nerves, and said, "I got this," so quietly it might've been a joke.

But then he reached for her foot and gently slipped on one of the shoes like the floor was a ballroom and not a battlefield of laundry baskets and unfolded towels.

The fit? Unfair.

She looked down at him, blinking, mouth parted but no words arriving.

Because they had a work party to throw. Co-workers to

impress. Potato salad to chill. And here he was, reenacting a fairy tale with bedhead.

The backyard party was just a little thing for the end of wedding season.

Fine. She wore the dress.

All day.

She floated through all the errands and folding and prep lists while swatting away Zach's smugness every time he caught her smoothing the fabric like she couldn't believe it was real. But then she got caught up with Babushka at the gourmet market, and by the time she finally showed up for final touches, it was almost time for the guests to arrive.

She stepped outside.

And the moment her foot touched the deck, she stopped.

There it stood.

The arch.

Twined in tulips with tulle catching the breeze.

Piper didn't say anything. Neither did her heart. That sucker skipped, like it suddenly had stage fright.

The fairy lights were twinkling against dusk like champagne stars. The flowers felt a little too intentional, the chairs arranged in two shockingly symmetrical rows around a path lined in petals. There was even a string quartet setting up. This wasn't a Bluetooth speaker with a wedding playlist.

There was Borodinsky set out next to a vodka-serving ice sculpture that could be qualified as a religious experience. The chocolate three-tiered cake was somehow both whimsical and Martha Stewart-certified.

And off to the right, the Dvornakov's legendary Tablitsa Sud'by stood proud beneath its obligatory sign.

Babushka bee-lined to the champagne flutes, wearing a grin that looked entirely too pleased with itself.

She paused near the Borodinsky and clapped twice, sharp as a starter pistol. "Vhere is the salt? You vant bad luck for marriage? Bring the salt here by Borodinsky. Eto katastrofa."

She adjusted an orchid centerpiece with brisk authority, then pulled a small square of embroidered cloth from her pocket. With uncharacteristic tenderness, she spread it over the corner of the main table.

"Vedding destiny," Babushka muttered, patting the cloth, eyes momentarily far away. "Tablitsa Sud'by always knows." Then she snapped back. "You. Vhere is salt? I asked for salt. No salt, no soul."

Piper blinked. Her feet refused to move.

Zach was leaning against the edge of the porch, now in a light-gray suit and white shirt, no tie. He didn't say anything right away. He slid his hands into his pockets, smile easy, eyes locked on her like she hung the damn moon.

She squinted. "What is this?"

Zach stepped closer, head tilting, voice warm as his gaze. "It's a wedding. Ours. If you're in. If you're not, then it's just a party."

Her mouth fell open. Somewhere behind her, Shelby made a choked sound that sounded suspiciously like a squeal.

Piper turned to glance to where her bestie stood with junior-event planner Abigail. "You were both in on this?"

They nodded. Then Shelby set down her drink long enough to root through her purse for her phone, muttering about the angle of natural lighting, but already snapping photos.

Piper's jaw worked soundlessly for a beat while her brain recalibrated. Because it was one thing to joke about surprise weddings. A whole different thing when the man you love made you a custom dress... and then gave you his forever in front of a Tablitsa Sud'by.

"You planned a wedding without me?" she asked.

"I had to," Zach said, shrugging. "You didn't want to."

She let out a stunned laugh, hands flying to her face. "Oh my God."

A lazy Sunday flashed in her memory. That morning months ago, sunlight slanting across the rumpled sheets, her head on his chest, the kind of morning that felt like it could last forever. She'd looked up at him and said with a sleepy smile, "When we get married, let's elope with a basket of tacos."

He'd laughed, warm and amused, but the way he'd looked at her lingered like a fingerprint. Quietly intense, like he was saving that moment for something.

"Also, I would like the extra bonus points I deserve because I handmade your wedding dress," Zach said with a grin.

This dress, with its careful details and delicate weight, felt worlds away from the cluttered Pinterest boards she'd made for the first weddings she'd planned. Those were weddings that happened to other people.

"Bonus points granted," she assured.

"It's legal. It's catered. And I present to you… zero doves," Zach continued.

That sealed it.

She surged forward, wrapping her arms around him before launching herself straight into what was, apparently, her wedding day.

Zach's family was all there. Even her parents and her sister showed up. Zach said he made them swear to be on good behavior. But honestly, she didn't care. Today was about her and Zach, not about them.

Guests arrived and trickled into the rows—even the D.I.C.K. crew showed up. Including Morty. Piper slipped Abigail aside to ensure she kept him and Babushka as far apart as possible.

That potential drama aside, the funeral directors had become more than clients to Piper. They were friends.

And they still refused to change their acronym. They liked it so it stayed.

The conference, for the record, was amazing and Piper was already working on the next one.

Babushka dabbed tears from both cheeks with a lace hanky that might've been passed down from the Romanovs. Probably.

Her mom stood by her sister with the rest of the Dvornakovs. And Piper held a bouquet of tulips that wasn't remotely wilting. Marrying into a family of florists did have its privileges.

Piper's dad took her hand gently as they stood at the start of the aisle. With a chuckle, he whispered, "Why do melons have weddings?"

"I have no idea," Piper said.

"Because they cantaloupe." He chuckled at his own joke.

Piper grinned. Then he scanned Piper's face, pride shining bright. "I still remember when you insisted on wearing your superhero cape to preschool every day. We knew then you were something special, but we couldn't have known how amazing you'd truly become."

"Dad..."

He squeezed her arm. "Let's go. We've got a long walk to get through."

He and her mom were dating.

Piper just stayed out of it. Someday those two deserved their own happily ever after. But it wasn't her job to plan or to coordinate.

Right before they reached the front, he leaned close and whispered, "The wedding is always my favorite part. There's so much happiness."

Piper gulped. "Zach's my favorite part. Same reason."

Brek stood at the end of the aisle with Zach. He'd actually asked if he could be their officiant.

Aspen assured Piper that he was legit and had been ordained by an internet church. She checked. Twice.

He mentioned something about coming full circle from

helping Aspen out in a pinch a long time ago by planning some weddings, to being the one to hold all the power at the end of the aisle.

He wasn't wearing a suit, but the black jeans weren't ripped, and his tattoos were barely visible under the sleeves of his black Henley. Honestly, Piper didn't care. She was only looking at Zach.

Brek cleared his throat. "You want traditional vows or your own?"

Piper glanced sideways to her almost husband. His eyes met hers like a vow that this one was totally her call.

"Our own," she said tenderly.

Her voice didn't shake. Somehow, it didn't shake.

"I never thought there'd be a wedding I'd want to attend," Piper began, her grip on her flowers loose and relaxed. "And then… you happened. You made space in my life I didn't know I needed. You saw every gross piece of me and still thought I was magic."

Zach swallowed. "Because you are."

She choked up at that.

"And you," he said when it was his turn, voice thick but steady, "you walked into my life and ruined all my plans in the best possible way. One minute, you're tripping on my keys and stepping in a wad of gum. The next? You're my forever."

They finished the ceremony with a kiss that came with cheers. Noah clapped the loudest from his spot beside Zach, and Shelby whistled one of those loud whistles that people do using their two fingers, their lips, and some kind of witchcraft.

It was flawless.

The reception unfolded in their backyard beneath glittering bulbs and a surprisingly competent string quartet who pivoted mid-song to a cover of "Sweet Child O' Mine."

Noah's toast was long, meandering, and involved a

metaphor about denim elasticity that no one fully understood, but everyone clapped politely anyway.

Tess, who had given up on the Stallions to go work with Noah and Zach, was never one to miss an opportunity. She was already brainstorming with Zach about a limited-run of bridal-themed Wild Sacks lace boxers embroidered with *Just Married* in glitter thread.

Piper raised one eyebrow. "Back. Off."

Tess winked. "Tomorrow, then?"

Zach chuckled. Noah draped his arm protectively around Tess—which was something that Piper was seriously going to take some time to get used to.

Midway through the fourth dance of the night, Zach pulled her close. His breath brushed her ear when he whispered, "You like it?"

And Piper, already head-over-heels for the perfect wedding day, tilted her face up to him and whispered back, "It's the best plan ever."

EPILOGUE

459 DAYS AFTER ANNA
& DRAKE'S WEDDING

BABUSHKA

There was nothing quite like a wedding in the backyard.

It smelled of grass and flowers smashed together in the heat, and people pretending to be surprised when everyone already knew a wedding had been brewing with those two idiots.

Honestly, I had money on it six months ago. Not with real bookies.

No, no. I am not an idiot.

But little psychic bets, I make with myself. One learned to do that in nine decades of being five steps ahead of people who think they are clever.

The vodka in champagne was a delicious decision.

The champagne dry, not sweet because I am not a child. I hide my smirk behind the glass.

It is a good smirk, too.

Had minor legendary status back in Saint Petersburg.

If the younger ones had seen it, they'd have known I was up to something. But I have mastered the old-lady look. That serene, possibly-senile sparkle that made people say, "Oh, she doesn't know what's going on."

I always know what is going on.

Across the yard, Zach and Piper are exchanging stupid and sweet vows. They hold back tears like it is a war effort.

Victory or nothing.

Someone blew their nose loud behind me. Maybe Cousin Irina?

Dramatic, that one. I taught her that when she was seven. *Still have it.*

With the wedding finished, thank God, we can finally eat.

"Nadzieja," Morty said my name and sat in the chair next to me like we were on speaking terms.

"I am not talking to you." I gave him a proper huff, nose in the air.

"I know." He folded his hands on his lap like a little schoolboy. "But we had a deal. And it's time for you to stop threatening me and start talking to me."

I shook my head. "No. I don't vant to talk. Deals change."

"You're telling me that you don't love me?"

I pursed my lips together. Old lips do not lie about love.

"That's what I thought." His eyes sparkled and his bald head glimmered. "Our deal is not dead, my darling. And I am tired of running from you."

I made this deal with him when I had been certain I would be dead before all of my grandchildren found love. Zachary was holding out, bless his heart.

"Now." Morty pulled out little glasses that made him dashing. Blast him. "You agreed that when all of your grandchildren were married off, you'd marry *me*."

"Married and happy. I said they must be married and *happy*." Which, they were. Curses.

He reached for my hand, and, dammit, the old fool I am, I allowed it.

"If you don't want to marry me, then we won't. But I want

that. I want you to be mine. Only mine. For whatever time we have left," he said.

"Okay, fine." Why spend my life alone? "Ve elope tonight."

"You don't believe in eloping," Morty said, bushy eyebrows raised high as the hairline he didn't have anymore.

"I don't believe in a lot of things that I do anyvay," I said. "Rules are like bread. You need to stretch them vhen they need stretching."

"I love you, my Nadzieja," Morty said with his stupid smile I loved so much.

"I know," I said, slyly. "It is mutual."

Tess came closer to us, smelling like fancy hair product. She was scanning the guests like she was looking for someone with a bazooka hidden under their blazer.

"Are you searching for the next disaster?" I asked.

She didn't yet know that I was the next disaster, and the solution. Always both.

"You can speak around Morty." I waved my hand to my fiancé. "He doesn't listen anyvay."

"I was worried our plan wouldn't work out," Tess said, glancing to Zach and Piper canoodling near the dance floor.

"Hold on. Stop." Anna hissed. She was too close; she was onto us.

Did she hear about my vedding? I hope not.

Her eyes sliced toward the bride and groom. "You did this?"

"Of course," I said.

"How much of it?" Anna demanded.

Morty chuckled because he was no fool. I would not marry a fool.

I tilted my head. "Darling, I started it."

"She did," Tess said. "I just helped her out. When you announced you were getting married so quickly and the Stallions wanted to run with the opportunity, Babushka reached out to me."

"Reached out to you?" Anna asked.

"She asked if I'd help find Zach someone to love."

"Aw, you do care." Morty grinned like a lunatic. "I knew you cared for me."

Our gazes locked, promising more than just a marriage. We would be happy, too.

"Perfect place to find love is in vedding," I said.

"Honestly, he and Piper made it easy. First meeting. Bam. The two of them were already hot to trot," Tess said.

Anna's eyes narrowed as she stared at me. "You manipulated this whole thing?"

I scoffed and jerked my thumb toward Tess. "No. I outsourced. I vas on cruise."

And it had been a glorious cruise, by the way. I'd meditated with llamas in Peru.

Yes, there were llamas. Yes, it was Peru. No further questions, please.

I waited a beat, savoring the moment.

Anna scrunched her face like she was solving algebra. Finally, I leaned in and whispered, "Don't think too hard. *Tch.* So vhat, I vent to Tess. She did a good job."

I grinned, stretching it out, all teeth. "I say to Tess, 'You find her. You make them fall in love. Quietly. No one interferes. I trust you.'"

And I had. Dvochka had taken my strategy and stuck the landing like a Soviet gymnast. Perfect.

"What does she have on you?" Anna asked Tess.

"No one needs to know that," I assured.

Morty laughed again. He knows these things.

Then I turned howard the married couple and clapped once, sharp. The couple was sealing the deal again with their good skin and strong bones. Good. I liked it when the people I meddled with became attractive together. It validated.

Anna was pacing beside me now. "Tess really knew this was a setup. She was in on it?"

"It vas not setup. It vas matchmaking espionage. Sophisticated. Romantic."

"Babushka," Anna said, deadpan.

I held up two fingers like I was swearing in at a trial and declared, "Vorth it. Now I vill die happy."

"But you're not really going to die, right?" Tess asked, one hand hovering as if she might have to catch me mid-faint.

"Vhen you love like I have in this life, you never really die, do you now?" I said, full of mystery and legacy. The type of line one should engrave on a bench or a vodka bottle.

Tess was undeterred. "But seriously, you're healthy?"

"That's vhat I say. I never die. You don't listen," I said with a *pfft*.

Anna leaned over, reassuring. "She's fine."

"Healthy as a strong Russian horse," I promised, flexing slightly. "Like Piper and Artyom."

Artyom had been the family's horse when I was young. He who kicked fences and lived mostly on fermented beets.

Inspiration came in all forms.

The kids who got married laughed.

Anna and Tess looked at me now with new respect and borderline fear.

Good.

For decades, I had played quiet.

A little mysterious. Always there.

Who was Babushka? Just the old lady knitting strange patterns that strangely resembled people's worst secrets?

I listened. I waited. I catalogued. Everyone came to me eventually, even the ones who thought they were too modern for tradition.

Truth was that family could become too noisy.

Everyone had an opinion.

And when my sweet, overthinking, soup-spilling grandson, Zachary, was finally ready and just on the cusp of having a crisis about dying alone? I didn't panic. I didn't knit him some sad blanket of solitude for his couch.

No.

I handled it.

Then I started with tradition. Booked a room on a boat to ask Morskoi of the sea to bring Zachary love. Was there a casino and a buffet? Yes.

But that's not why I did it. Just extra benefits.

And I met Tess. Peggy's granddaughter.

Tess had the eyes. Not simple "I love dogs" eyes.

She had curious eyes. Eyes that noticed what wasn't said.

I watched her—always on the edge, listening. Smart girl. Not afraid of Babushka.

Not yet, anyway.

I had offered her a proposition. "Help me find someone for my grandson. Make it natural. You're clever. You can make it seem like accident."

In return I gave her... *well that is between us, yes?*

Tess had looked at me like I'd asked her to rob a bank. But after two shots of cranberry vodka (the weak kind, for Americans), she'd said, "Okay, but I'm not guaranteeing anything."

"Yes, you are," I had replied.

"Excuse me?"

"Vhat?"

"Did you—"

"I said vatermelon is good in August."

Language was flexible.

And now look. Backyard. Vows. Flowers everywhere. Guests weeping.

I took a long sip of my champagne as Zachary dipped Piper for a dramatic kiss. They nearly fell.

Excellent. Must keep them humble.

Later, people would toast.

People would ask, "How did this happen?" and "How did

fate know?" and "Didn't Zach have a weird thing with that doctor lady?"

And I would sit, perfectly composed, and tell them: "Love finds a way."

My gaze trailed to Morty. Love does find a way. But only if Babushka gives it a little push, da?

They wouldn't even know where to start asking follow-up questions. Which was, of course, the point.

I stood and went over to squeeze Piper's hand. Piper looked at me like she wanted to cry and laugh and maybe throttle me just once, for balance.

"You did good," I whispered.

Piper exhaled. "I have a question."

"Yes?"

"Did you lock us in the AV room that day on the terrace of The Falcon?"

I made sure to look affronted. "No."

Piper stared at me for a deliciously long second.

"I had Tess do it." I grinned. "Throw you all off of my trail."

A pause.

"You're an absolute maniac," Piper said.

"Yes," I said proudly. "But now you are family. So... too late."

Enjoyed the story?
There's more Zach and Piper in a
special bonus scene!

Grab your copy here:
christinahovland.com/cbycbonus

ACKNOWLEDGMENTS

My family continues to be amazing. Steve and my four kids are always so supportive of my career. I am so grateful to each of you.

Thanks to my mom, Shirley, for always keeping me on my toes. She is my book event buddy and is always ready to sell you a copy of my stories. (Seriously, if you don't want to end up purchasing a copy, you should avoid her.)

Sereneti, my sister, you are just amazing. Thank you for being an awesome friend and the best sister I could ever have.

Karie, I love you. You are are bestie for life and I am beyond grateful we bonded over a mutual love of cupcakes.

Thank you, as always, to my agent, Emily Sylvan Kim.

Gina, thanks for being my movie buddy and always having a listening ear.

Courtney… girl. Thank you for reading an early copy for me. You deserve all the good things.

Thanks to Serena Bell and Dylann Crush for the early reads and staunch support.

My editorial team on this book went above and beyond, as always. Thanks to Holly Ingraham, Cathy Yardley, Shasta Schafer, and Tara Wine-Queen.

But the team's not complete there:

Terri Mutell! Thank you for being amazing and sending in the mistakes you caught in the early version of this book.

Suzie Waggoner, thank you for being my Typo Terminator. Make no mistake, if you've found a typo in the book it's because I made a change after Suzie's thumbs up.

Beth Carbutt—you are the best editorial goddess a writer could ask for. Thank you so much for your kind notes and thoughts on this story.

And thank *you*, yes YOU, for making my dream of being an author a reality. This is a pretty great gig I've got!

The Mile High Matched Series

Rock Hard Cowboy, Mile High Matched, Book .5

Going Down on One Knee, Mile High Matched, Book 1

Blow Me Away, Mile High Matched, Book 2

Take It Off the Menu, Mile High Matched, Book 3

Do Me a Favor, Mile High Matched, Book 4

Ball Sacked, Mile High Matched, Book 4.5

Can't Believe You Came, Mile High Matched, Book 5

The Mile High Rocked Series

Played by the Rockstar, Mile High Rocked, Book 1

Knocked Up by the Rockstar, Mile High Rocked, Book 2

Married to the Rockstar, Mile High Rocked, Book 3

Tapped by the Rockstar, Mile High Rocked, Book 4

Reckless with the Rockstar, Mile High Rocked, Book 5

Mile High Stallions

On the Map

In the Friend Zone (Coming Soon!)

Standalone Novel(s)

The Honeymoon Trap Confessions

ABOUT THE AUTHOR

Christina Hovland lives her own version of a fairy tale—a retired artisan chocolatier turned romance writer. Born in Colorado, Christina received a degree in journalism from Colorado State University. Before opening her chocolate company, Christina's career spanned from the television newsroom to managing an award-winning public relations firm. She's a recovering overachiever and perfectionist with a love of cupcakes and dinner she doesn't have to cook herself. A 2017 Golden Heart® finalist, she lives in Colorado with her first-boyfriend-turned-husband, four children, the sweetest dogs around, and Mayonnaise the wonder cat.

GET YOUR PLAYED ON!

**Turn the page for chapter one of
Played by the Rockstar!**

**He's a rock star.
She's a waitress.
He's about to rock her world.**

Certified behavioral counselor (and former band groupie) Becca Forrester needs a break. Taking a leave of absence from her job, she moves into the apartment over her parents' garage, and clinches a gig waitressing at a dive bar known for bringing in big name musicians.

Cedric "Linx" Lincoln is a certified rock star. Bassist for the hugely popular rock band, Dimefront, he's in Denver while the band is on hiatus a-freaking-gain. He's looking for something—anything—to keep him occupied until they can all get back to making music. When he saunters into his friend's bar, he finds the perfect diversion.

Becca's presence is a breath of fresh air. The sizzle she ignites in him is precisely what he needs. Bonus: no-stress, no-strings hookups are his specialty. But when things between them tip toward serious, his band implodes, and Becca's leave of absence ends, they're forced to decide what their "real" lives should look like. Maybe there's room for an encore…

CHAPTER ONE

Neon beer signs totally signaled a new beginning. Sure, a girl might not think it possible, but Rebecca —Becca—Forrester was out to prove they could. The scent of hops and bourbon paired with the blast of music through the speakers and constant hum of life in the background at Brek's Bar in Denver, Colorado. Outside, the snow had turned to a slushy mess. Inside, the bar warmed her like she'd taken a shot of top-shelf whiskey.

Oh yes, this joint was the perfect place for a fresh start that did not involve anyone else or the baggage they dragged along with them.

"Why do you want to wait tables here?" Brek asked, giving a dose of emphasis on *here*. "I'd have thought you'd prefer some place with tablecloths."

Becca laughed. Brek was as biker as biker got—long hair, leather, and an abundance of tattoos. His wife was...not. She was a financial planner, and Becca's friend.

Becca shook her head. She definitely didn't want to wait

tables anywhere else. "I'm looking for the diviest dive I can find."

The idea to wait tables was a complete one-eighty from her recent past as a certified behavioral counselor, but she wouldn't go back. Not yet. Especially not when she was having a perfectly lovely time at the local go-to spot for great music in Denver, hanging with her friends, and harassing Brek into hiring her as a part-time waitress while she took a life break.

"Diviest dive? Well, I guess this is your place." Brek flashed her a smile.

"Exactly." Becca tucked a lock of her thick, brown hair behind her ear, where it belonged but never stayed. "Until I figure out what comes next for me."

"You can live the dream right here with me." Brek patted the bar top like it was a living, breathing thing. Something he adored.

Sigh. Someday she wanted someone to look at her like Brek looked at his wife and his bar top.

Not now. She was on a break from all of that—the relation-ships, the responsibility, everything—but, someday, the adoration thing would be fun to have, too.

He'd created the perfect dive bar atmosphere—neon lights on the dark wood over the bar with his name lit up in blue. The wood paneling covering the walls was new enough to make the place look well-kept but beat up enough that it didn't look like he had tried too hard. Aesthetically, nothing matched. Yet everything still worked together. The place was definitely Instagram-worthy.

The darkened room hopped in preparation for the band to take the stage. A vibe she loved pulsed through the air. That feeling right before music blasts and the lights come to life. Yep. This was exactly what she wanted for her present life: loud music and the familiar faces of the bar's regulars, with no further obligation for the mental or physical well-being for those around her.

Also, the best bands played at Brek's Bar. Sometimes, because he had the connections, Brek brought in huge names. Like *huuuge*. Waiting tables here was perfect for a recovering groupie on hiatus from life.

"You can start next weekend?" Brek asked.

"Next weekend would be perfection." Becca glanced at her friends, mingling across the room.

Then *Linx* entered Brek's Bar. Becca choked on nothing but air.

Linx. Walked. Through. The. Door.

Bassist for Dimefront. Hot as all hell. Heartbreak in leather pants when he took the stage.

She, on the other hand, was only hot when she wore a sweater. Definitely not heartbreak in any kind of clothing. Unless… Could a woman be heartbreak in yoga pants? She was sure that wasn't possible. She shook the thought from her head as he moved her direction.

Her mouth didn't just go dry; her entire body froze in time.

Tonight, he'd ditched the leather and wore shredded blue jeans instead. Lanky, with ridiculously long dark hair, stubble that was a half day away from being a full beard, and all the charisma of a man who could get tens of thousands of screaming fans on their feet with one chord on his guitar. He scanned the room like he owned the joint.

Brek may have owned the bar, but Linx owned the room.

"Looks like my current assignment is here," Brek said, offhand with a touch of growl.

"Linx is your assignment?" Okay, she tried to resist sliding her gaze back to Linx, but she failed. Every woman in the house got the Linx grin as he continued his slow saunter through the room.

"I'm his babysitter..." Brek said, glowering in Linx's general direction.

Crumpet crap-ola. Her blood seemed a whole lot thicker and her skin a whole lot thinner when he sauntered toward Brek... and her. The blue neon halo was a nice touch. Well done, universe. Well done, indeed.

She sighed because.... Linx.

All eyes were on him. Every woman in the room got a solid eye canoodle as he strutted right up to where she stood across from Brek. His eye canoodle could likely get a girl pregnant. She sucked in a breath and braced for her turn.

Linx moved less than an arms-length away, and her heart stuttered like he'd asked her to remove her panties. Surely, he wouldn't recognize her. It'd been years since they partied in the same circles.

She held her breath because she couldn't take the risk of his scent. Not because she had any special superpowers that involved scented rock stars—that she was aware of—but she knew he smelled amazing. Rock star heaven and concerts and something musky, like oak trees in the rain.

"Do you want me to wait for the drinks, or do you want to send them over when they're done?" Becca asked Brek, ignoring the fact that Linx was right-freaking-there doing some kind of intense handshake thing with him.

"You should definitely wait," Linx said, blasting her out of her knickers with that smile of his.

Yes, she often thought in British slang that she'd picked up one summer on a European Dimefront tour. She really took to their language choices. Refined, but still rather raunchy.

Like her. Rather, who she wanted to be.

She slid her gaze up the length of Linx—long and lithe. Not beefcake, but definitely built. He had more of a runner's build. Muscle and sinew, but not overdone.

He leaned against the bar top, a look of pure happiness on

his face. This wasn't a cat's-got-his-cream smile. This was a cat's-about-to-play-with-his-dinner-before-devouring grin.

"Becca, this is Cedric," Brek said, slinging drinks like a pro. Cedric?

Right. Sure, yes, she knew that was his given name. Cedric Sebastian, wasn't it? Last name was Lincoln, and all the original members of the band took a nickname that had an x at the end. Together, they made a triple-x, which they found hysterical, as pointed out in multiple Rolling Stone articles.

"Becca," Linx—er, *Cedric*—stretched her name across his tongue and played it like an instrument.

He held his hand out to her. *What to do? What to do?*

She could touch him. She should touch him. He was expecting her to touch him.

Do something already, Becca.

She was overthinking this way too much. So she gave him a solid handshake.

The way he squeezed her palm was nearly erotic. For no good reason, either. It was just a handshake. He didn't make any lewd gestures or anything.

Still, the bar seemed to zip to a pinprick and focus on Linx.

"Becca is a friend of Velma's." Brek tossed Linx a look like her dad used to give her when he thought she was going to use very poor decision-making skills.

Becca extracted her hand from Linx's grasp. She noted how he kept the touch for as long as she'd allow.

"I like Velma." Linx grabbed a pretzel from the bowl on the bar and flipped it into his mouth.

"I do, too." Brek continued working. "That's why I'm making it clear to you that *Becca* is a friend of *Velma's*. Which means stop looking at her like that."

"Like what?" Linx held up his hands.

"Like you want to make her Denver," Brek said with a growl.

What the heck did that mean?

Linx popped another pretzel into his mouth. Somehow, he chewed, smirked, and smoldered, all at the same time.

"She's not Denver. Denver is Denver. Becca is Becca."

Brek crossed his arms. "You and I need to discuss what you're allowed to do and not do while you're visiting."

Linx held his palm to his heart and wobbled dramatically. "I am offended."

For the record, he didn't sound offended.

"It's not visiting if I bought a house. That makes it my home," Linx said to Brek.

He bought a house in Denver? Huh.

Perhaps Becca wasn't the only one in the midst of reconsidering life choices.

"You *bought* a house in Denver?" Brek asked. "I thought it was a vacation rental."

"It was," Linx said with a shrug.

"The landlord was being a total dick about Gibson, so I made him an offer." Linx did the pretzel thing again.

"Who's Gibson?" Becca asked.

Not that she had any real reason to be part of the conversation, but Linx hadn't asked her to leave.

"His cat," Brek said, arms still crossed.

"He's more than a cat." Now Linx crossed his arms. "So what if I bought one little house so he has a place to live?"

Brek shook his head. "Whatever, man. You do you."

"That's my plan." Linx slid his gaze to Becca. "Unless Becca wants to sit here and have a drink with me? Then we can see what happens."

Linx gave her a charisma-soaked smile.

Ah. There it was, her eye canoodle. She felt that stare deep down in her soul.

Yeah. Total player.

A player who went through sex partners like they were potato chips. This was according to his bandmate, Bax, and general female knowledge when meeting a player of his magnitude.

Back when she'd followed Dimefront concerts she'd had her eye on Linx. Something about him was like a magnet, pulling her in his direction. She had wanted him. Full. Stop.

But Linx was bad news for her. He rocked a total love them and leave them vibe. The kind that made a girl like Becca—someone who tended to see only the good in people and, therefore, fall for the wrong men—step away. He had just the right amount of baggage for her to want to unpack. And he was exactly the type of guy to pick up those suitcases and leave town right after she committed to the unpacking.

So she kept far away from his wandering gaze, preferring to observe him in his natural rock star habitat, and not let her heart, or body, get involved.

Brek handed a bottle of Coors to Linx.

"I've actually..." Becca jerked her head toward her group of friends. "Got to get back."

"That's a drag." Linx shrugged and gave Becca an extra-long, excessively thorough glance.

She shouldn't have done it. But she did. Yes, she totally canoodled him back.

"Becca?" Brek's voice cut through whatever the heck was going on between the two of them.

Brek had, of course, known Becca during her groupie days. Back then, he'd managed Dimefront and she'd been a Ten, the pet name they called their groupies. The Grateful Dead had Deadheads, Justin Bieber had his Beliebers, and Dimefront had their Tens. She'd spent a summer being Queen of the Tens.

This was not something she shared regularly. With anyone. No one else in her real life knew. Not even her best friends. That summer had been her first attempt at a life vacation. And it'd worked. Lucky for her, Brek didn't, and she was quoting here, "Broadcast shit that wasn't his to tell."

She let out a long breath and turned to Brek. He glanced pointedly to the order he'd prepared.

"Thanks." She snatched the remaining drinks and—and this was the hard part—she walked away without looking back at Linx and his neon halo.

Enjoyed the sample?
Played by the Rockstar is Available Now!